WORTH THE WAIT

ETERNITY SERIES

BOOK SIX

JENNIFER J WILLIAMS

JJW PRODUCTIONS

Cover Designer: KB Barrett Designs

Photographer: Katie Cadwallader Photography

Model: Cole

Editing: Brenda Bastien

Proofreading: Bookworm Yogi LLC

This book is for every veteran, whether you've been deployed or not. If you've said goodbye to your spouse or children for deployment, TDY, or a remote. If you've dealt with getting medical care from the VA in your area, or had to tell your spouse about a short notice deployment or PCS. If you've shopped on a Friday payday at the commissary, sat through a promotion ceremony in an Air Force hanger in 100 degree heat, or participated in a base exercise that, honestly, didn't make a lot of sense: this book is for you.

A NOTE FROM JEN

Hi Friends!

Your mental health is important to me. This book deals with some very heavy topics surrounding military deployments, injuries from an IED explosion, death of a sibling (off page), depression resulting in suicidal thoughts, miscarriage (in flashback), and both main characters going through therapy.

As always, take care of yourself first if you feel this book may be upsetting to you. You can reach out to me at jennifer@author-jenniferjwilliams with any questions or comments. Happy reading!

Play List

You can listen to the playlist on Spotify.

you broke me first Tate McRae

That's So True Gracie Abrams

I miss you, I'm sorry Gracie Abrams

I Can Do It With A Broken Heart Taylor Swift

Golden HUNTR/X, EJAE, AUDREY NUNA, REI AMI

The Fate of Ophelia Taylor Swift

Die With a Smile Lady Gaga, Bruno Mars

Ordinary Alex Warren

BIRDS OF A FEATHER Billie Eilish

Lose Control Teddy Swims

make you mine Madison Beer

Beautiful Things Benson Boone

Belong Together Mark Ambor

End of Beginning Djo

Man I Need Olivia Dean

Chapter 1

ELLA

EIGHT YEARS AGO

"This is dumb, El. You shouldn't do this. You're going to regret it," my sister, Ember, says bluntly. With matching blonde hair and athletic builds, my older sister Ember and I could pass as twins. Our main difference is our eyes, with Ember's eyes a much lighter blue than mine.

"I don't see a reason to keep the relationship going," I confess, my voice only slightly louder than a whisper. "I can't move with Mom's health the way it is. I know he's going to ask me to move again, and since he reenlisted, I know he can't move home. We're in this relationship stalemate where we either break up, or one of us has to settle and be miserable."

"You don't know that you'd be miserable in North Carolina," Ember says with a laugh. "You're assuming you will be."

"I will be miserable. I'll be a nervous wreck being so far away from Mom. When Leo deploys, I'll be alone, and it's already a struggle to handle my emotions when he's overseas. At least here, I have Mom, you, friends, the bookstore. I'd have nothing but him in North Carolina. And I don't think it's a good idea to start off living in North Carolina on that note."

"That's pretty dramatic, even for you. You've been dating since you were teenagers. You aren't starting anything. You're continuing it. He's the only person you've ever loved, and you're throwing it away! Men like Leo Santo don't come along too often."

"Oh, I know. I won't meet anyone even remotely like him," I reply.

"And you're still set on breaking up with him?" my sister asks.

I nod. "I'm doing this for him. He's always wanted a family. Now he can meet someone local. Get married. Have a kid or two. He won't have to worry about the panicked woman in his hometown who can't seem to get out of Colorado."

"Hadn't you guys ever talked about having kids?" she asks.

"Yes and no. I'd always assumed he'd be back here if we had kids. I don't want to be thousands of miles away from family, with no support structure, and try to juggle motherhood alone. I'm sure there are tons of women in the world who can handle that, but I'm not one of them. I can't even handle the thought of moving an hour away from Eternity Springs."

Ember sighs, stretching out on the well-loved couch in the middle of our bookstore. Purrfect Books has been a dream of mine for as long as I can remember. Ember reluctantly came along for the ride, but I'm pretty sure she's here more for the cycle of cats that take up residence among the book stacks. I work with a local rescue by showcasing the cats who are available for adoption. In our first year, we were responsible for ten cat adoptions. Each year since, we've met, or beaten, that number.

"El, you're making this decision without having a conversation with him. It's not fair to him, and you know it."

Oh, I know. I can already visualize how he'll respond. The look he'll get in his eyes as he cocks his head to the side and pleads with me to reconsider. It'll be the same look he's used on me when he wants to have dinner somewhere else, stay in instead of meeting friends, or watch a different movie. But he's also given me that look every time we've broken up, and I know he'll do it again.

Those beautiful, dark brown eyes will beg me to think about things. His look will make me have second thoughts.

But I've been assessing our relationship for the past six months. The things we've said, and what we haven't. How much anxiety it gives me to think about moving away from home, but also the crippling fear I have every time Leo deploys. We're clearly in different places in our lives, and it's time to move on. Leo will always be the greatest love of my life. No one will ever compare. I know this. Although I don't see myself getting married or having children, I want him to have that opportunity.

"You're going to regret this, El," Ember says quietly, then nods toward the door as the bell rings, signaling someone has entered. "He's looking way too happy, and I can't sit here and watch you break his heart."

Pain settles in my stomach, like I've swallowed a cement block. I turn to find Leo smiling happily as he strides toward me. "You ready, Ladybug? I've got something special planned for tonight."

"Leo, can we talk first?" I ask tentatively. Standing, I walk toward the register where my sister keeps her head down, busying herself with unnecessary paperwork.

"We can talk when we get there. Come on, El. Time's a-wasting." Once I have my purse, Leo grabs my hand, pulling me toward the door.

As we get in the car and drive west toward the far outskirts of Eternity Springs, I notice how nervous Leo is. His left leg bounces, and his right hand taps the steering wheel in a repetitive pattern. And he talks nonstop. Leo is not a talker. He talks when spoken to, and he'll inject information into some conversations, but his focus has always been on observation. He doesn't give me any time to change the subject, and I certainly don't have an opportunity to explain how I think we should stop seeing each other.

When he finally stops the car, I see that we're at one of our favorite trails. Leo and I have always enjoyed the outdoors. Every time he's been able to come home, we've hiked at least once. When

I turn to see his boyish smile, I can't help the words that tumble out of my mouth. "I can't do this anymore."

His smile slightly drops, confusion evident in his eyes. "Do what anymore?"

"This," I say, gesturing back and forth between us. "You and me. It's not fair to either one of us. You deserve someone who can meet you where you're at. I'm not that girl."

"What are you talking about? Yes, you are. I've known since the eighth grade that I wanted to marry you, Ella. I'd have done it years ago if I'd thought you would've said yes." He grabs both of my hands, holding them tightly in his. "We can figure everything out in time."

I shake my head, tears filling my eyes. "We've had enough time. We've never taken the next step because I think we've both known, subconsciously, that it would never work. I can't leave Eternity Springs, Leo. And I don't want to. I love it here. But I know you've always wanted to be elsewhere. We want different things."

"I want you," he says passionately, dropping my hands so he can cradle my face. "Just you, Ladybug. I'll get out. I promise. I'm in for two more years, then I can be discharged. Just stick with me for two years."

A tear cascades down my cheek, and he tenderly wipes it away. "You promised me you wouldn't reenlist the last time, Leo. Then you didn't even tell me you had. I read it on *The Eagle Has Landed*. I was heartbroken. Then when we had dinner, I had to confront you about it." Originally created as a town website, *The Eagle Has Landed* morphed into a gossip site for our small town some time ago. While it's routinely wrong, retractions are rarely issued, and I have no doubt some of their stories have caused breakups for no reason.

"Shit, baby," he says quietly. "I'm so sorry. I didn't know that's how you found out. You never told me that detail. I assumed one of my siblings told you."

"That wouldn't have been any better, would it?" I ask, my tone full of accusation. "Your whole family knew before me, like I'm just some afterthought. I can't take that heartbreak again. I know what will happen. You'll get news of some village that needs to be occupied. Or you're really close to ranking up. Or you want, or need, to avenge someone's death. There will be some reason you have to reenlist."

His wide eyes dance back and forth between mine, as he searches for the words. "It wouldn't matter if I could just get you to North Carolina."

"I can't. You know that," I whisper.

"No, you *won't*. There's a difference. Your sister is here. Your brother could help too. Why does it all fall on you?" Leo asks angrily. He lets go of my face, ripping one hand through his hair aggressively. His jawline clenches under the thick beard covering it, and I fight the urge to drag a finger across it. He's usually clean-shaven, especially when on active duty, and I've always loved the beard he grows on leave from the Army.

"Because I want to be the one to care for her. And you know damn well my brother won't help our mom. And Ember is too scatterbrained to keep track of all the medications, appointments, and schedules." Our father died about ten years ago, and our mother was diagnosed with early-onset Alzheimer's only a few years later. We were hoping to keep her out of an assisted-living facility for as long as possible, but I don't think we can hold off much longer. Even with me living with her in the house we moved into from Silver Mist Falls, she's constantly getting into trouble. Mixing up medications, leaving things on the stove as it's heating up. We took away her car keys, not knowing she had a spare. She crashed into a shallow pond only a mile from our neighborhood.

"I want to be with you, El. I don't want this to end," Leo confesses, closing his eyes as pain flashes across his face.

"You deserve someone who will excitedly wait for you through every deployment. Who you'll marry and have kids with. Someone that loves you so much, and loves North Carolina, and supports you unconditionally."

His eyes open, and they're filled with anger. "Are you saying you won't do any of those things? That you don't love me, or support me? What the fuck, Ella?"

It's time to admit where my mind has been all these years. "I've had recurring nightmares for years, Leo. *Years*. It's usually Alex coming to the door to tell me you're dead. Or I find out on that stupid gossip website that you've been injured. I dream of your funeral. I wake up screaming most nights of the week. I am petrified of everything. I think about living in North Carolina, with no support at all, and finding out you're dead. Then what do I do? How do I survive that? What if we're married, and the chaplain arrives to tell me you've passed? Then I'd have to be the one to tell your family. I can't do that. I can't give them the worst pain they'll ever experience. I thought, with time, I'd get used to military life. But it just gets *worse*."

"I've been active duty for over ten years, and you're just now admitting you've had nightmares? What the fuck, Ella? How can I help when I don't even know there's a problem?" Leo scrubs a hand over his face, taking his eyes off me to glance out the windshield. His head drops back against the headrest as he blows out a ragged breath. We're still buckled in our seatbelts. He hasn't even turned off the car. I just dropped all of this on him as soon as he stopped talking.

"I thought I could fight it all," I confess, my voice trembling with emotion as I take in his profile. I desperately want to reach out to drag a finger along his jawline. Commit the feeling to memory. Tears fill my eyes as I realize I'll never touch him again. Never kiss him. Feel the safety of his arms.

But I know this is for the best. Leo was made to be in the military. He's a natural leader, incredibly brilliant, and thrives under pressure. Could I give him an ultimatum, and tell him to come home? Maybe. But he'd be miserable, and I can't do that to him. I want him to do all the things he's ever dreamed of. I don't know what the future holds for me, but forcing Leo to come home so he can watch me care for my slowly dying mother won't be happening.

"I can't believe you're doing this. Again. Right when I think we're on the same page, you rip the rug out from under me. Again and again, El. Breaking up in high school was because of stupid shit, but the times you've ended things since then? Same song and dance about Eternity Springs, your mom, and having no friends in North Carolina. It's always been your decision. Well, now it's going to be mine. If you end this, it's done. Forever. I'm not going to forget. I won't come crawling back. I swear to you, I'll never speak to you again."

Another tear slides down my cheek, but Leo makes no effort to swipe it away. His gaze has turned cold and bitter. He knows what's coming. I've never been one to handle ultimatums very well, but it wouldn't matter if he hadn't just given me one. My mind was made up before I got into his car.

"It's time we move on," I whisper, emotion clogging my throat. "You deserve to find a woman who meets all of your needs. I'm not the one."

He chuckles sardonically. "What about you? You haven't said one damn word about finding your perfect match."

I shrug. "I have no intention of looking."

His eyes widen. "So you're claiming this is solely for me? So I can find someone else?"

"Yes and no. It's for my peace of mind. I've started having panic attacks, Leo. I get so anxious I throw up. I can't keep living like this, in a constant state of fear. I know I'll never find a love like ours, and I don't intend to try."

He throws up his hands in frustration. "Are you fucking serious? You can't be. This is complete bullshit."

"I've never lied about how I felt about you. I just didn't tell you about my fears."

"Don't act like you're innocent because of a technicality. An omission is still a lie. This is unbelievable." Unbuckling his seatbelt, he throws open his door. "I have to get some air."

"What? Wait!" I shout, scrambling to get out of the car. I have to run to catch up with him, his long legs carrying him fifty feet up the trail before I grab his arm. "That's it? That's how this ends? What am I supposed to do?"

"Take my car and put the keys under the seat. I'll get it later. I can't be near you right now, Ella. You just broke my fucking heart, and I was about to … you know what? It doesn't matter. None of this fucking matters. Go home, Ella. You got your wish. We're done."

I watch as he stalks away, and I silently cry. God, I love him so much. But I can't keep doing this to myself. He shouldn't want this for his life either. I know there's a woman out there that's perfect for him. She'll have dinner on the table every night when he gets home from work, and she'll excitedly welcome him home with a huge poster after a deployment. They'll have gorgeous kids, and I'll painfully smile as I see them around town when he comes back on vacation.

I wait for ten minutes, long since his silhouette slipped around a grove of Aspen trees, feeling the fraying of the invisible tether that has held us together. I send up a silent prayer. Am I doing the right thing? Sacrificing my happiness for his? I want so many things for Leo. He deserves the world. I hope he understands I'm giving him the opportunity to find a partner who matches him exactly where he is, instead of a childhood sweetheart who can't seem to leave home.

I pull out my phone and call Gianna.

"Ella."

"G. You need to talk to Leo. He needs you," I say quietly, willing my voice to remain calm.

"I just spoke to him, Ella. What the hell did you do?" Gianna says angrily.

"I ended it. For good this time. We were living in a fairytale, thinking it would work. But we're up at the trailhead for Elk Meadow Park. He told me to take his car back to town." I sniff hard as I imagine Gia's expression. "I want him to find happiness, G. He deserves to find someone who can give him everything he needs. Can you make sure he tries? That he gives up on me?"

"You're forgetting how stubborn my brother is. If he doesn't want to give up on you, there's nothing I can say to change that."

"Wait a few months, then tell him I'm dating someone new."

"Ella!" Gianna gasps. "I'm not going to lie to Leo about you! He comes home. He'd figure it out."

I chuckle bitterly. "If he thinks I've moved on, he won't ask anyone about me. You won't even be able to say my name."

"Fine. I'll handle it," she snaps, then ends the call.

Great. I knew this would happen. That I'd lose both Leo and Gianna. But what choice did I have? I can't fault her for siding with her twin brother. I'm glad Leo has support, just like I have Ember.

As I slide into the driver's seat of Leo's car, I take a deep breath. The air is permeated with Leo's cologne, a Nautica scent of bergamot, lemon, and sage. He's still using the same bottle I gave him for Christmas a decade ago, because he only uses it when he's with me.

Correction. He only *used* it when he was with me.

I frown as I imagine him spraying it on for a future date, and another woman complimenting him on how nice he smells. The thought makes my stomach churn. I shake my head, forcing the images out of my head. This is what I asked for. He deserves someone who can give him exactly what he needs, and I know I'm not the one.

A sound of tires crunching on gravel makes my head pop up, and Leo's very angry brother, Dominic, jumps out of his car. He motions for me to roll down my window. When I do, he leans close and whispers, "You're lucky you aren't a man. When men break our sisters' hearts, we show them how bad that decision was. But stay the fuck away from Leo, and stay away from my entire family."

I nod numbly as he stalks up the trail. I deserve that too.

I don't remember the drive back to Eternity Springs. Nor do I remember parking in front of my house, or relieving the home health aide who sits with my mother during the day when I'm working.

In fact, the only thing etched into my memory, in fact, is the empty road the next morning, after Leo retrieved his car.

And that was how I made the worst decision of my life, one that I regretted almost immediately. I figured it would get better. I needed time to grieve our love story. But life wasn't kind to me or my family, nor was it kind to Leo. Eight years later, and I'm still regretting leaving the only man I ever loved.

Chapter 2

LEO

"Stupid fucking marmot," I mutter as I pick up more debris to place in a large trash bag. Yes, it's a marmot. No, he isn't supposed to be this far down in elevation, as marmots typically live above the tree line. I don't know why this exact marmot has decided to wreak havoc on my hometown of Eternity Springs, Colorado, and especially my family's boutique hotel, Everlasting Inn and Spa, but I know he has fun.

Picking up a ripped hockey jersey, I shake my head. "Luca is gonna skin your damn ass if he finds you, Mason."

I didn't name the marmot. The town did. He's become our town mascot, with many of the residents — mostly the women — thinking he's so cute and don't care that he destroys stuff. But my brother, Luca, is ready to shoot the marmot dead as soon as he finds him, because Mason has an affinity for Luca's old hockey memorabilia. Now retired, my brother spent many years with the NHL Denver Wolves hockey team, and now coaches the Eternity Springs High School hockey team. He still likes to look at his old things, though, and I really hope this isn't a one-of-a-kind jersey that can't be replaced.

"Leo? Are you out here?"

Fuck. I stand still, hoping like hell my body is lined up perfectly with the tree I'm next to. It's not that I'm avoiding my sister, Gianna, but I totally am.

"Leo. You're getting rusty. I'm following your footprints in the snow, dummy."

Well, God dammit. I sigh loudly, making Gianna giggle. It's one of my favorite sounds in the world, and I even had a recording of her giggle saved in my phone to play when I was deployed. Our mom often fondly tells people how I would make Gia laugh as a toddler, over and over again, just to hear the sound.

That little trip down memory lane is abruptly stopped when a snowball hits me square in the face. "God, you really are getting rusty! I thought you'd stop that before it hit you!"

"I guess I am rusty," I mumble, swiping snow from my cheeks and eyelashes. It's not like I have any reason to stay on top of things. The Army booted me out as soon as I got injured, and they don't even want me to help train new soldiers. A mangled leg and a traumatic brain injury aren't good for the Army's public image.

"Want to come over for dinner? Your nephew misses you," Gianna says lightly. Looking down at her, with her curls shooting out from under a hat, I marvel at how we're twins. Fraternal twins, obviously, but we're nothing alike. Gia tops out at maybe five-six, whereas I'm six-three. Her hair is a lighter shade of brown than mine, and tight curls surround her face. But we have the same eyes, and that fascinating connection that all twins seem to have, because whenever I'm really struggling, Gia shows up.

"I guess your husband is working tonight?" I ask wryly.

"Yes, but that's not why I'm asking you over," she huffs. "I found a new recipe I want to try. You've always been my favorite guinea pig."

Ain't that the truth. She's been force-feeding me since we were teenagers. Every time I came home from deployment, or the rare times I visited on leave from the Army, Gianna was ready with a binder of recipes to try. She's not a baker like our sister Isabella, or someone who wants to feed the masses, like our mom. Gia likes to experiment in the kitchen, and she has an eclectic palette.

"Alright, I can come over. Do you want me to bring anything?" I ask, as I rub a hand against the back of my neck. A tension headache is coming on. I get them fairly often since the TBI, but only Gianna knows. My family knows I was injured, but Gianna and our parents are the only ones who know to what extent.

I'm a private person. I always have been. I kept my circle of friends small, even as a child. Going into the Army, it was easy to transition into a top secret career field where I couldn't share anything, even if I'd wanted to. Our tasks were usually of the "get in, get the job done, get out, and don't ask questions" type. I fucking loved it. The group of guys I was with became a second family. Ride or die. Until that last op, when only half of us came home.

"No, you don't need to bring anything," Gianna says quietly. "Did you ever go to that acupuncturist I found?"

"No," I answer bluntly.

"Why not?"

"Because I don't need some new age woman talking about my aura and claiming she's rid me of the ghosts of my past while she jams needles into my body."

"That's not ... well, I don't think that's what happens during acupuncture, but I honestly don't know. So what if they do all of that, Leo? If it helps your headaches, does it matter?" Gia asks.

I shrug. "I don't see how it'll help. The military doctors said this is just who I am now. My head is fucked up even more than it was."

"Have you been going to the therapist Dom recommended?" she asks, but I don't answer. No. I'm not in a place to even think about therapy. I'm still too pissed off. I'm angry that I'm hurt and that the Army didn't care. I'm angry that my career was taken from me in a split second. And I'm so fucking angry that I watched some of my best friends get blown up. So no, not ready for therapy.

"Leo," Gianna whispers.

"Leave it alone, Gia."

"No," she snaps. I look down at her to see a murderous expression, hands on her hips in annoyance. "No, I will not leave you alone. I've walked on eggshells for too long, letting you traipse around like you're in purgatory."

"Maybe I am in purgatory! Maybe this is exactly what I've been given because I deserved it!" I shout, throwing up my arms in frustration. I lost everything. People have broken hearts because of me. Surely this is my penance.

I hate when my mind plays the "what if" game. What if I hadn't turned right? What if I'd stopped twenty seconds prior? What if I hadn't reenlisted? What if I'd proposed that night? What if she hadn't moved on? What if I was still with her, and we were married today?

Ella Langley stole my heart from the moment I saw her in eighth grade. Wavy blonde hair that seemed to sparkle under the sun and crystal clear blue eyes that made my heart beat faster when they looked at me, I was a goner from the beginning. She'd been a transfer, immediately pulled into the popular crowd, far away from me. But I couldn't take my eyes off her. Always the loner, I mostly kept to myself, or hung with Gia. I was always aware of Ella, feeling like the air shifted whenever she was near me. It only took six months before I spoke to her, courtesy of Gia befriending her, and I was even more captivated by her soft and steadfast personality. Ella pulled me out of my shell, but in a quiet and patient way, never making me feel like I wasn't enough.

"I think we should talk about her," Gia comments, reading my thoughts. Stupid twin thing.

"No."

"Leo," Gianna protests, but I throw up a hand to stop her from speaking.

"There's nothing to talk about. She broke up with me. She moved on. That ship sailed, and I've come to terms with it," I lie. I haven't come to terms with jack shit.

I'd only been home in Eternity Springs for a few months when I ran into Ella. My mom had convinced me to go into town with her to pick up some baked goods at Bake, Batter, and Bowl, my sister Isabella's bakery. Begrudgingly, I went, keeping my head down as I stiffly walked behind my mom. That's probably why I didn't see Ella until she was right in front of me. I didn't have time to prepare myself. I saw her beautiful face, with an infant bundled up against the cold January temperatures, huddled against her chest, and I thought I was having a heart attack. She'd stammered my name, but I didn't give her any time to continue. Rushing past her, I stalked into Isabella's bakery, walking past the counter, and straight into the back.

I've always hated getting "the look" from people. For me, it comes for a variety of reasons, but it almost always comes quicker than I'd like. Hearing I was injured overseas, or that I lost many friends in our failed mission usually gets a gasp, a sympathetic hand on my arm, and the look of sadness. Explaining I had no intention of moving back to Eternity because I wanted to continue working in some capacity for the military gets a look of sympathy mixed with consternation, like they think I couldn't possibly know what I want in my life. Finding out I have a traumatic brain injury because of my last mission makes people somehow feel guilty, and that look usually leads to them skedaddling pretty quickly. How my injuries in a war overseas becomes about them, I'll never understand.

But when I got a mixture of the first and second look from Ella, I peaced out of there as fast as possible. I knew she didn't want me to stay in the military. Our last fight, and subsequent breakup, had been about just that. I'd begged her to join me in North Carolina, but she'd refused. She begged me to move home, and I said no. We were in a stalemate, and she'd dropped the bomb on me about a breakup. I shouldn't have agreed to it.

I went back to North Carolina an emotionally broken man, and threw myself into work to avoid thinking about her. Ella only reached out once, a few months after we broke up, but I'd been deployed and out of range. I didn't get the message for a few weeks, and when I tried to return her call, she didn't answer. Did she regret the breakup? Was there something she'd needed from me? I never found out.

"… I don't think it's healthy for you to avoid everything having to do with Ella. You're bound to run into her again," Gianna says quietly, bringing me back to the present.

"Not if I never leave Everlasting's property," I mutter.

"Oh, that's a super mature response," Gia snaps.

I shrug. "There aren't many reasons to leave. Anything I might need from town can be delivered these days, and I'm sure as hell not going to go hang out at bars to try and pick up women."

"A date might do you some good, actually. When's the last time you took someone out?"

An actual date? Ella. Eight years ago. "What the hell does that matter?"

Gia steps in front of me, lightly poking me in the stomach. "Look. I don't like talking about this either, but maybe you need to find someone who can help you … loosen up a little bit."

Jesus Christ. "Are you seriously suggesting I find a fuck buddy?"

She throws up her hands in frustration. "I don't care what you call it, but you're wound so damn tightly! There has to be a woman out there who you can enjoy for a night, without getting attached, and who doesn't talk too much. I know you hate chatty people."

She's right about that. "I know your heart is in the right place, but talking about my sex life with my twin sister isn't my jam. But if you must know, I don't want to have to explain my injuries to a woman. To have sex, you have to remove clothes. Women don't seem to have the ability to keep quiet."

"We are typically chatty bitches, huh," she muses with a smile. "I have to think there's at least one woman out there who will respect your boundaries, Leo. Both emotional and physical ones. Have you thought about looking into a, uh, service?"

My mouth drops open as I stare at my twin incredulously. "You did not just suggest I find an escort or prostitute."

Gianna's eyes fail to meet mine as she glances all around us. "When you word it like that, it sounds much worse than what I intended."

"Whatever you intended, the answer is no. I will not use a 'service'" — I use air quotes — "to find a woman to sleep with me. If, and when, I want to fuck, I'll figure it out."

"If?" she screeches. "Holy shit, Leo! *If*? Have you not had sex since?"

Well, fuck. "Go home, Gia. I'm not talking about this with you."

I feel her hand tentatively grip mine, and I look down to find her studying me. "You know you can talk to me about anything, right? Or Travis. We're a safe space for you."

I know she means well. Truly. But the demons hounding me from the past eight years are too much for her to handle. That's why I stay alone. Cut off. Isolated. Because no one will ever be able to fix me.

Chapter 3

"I know, sweetie," I soothe, jostling Violet. Her face resembles her name, a reddish-purple, as she screams her lungs out. "If I could put you down, I'd be able to make your bottle faster."

Her hands grab onto my shirt tightly, as if she understands exactly what I said. Violet is only six months old. I'm fairly sure she doesn't comprehend much of anything except for milk, sleep, and her favorite pacifier.

Well, that's not entirely true. Violet clearly knows that I'm not her mother. My sister, Ember, is. I mean was. My sister was her mother.

Ember was my best friend. I was there through everything. When she found out she was pregnant by a one-night stand — and then a second time — I stood beside her. I was with her when she delivered Violet. I was there when Violet smiled at Ember for the first time, and I was there when Ember told me she'd had a will written up, as a precaution, listing me as Violet and her older brother Oliver's, guardian.

I just never thought it would happen so soon.

Ember was killed in a car accident when Violet was two months old. Fortunately, Violet wasn't with her. She was with me, while Ember ran to the next town over to grab some supplies for our cat showcase/bookstore, Purrfect Books. On the way back, she was hit by an elderly driver in the midst of a medical emergency. I was told she died instantly.

Violet hasn't really smiled since. She'll smirk on occasion. But a beautiful gummy grin? Nope.

"Okay, baby girl, I got it. Here you go," I say quietly, then laugh as she grabs the bottle with gusto. Her eyes don't leave mine as she begins to inhale the formula. Eyes the exact same shade as her mother's. While mine are more sky blue, Violet has ice blue eyes. They're almost unnerving when she's focused on you, like she's systematically dissecting every part of your psyche.

Quickly walking to the rocking chair in the corner of my living room, I sit with a long sigh. Life hasn't exactly gone to plan. I'm raising my sister's children, living in a three-bedroom apartment I can't really afford, and am in danger of losing my bookstore because it's falling apart around me, but I don't have the funds to fix everything up.

I don't know where I can go to wave my tattered, white flag, but I keep looking. Things have to get better, right?

I always knew I would live in a small town. Growing up in Silver Mist Falls, a town a couple hours west of Denver, I loved the quaint area. My best friends and I would play on my cousin's ranch, oblivious to anything around us. My cousin, Ally, knew she'd inherit the ranch someday, and had detailed plans for what she'd do to it. Some little girls play wedding, mom, or teacher. We played veterinarian, barrel racer, and animal rescue. Surrounded by those girls, I was at my happiest.

So when my parents announced we had to move to Eternity Springs because my father had lost his job, I was devastated. I may not have known what I wanted to do with my entire life like Ally, but I knew I wanted to live in Silver Mist Falls forever. I cried for weeks after we moved, and barely made any friends at my new school that year. It wasn't until the following year that I opened myself up to friendships and began to show interest in the opposite sex. Specifically, one person of the opposite sex.

Leo Santo.

I saw him before he saw me. I watched how alert he was, how he seemed to memorize things around him without saying a word. It took months before I gained the courage to smile at him, and even longer before we spoke. I was halfway in love with him before we had our first date, and could barely contain the words once he admitted his feelings toward me.

Then he joined the Army, and life seemingly got harder and harder. I begged him to come home, he begged me to move away from Eternity Springs. We'd break up, last a few months, then get back together. I felt like I could barely function without Leo, but it was even worse when he was deployed. I had nightmares all the time. I'd imagine the impeccably dressed soldiers coming to my door to tell me he was gone. Ridiculous, honestly, because we weren't married, so they'd have to go to Leo's parents to deliver the news. Then I'd wonder which of Leo's brothers would be tasked with telling me about his death. Years ago, I'd been close with his twin, Gianna. We drifted apart, mostly due to the constant break ups and make ups, undoubtedly.

Eight years ago, when he hinted at a reenlistment, and again suggested I move to North Carolina, I'd had enough. I couldn't do it anymore. I was withering away, spending days like I was walking in a fog, waiting for what I'd deemed as the inevitable. How could I survive losing him? I decided my only option was to do it on my terms. End the relationship and move on. I figured since he was two thousand miles away, I could manage it.

Honestly, I never thought he'd end up at home again, after almost losing his life.

That first time I ran into him, while babysitting Oliver, had rocked me to my core. Leo had looked down at Oliver, and the shutters that he'd immediately put up had been a shock. Eyes that had appeared full of pain were then completely devoid of emotion. He addressed me by name, and then stepped around me. "Ella."

I hadn't spoken to him since, three years later. I'd only seen him a handful of times, and he completely ignored me. He looks almost the same, but harder. And he limps. For the most part, he covers it up well. But I know him. Well, I knew him. I memorized every inch of his skin, all of his mannerisms, and his moods. No one knew him better than me. I can tell when he's hurting. And every single time I've seen him in the past three years, I know he's hurting more than he'll let on to anyone.

If I had to guess, he's hurting more emotionally than physically.

My phone rings, jarring me out of my trip down memory lane. Shit. It's the preschool. "Hello?"

"Hi, Ella, it's Marie," the woman says. Marie is the teacher in the four-year-old room at the main preschool in Eternity Springs. "Oliver had an accident again, and there aren't any spare clothes in his backpack."

Dammit. I knew I forgot to do something this morning. It's rare that I take a day off during the week, and I kept Violet home with me. Oliver absolutely loves day care, and would never choose to stay home on my off days. "I'm so sorry. I'll be there in ten minutes."

"No rush. He's hanging out in a pull-up right now, totally happy. It's almost time for pick up anyway, so you're more than welcome to grab him early."

"Okay. Once Violet finishes her last ounce of formula, I'll head over."

At four years old, Oliver has been regressing quite a bit lately. His pediatrician told me not to be concerned, because he'd lost the only parent he had. Violet and Oliver had different fathers. If Ember knew Oliver's father, she'd never told anyone, and he wasn't listed on the birth certificate. Only after her death did I find a paper shoved in the back of her filing cabinet for a guy I'd never heard of, relinquishing his rights to Oliver. It was a relief, honestly, to know I wouldn't have to fight any birth parent for him.

While Violet has seemed to struggle to find joy as a baby, Oliver has lashed out in other ways. He has impeccable speech, but now uses a lot of baby talk to display his emotions. Regression in potty training has been quite the issue. Before Ember's death, Oliver was one of the first boys in his preschool class to triumph over pull-ups. Especially within the past two months, he's been having accidents on a more consistent basis. The pediatrician says there's nothing wrong with him physically. He suggested a child therapist, and we're on a waitlist for a highly recommended one on the outskirts of Denver.

I'm convinced I'm doing an awful job of raising my niece and nephew. I didn't even want kids. I liked being the fun aunt who could have Oliver over for a sleepover, then send him back to his mom's house, so that I could recover. I had visions of grand adventures I'd have with Violet, but always with the assumption she'd go home afterward. It's been a challenge to come to terms with the fact that I am now the mother. A second-rate one at that. And I feel like I'm failing my sister every day.

After a large belch from Violet, I walk out to my SUV. Securing her safely in her rear-facing car seat, I begin the short drive across town to the Rising Stars Preschool. It's a cold and blustery February day, and dark clouds promise more snow on the way for Eternity Springs. I'm thankful I only live one block away from the bookstore, and my childcare provider lives next door, so even when the roads get dicey, I can get to and from work safely.

"Alright, pretty girl, let's go get your brother," I sigh, as I pull into the parking lot at Rising Stars and turn off my car. I see the very old sticker in the upper lefthand corner of my windshield, noting how many thousands of miles I'm overdue for an oil change, but I don't have any money to spare right now. My sister didn't have any savings or life insurance, and infant formula is ridiculously expensive. Violet had difficulty gaining weight at birth, and her pediatrician put her on Nutramigen hypoallergenic baby formula. I love that she immediately began gaining weight, but the formula is at least thirty bucks a container! Occasionally the pediatrician has samples he gives me, but it still costs a ton. I recently began trying solids with her, and it has not gone well.

I quickly pull Violet from the car and briskly walk toward the building. As I open the door into the lobby, I see Oliver waving at me from behind the desk. "Auntie Ella! You're early!"

"That I am," I mumble, jostling Violet on my hip. Her head is on a swivel as she takes in all the action. We can hear music from one room, loud squealing from another, and multiple phone lines ring as a frazzled Marie strides around the corner.

"I'm so sorry to just throw him at you, but another kiddo just threw up, and we're down a teacher already," she says.

"Stomach flu?" I ask, my heart dropping. She gives me a grim nod. "Great."

"Hey, maybe you're getting out of here in time. I'll cross my fingers Oliver doesn't get sick." A crash sounds from behind Marie, and she winces. "Crap. I gotta go."

"Good luck," I murmur, then look down at Oliver. He peers up at me, suddenly pale.

"Auntie, I don't feel good."

Shit.

"Come on. Let's get home before anything else happens."

"Auntie, I feel yucky …" he trails off, and I know. I feel it in my bones, two seconds before it happens. Then I literally feel it, when it hits my shoes. Tears fill my eyes as I take a deep breath, acutely aware of how much my life is going to suck for the next couple of days.

"I spoke too soon. So sorry, El! Take him home. I'll clean up," Marie says hastily from the desk. I nod glumly as I grab Oliver's hand.

"I frow up," Oliver says. "I don't like that."

"I know, buddy. I don't like to throw up either."

"Why, though? Why I frow up?"

Thankful I left the car unlocked, I usher Oliver into the car, then round it to put Violet back into her seat. "Well, some germs got into your tummy. When your body doesn't like the germs, it wants to get them out. Throwing up is the fastest way to get the germs out."

"Am I gonna frow up again?" he asks.

"I don't know. Maybe. Let's get home, get you in a warm bath, and we'll take it a step at a time. Okay?" He nods, but his lower lip quivers. I'm close to crying as well, and Violet's gaze bounces between the two of us as I snap her into her seat, then hustle back to make sure Oliver is in his booster.

I take deep breaths as I drive home, slightly above the speed limit, willing myself not to focus my attention on the smell in my car, or how my feet feel. Oliver missed his entire body, seemingly focused on hitting just me. In a normal situation, I'd admire that feat. But right now, I'm two seconds away from having a break-down. I don't like vomit, especially when it's someone else's.

My tires squeal as I come to a stop in front of my building, and I get both kids out of the car in record time. As I'm pushing Oliver through our door, my phone rings. Right as I pull it from my pocket, seeing Gianna's name, I go to hit the "decline" button, and Oliver throws up again.

"Shit!" I shout, putting Violet in her bouncer. I grab a trash can and shove it under Oliver as he continues to retch.

"El? What's going on? Are you okay?" I hear, and I realize I somehow connected the call to Gianna. God. Now is not that time.

"G, I can't talk. Oliver is throwing up." Violet lets out a scream, and I swivel to see her covered in what I assume is her last bottle. "Now Violet is throwing up too! What am I supposed to do? I'm not equipped to handle this! The stupid washing machine is broken, and the dryer broke months ago, so how am I supposed to wash anything? I don't even have anything bland for Oli to eat, and what if I get it? Is this how parenthood is? I didn't sign up for this! It isn't fair, my sister should be here! I don't want to do this!"

There is silence on the other end of the line, and I begin to cry. I never thought it would be this hard. I love these kids. I'd do anything for them. But it is hard! I'm not their mother, and I know I'll never be good enough to take her place. They'll always wish she were here instead of me. I'm making mistake after mistake, and nothing I do seems to be enough.

"I'll be there in fifteen minutes."

"What?" I ask, my voice meek and shaky.

"I'm coming. You need help. I've been there. I'll bring cleaning supplies and bland food. We got this, girl."

"Okay." I don't even argue. I don't have the energy.

Fifteen minutes later, Gianna charges in, arms laden with bags of items. "My entire family just had norovirus a couple of weeks ago, and we stockpiled a bunch of things. I also ordered some groceries to be delivered in about an hour."

Fresh tears fall from my eyes as I wipe a lock of hair off my forehead. "You didn't have to do all of that."

Gianna shrugs. "If the roles were reversed, we both know you'd have done the same thing. Where are the kids?"

I point toward the bathroom, where I can see Violet reclining in her infant bathtub, and Oliver stacking empty cups on the edge of the tub-shower combo. It's a rare time I'm thankful I can see the tub from the front door. "In the shower. I just got them stripped of their clothes, and now I need to go bathe them."

"I'll handle that. You go clean yourself up. What's wrong with the washer?"

"I really don't know. I'm not adept at those things. The dryer stopped heating the clothes a while ago, but I figured I could just hang things to dry for now. The washer seems to drain all the water without soaking anything, so nothing actually gets clean."

She whips out her phone. "Okay. I'm on it. I'll get someone here to repair them this evening."

"G, no," I say hurriedly. "I don't have the money to fix them. I'll just have to use the laundromat by the bookstore for now. I was complaining earlier, I didn't expect you to roll in here and fix everything."

"Ah, but fixing things is what I'm good at. Just ask Travis. It's the type A personality. I've got this. Go get cleaned up. The kids will be fine with me for thirty minutes."

Thirty whole minutes to shower? I'm not sure the last time I had that long of a shower. I shouldn't take the whole half hour, but I do. I need the time to get my head on straight. Think of ways I can make ends meet for the time being.

As I shampoo my hair, I start doing the math. I only have a couple hundred dollars in savings, and a new washer and dryer set will run well over a thousand. I have good credit, so I can probably get approved for a card somewhere. But what will the monthly payment be? I'm already tapped out on utilities, food, and general expenses.

I have a handful of old baseball cards of my dad's that I know are worth some good money. I hate to think about selling them, but difficult times call for difficult decisions. Wait, is that the saying? Crud. I don't know.

Another option I have is to open up the bookstore for events. I could charge a flat fee per hour. But how will that impact the well-being of the cats that currently live there? And would events change the insurance premiums I pay for the space?

I could also start volunteering to babysit nights and weekends. I'm thankful the bookstore keeps regular hours, and I split the shifts with my best friend, Whitley. Her focus is mostly on the attached café, but we cover for each other so we can have another day off during the week. We're closed every Sunday, so I could pick up babysitting then. But it risks the chance of bringing more germs into my home, and if the kids are sick, I can't work.

After taking the longest shower in recent memory, I'm more relaxed, but no closer to any answer. Wrapping my hair in a towel, and my body in my well-loved chenille robe, I pad down the hall to check on the kids, but the doorbell rings.

"That's probably the groceries!" Gianna calls out. "I'm almost done in here, can you get the bags?"

"Okay!" Well, I'm in a robe, but considering I walked through the parking lot of Rising Stars with puke in my shoes, having a grocery delivery person see me this way is nowhere close to topping my humiliation for the day.

To my dismay, it's not the groceries.

It's much worse.

"Leo?"

Chapter 4

LEO

I'm going to murder my sister.

Nowhere in our text messages did Gianna say anything about Ella. She said she had a "friend" who was going through a rough time and needed help with fixing a washer and dryer.

"Did you set this up?" I blurt out, furious at being played.

"What? No? I'm not sure I'm following what you think I set up," Ella says hesitantly. I'm trying valiantly to keep my eyes on her face. Behind her head. On the wall. Wherever. But she answered the door in a fucking robe — the robe I gave her ten years ago — and she looks so goddamn perfect I can barely see straight.

"Is my sister even here, or is this all a trick?" I say through clenched teeth.

Ella's eyes widen. "She said she was going to get someone to fix my washer, but she never said it was you! I swear, Leo. No games."

"Leo?" I hear Gianna call, and I push past Ella, groaning when her vanilla scent fills my nostrils. She's smelled of coffee and vanilla for as long as I can remember: coffee from working at the bookstore, and vanilla from her favorite products.

"What the fuck, G?" I say, then stop dead in my tracks. My sister stands in a bathroom, sopping wet, with a big grin on her face. She's holding an infant wrapped in a fluffy blue towel, and a child splashes behind her in a tub.

"Watch your mouth, Leonardo," she snaps, the smile wiped off her face. She points into a room on the right. "There's the washer and dryer. El said the washer keeps draining, and the dryer won't heat. Figure it out. As a favor to *me*."

Fuck.

I know that tone. That's the "I might be smaller than you, but I'll rip your balls off if needed" tone that Gianna has saved for me from time to time. When my eyes meet hers, she purses her lips at me. Our weird twin connection thing tells me that she's even more pissed than she's letting on, and that Ella isn't to blame for any of it.

I sigh, then speak to Ella, but I don't turn around. "Do you have any tools?"

"Not really, no," she stammers.

What kind of mother doesn't have tools? How the hell is she supposed to take care of her kids when something breaks? And where the fuck is their father? I take a quick peek at the child in the bathtub. He looks to be around six, but maybe he's on the larger side? Wait. If he's older than six ...

I whirl around, fury emanating from me in waves. "Is he mine? Is that kid mine?"

Ella's mouth drops open. "Are you being serious right now, Leo?"

"Jesus Christ, Leo!" Gianna scolds.

Ella's face reddens. "No, he's not yours, you asshole. He's not even mine. They're both Ember's. But you'd know that if you didn't run away from me every time I've seen you over the past year."

Confused, I study her. "Why the hell do you have your sister's kids?"

"Because she's dead, Leo. That's how." Ella's eyes fill with tears, and she steps into a room on the left, slamming the door.

A tiny voice pipes up behind Gianna. "Auntie Ella never gets mad. Is she mad cuz I frowed up in her shoes?"

"No, sweetie," Gianna says calmly. "She's mad because my brother is dumb."

"Oh. Okay." And the child goes right back to playing in the tub, completely unaware that a bomb has just gone off in my life.

"Leo," Gianna whispers. I turn to find her looking at me with sympathy etched on her face. "I tried to tell you. Every time I've brought up her name, you've shut me down. Ember died four months ago. Ella is their guardian."

"But I saw her years ago …" I trail off, remembering every minute detail of running into her in town. How perfect she looked with a baby. How, for just a second, she looked overjoyed to see me. And then the walls went up, closing her off to me. Just like every other time I'd seen her after a breakup.

"You know how close she and Ember were," Gia says quietly. "The time you saw her was probably when she was babysitting Oliver."

Oliver. I nod at the little one in Gia's arms. "And this one?"

"This is Violet. She's six months old."

"She was only two months old when Ember died?" I ask softly. I lift a hand, rubbing my forehead. I can feel a massive headache coming on, and I can only hope it doesn't turn into a full-fledged migraine.

"Listen," Gianna whispers. "I know you don't want to be here. But frankly, Ella doesn't either. She would never have approved of me calling you. There's no one else in town who would be available to fix this tonight, and everyone knows you're the best at tinkering with things like this. It's about to snow, she's got two kids with the stomach bug, and she's struggling. We have the means to help her."

"Alright," I reply with a nod. I quietly head into the laundry room, looking at the machines. They're quite old, not a high efficiency set, but that can be a good thing. It still has the agitator, and it looks to be in fairly good condition. Taking it apart, I find that the pressure hose is caked with detergent, but doesn't have any cracks. The drain hose appears to be pushed too far into the stand-pipe, which can make the hose siphon the water out of the basin immediately. Two easy fixes. I put the machine back together, then fill the basin with water, watching to see if it empties.

Moving on to the dryer, I begin to take it apart. Usually dryers won't heat because a heating element has blown. To ensure it is still tumbling, I remove my sweatshirt, placing it inside. Turning it on, I hear it immediately begin to tumble. In a moment of clarity, I look to the left, where the breaker box is inset in the wall. Opening it, I immediately see a tripped breaker. Dryers run on two break-ers: one for the motor, and one for the heating element. The breaker controlling the heating element is tripped. I pop it back on, then run the dryer again. It immediately begins to heat.

Satisfied, I take my time in checking every last element of the dryer, removing all the lint I can see, and ensuring it'll continue working safely for Ella for the foreseeable future. I quietly clean up the space, then shuffle out to the main living space. I find Ella and Gianna quietly talking on the couch. The baby appears to be napping in Gianna's arms, and the little boy sits at Ella's feet, eyes focused on the television.

"Uh, they're fixed."

Ella jumps up. "Really? What was it? Both of them? I can do laundry?"

I struggle to withhold my smile. "The washer had a hose that was full of detergent gunk, and the drain hose was jammed too far into the standpipe. Once I fixed those two things, it works fine. The dryer was a tripped breaker."

Her look of sheer confusion makes me snicker. "I don't under-stand. The dryer was working, just not heating."

"Dryers work on two breakers. The tripped one controlled the heating element. The other one was fine."

Her eyes close in frustration. "I hate living here. Stuff like this happens all the time."

"Why live here then?" I blurt out.

"Because it was Ember's place. It made more sense for me to move in here than for the kids to move in with me. Besides, this is bigger than my place. Not that I can afford it," she grumbles.

"How many bedrooms is this?" I ask, looking around. It's a good space. Probably close to fifteen hundred square feet.

"It's three, but one is tiny." A loud noise sounds from above, making me wince. "What the hell was that?"

Ella rolls her eyes. "That's Jeremy. He's an idiot. Mostly harmless."

"*Mostly?*"

"I mean, he's suggested some things to me, but I shut him down every time. And sometimes he knocks on the door in the middle of the night."

"Have you called the police?" Gia asks.

"No. I'm telling you, he's harmless." Ella stares defiantly at me, arms crossed over her chest, her chin jutted out. I fight a smirk as I study her. This is the Ella I remember. The one who had stubbornness as she fought for things, and people, she believed in. It's a stark reminder of my past, and my smirk dies as I'm reminded of how different we are now. She's a mom, and I'm a fragment of the man I used to be.

"What else is broken here?" I ask curtly.

"Not much, really. Nothing I can't manage."

I growl in frustration. "Ladybug, that's not what I asked you."

Her eyes widen at the nickname. The nickname I gave her our senior year of high school. She'd been obsessed with finding ladybugs, and they always brought her such happiness. Since red had always been her signature color of choice, calling her Ladybug was fitting.

"I'm sorry —" I begin, but she cuts me off.

"No. You don't get to call me that right now. I do not have the headspace to deal with that. I'm doing fine, Leo. I'm managing. Don't think you can come in here and be a knight in shining armor. I know rescuing the little guy has been your life's mission, but I don't need rescuing." Her eyes shine with a sheen of tears, but there's fury in her gaze. Honestly, I'd rather her look at me in anger, then look at me with a dull look of sadness and surrender.

So I decide to poke the bear. "Your fridge is making an odd sound, and your kitchen faucet drips. Multiple cabinet doors aren't hung properly, and I bet if I looked closer, I'd find wiring problems in the light above my head, because it sounds weird."

Ella's eyes narrow. "You cannot tell if a light is wired wrong by its sound."

I shrug. "Didn't know you were moonlighting as an electrician."

"I'm not. Are *you*?"

"I have more experience than you," I point out.

"But you're still not a licensed electrician. I can call someone to fix it if it becomes a problem."

"For free?" I ask. I feel a hand latch on to one of my fingers, and I look down to find the boy staring up at me. "What's up?"

"How do you know when a sound means something bad?" he asks.

I crouch down. "What do you mean?"

"The sound the light makes. I can hear it too. The light in my room makes the same sound. I don't like it." He shudders, and I immediately stand.

"Show me your room," I tell him, then follow him as he shuffles into a small bedroom. I sure hope this is the tiny room Ella mentioned, because if not, I can't imagine the smallest room size. "Wow. This is … wow."

Oliver points to the light switch beside me, and I turn it on. The same noise as the hall light comes out. It's a mix of a hum and static. "I'm glad it doesn't make that sound while I sleep. I don't think I could sleep if it did."

"Me neither," I comment. Looking back at Oliver, I nod. "I'll get it fixed for you, kid. I promise."

Oliver studies me. "Auntie Ella doesn't like you."

I frown. "Maybe she doesn't. But it's okay. I'll get the light fixed so it doesn't make any more weird noises."

"You should check the dishwasher too."

"Oh yeah? What's wrong with that?" I ask, mentally making a checklist. I should look online, see if there's any kind of list for new renters or homeowners on things they should check during an inspection. While I do a tremendous number of odd jobs around Everlasting Inn and Spa, becoming a jack-of-all-trades for my family's boutique hotel, I've never done an apartment inspection. I might miss some things that Ella should check on every year.

"The dishwasher screams," Oliver says bluntly.

"It screams."

He nods. "I don't like it, and it makes Violet scream too."

"That sounds less than ideal," I say with a sigh, right as Ella stomps into the room.

"It doesn't scream, Oliver," she says with her hands on her hips. "It just makes a high-pitched sound. It's done that for as long as I can remember, but since it still cleans dishes, I haven't felt it needed to be addressed."

"I don't work on dishwashers too often, but it could be something easy like a piece of debris is in the filter, or even lodged in the drain pump."

Ella stares at me blankly. "There's a filter in the dishwasher?"

I muffle a laugh. "Yeah."

"One that I have to replace every so often? Because I guarantee that if I didn't know about it, my sister didn't either."

"Usually you just need to dump it out, or wash it out. It's plastic. Shouldn't need to be replaced. I can take a look at it if you want," I offer.

She looks at me, studying me in a knowing way that unnerves me. Ella was always the one who could make me be uncomfortable in silence. Usually I appreciate silence and solitude. But when she was quiet, I knew her mind was racing. Finally, she speaks. "No.

It's been a long afternoon, and I need to get these two settled down for bed. Thank you for all of your help, Leo."

Ella walks away, and I have no choice but to follow her. Gianna is already getting her coat on, and she gives me an apologetic smile. As Ella opens her door, motioning for me to walk outside, I realize I've been excused. She doesn't want me here in her space. She whispers goodbye to my sister, then closes the door without another word. Gia gives me an awkward pat on the arm.

"I'll walk you to your car," I murmur.

"Pretty sure I can do it myself, but okay," Gia teases. "How mad at me are you?"

"I'm not mad, G. A little confused. Frustrated. You could have warned me."

Gia sighs. "I couldn't. I knew you wouldn't come. You'd have paid someone to show up in your place, and Ella would have been even more mortified had that happened. You saw the state of her apartment. She's struggling. She needs support."

"I'm mad at myself for assuming the worst," I confess. We reach Gia's car, and she turns to me. "I saw her with a baby all those years ago, and I was so hurt that she'd moved on. I couldn't stand the thought of her being with someone else."

"If it matters, I don't think she's dated anyone, Leo," Gia says quietly. "Especially since her sister died. But I haven't heard anything about a relationship. Granted, she and I haven't talked that much in the past few years. When she ended things with you, I said some things. I probably hurt her, then didn't reach out at all. So she lost me as a friend as well."

"Why?" I ask. "That's such bullshit. You were her best friend for a time."

Gia shrugs. "We've talked occasionally since then, but not as often as before. I assumed it was too hard. Maybe she feared I'd tell her you had moved on."

I look back at Ella's building, watching as a curtain moves almost imperceptibly in her living room window. "I don't know how much I can be around her without blowing up. I want answers. At the same time, I'm not ready to hear what she has to say."

"I know. You don't have to make any decisions tonight. You were instrumental in helping her today, and maybe that's all she needs right now. I'll keep in touch with her to see if, and when, she needs more support. You don't need to take point."

I let out a relieved breath. "I don't think I can do anything right now, G. I'm not in a good head space."

My phone vibrates in my pocket with a text. Pulling it out, I frown when I see it's from my brother-in-law, Sebastian. I say goodbye to my sister, then walk to my truck as I open Seb's text.

Seb: You busy tomorrow?

Me: Why?

Seb: Are you always this paranoid?

Seb: You know what? Don't answer that. I've got a guy coming to the Clubhouse to speak about his transition from Army to civilian life. I think you should come.

Me: I don't know. I've acclimated just fine.

Seb: I know I don't know you THAT well, Leo, but you're full of shit.

Seb: You may think you're acclimating, but your loved ones don't. Isabella wants you to attend. So do it for her.

Me: That's a low blow, pulling out the sister card.

Seb: I never said I played fair. Besides, it'll get you out of Eternity Springs, and you can meet the rest of the guys. Almost every single club member has deployed. You'll be around guys who know what you experienced.

Me: I don't ride.

Seb: It's not a requirement, but if you're interested, we can get you on some wheels.

Me: I don't know if my leg will handle a motorcycle well.

Seb: Let's cross that bridge when we come to it.

Me: If we come to it.

Seb: Nah. WHEN we come to it. I'll get you on a hog, Santo. Trust me.

Me: I don't trust easily.

Seb: It took me ten years to get your sister to trust me, and now I'm married to her. I'm ridiculously patient.

Me: I'm not marrying you.

Seb: You'd never be that lucky. I'm a hell of a catch.

With a snort, I toss my phone on the passenger seat, then start my truck. Looking up, I catch Ella's eyes right before she whips the curtains shut. We definitely have unfinished business to discuss, but I have no idea if I'll ever be ready to have that conversation.

Third — Fourth — Sixth Time's a Charm?

Sources tell me our most eligible Army veteran — and only single Santo left — Leo, was seen leaving Ella Langley's apartment late last night with his twin sister in tow. Is Gianna Santo Anderson playing matchmaker between her long-lost best friend and her brother? And how long do we think they'll stay together this time?

Chapter 5

"So, how was it?" Whitley asks.

"How was what?"

"Leo."

I give her a glare as I pull stacks of books out of a shipment. "You're acting like it was a date. He didn't even know he was coming to my apartment, Whit. It was awkward and uncomfortable and I couldn't relax until he left."

"Did he look the same?" she inquires.

"Yes and no."

"What the heck does that mean?" she mutters.

"Physically, yes. Same hair and eyes. Same intensity. Same full lips. His build is different, though. He limps a little, and I know he was injured in Afghanistan, but I don't know the extent of his injuries. Overall, he's more muscular than he was the last time we were together. It's his gaze, though. His eyes are full of pain. I don't know if I'm partially to blame for that, and it guts me to know I might be."

"You can't possibly be to blame for him being angry or upset. The breakup was so many years ago. He's made no effort to contact you, so maybe he moved on. Something you should have done as well, you know," Whitley points out. Her eyes are laser focused on mine as she waits for my response.

"You've made your opinion of my choices very clear," I finally say.

"I still can't believe you've gone this long without sex. Who the hell does that in their thirties? It's not realistic at all," she comments.

Yep. I know. It's been years since I've been with someone. Leo was the last guy I was with. Actually, Leo is the only man I've ever been with. I fell for him when I was still a child, and even when we were broken up, I couldn't fathom the thought of moving on. He was always it for me.

And, frankly, he still is.

I knew the moment he stepped into my apartment that I was still a goner for the man. I wanted to collapse into his arms, beg for forgiveness, and let his steady heartbeat calm me. Leo was always the calm in my storm, and I know I was for him as well.

But the Leo I loved as a teenager, and the Leo I knew in my twenties, is not the Leo of today. Now he's jaded and guarded. He's seen things I can only imagine in my worst nightmares.

"Are you going to see him again?" Whitley asks.

I shrug. "I guess I'll see him around. He said he'd fix a couple of things around my apartment, but I'm not holding him to that. Oliver has asked about him every day, though. He's pretty taken with Leo."

"Of course he is," Whitley says with a smile. "They have the same analytical brain. See a problem, figure it out, and fix it. No gray areas there. It's been a few days since he was there, right?"

"Yeah. I don't want to force Leo to interact with Oliver. I can already imagine what they'd be like, teaming up against me." I laugh quietly. "Leo asked if Oliver was his son. Honestly, based solely on personality, it wouldn't be far-fetched to say yes. They are remarkably similar. If I didn't know where Leo was when Oliver was conceived, and the fact that Ember would never sleep with Leo, I'd wonder if there was a relation."

"You told me once that Ember was ready to fly to North Carolina and yell at him one time, right?" Whitley didn't know my sister very well, but has heard many stories about my big sister. Ember would have burned down the world for me if she thought it would help me in any way.

"She was," I say with a grin. "The last time I broke up with Leo, she felt like he gave up too easily. I was heartbroken, and since she couldn't really yell at me, she wanted to go rip him a new one."

"Why did you guys break up? What was your thought process?" Whitley asks quietly as she watches me break down the shipping box.

"Leo wanted me to move to North Carolina, and I didn't feel comfortable leaving my mom. He'd admitted his last deployment he hadn't felt fully focused because he was worried about me. I felt like I'd be even worse away from home, and he definitely couldn't focus then. We were in a stalemate. I wanted him to feel like he could move on with his life, even if I knew I couldn't move on with mine."

"So you knew you'd struggle?" Whitley asks, and I nod. She sighs. "That's no way to live a life, El. And honestly, that's not a reason to end a relationship, either. But your mom died not too soon thereafter, right? Would you have moved then?"

Emotions clog my throat as my vision clouds. As if I haven't thought about that. I racked my brain for months trying to find a suitable outcome where we were both happy. After my dad died, my mom was a shell of her former self. Ember was all over the place. Our brother moved out of town as soon as he could. I was the stable one. I needed to provide the safety and security my mom desperately needed. I knew I couldn't do that from across the country.

There are thousands of women who manage deployments well. They're independent, go-getters, and can thrive when their partners are overseas for months at a time. I was never one of them.

Every time Leo deployed, I was miserable. Every time the phone rang at an odd hour, I was convinced it would be someone from his family tasked with telling me he'd been killed. I lost track of the number of nightmares I'd had. I couldn't go on social media, or watch television, because I'd inevitably see a report about a soldier's death, and convince myself it was Leo.

For the majority of my twenties, I kept those fears to myself. Leo had no idea I struggled as badly as I did. Or, if he did, he didn't talk to me about them. He didn't know I'd been diagnosed with depression and anxiety, or that I had started meeting with a therapist. I'd only asked him a couple of times if he'd ever thought about a discharge and moving home. Once I realized he had no intention of getting out of the Army, I began to realize our relationship had a timer on it. I wouldn't move to North Carolina, and he wouldn't move home. There was no reason to continue, even if I knew my heart would never be the same.

"I couldn't leave. Even after my mom passed. It was like being here kept the connection to my parents alive," I finally say, clearing my throat. "And Leo didn't want to get out of the Army. We were at two different points in life. I knew I couldn't demand he move home. I'd never do that. Leo loved being in the Army. I would never want him to regret moving home for me. I'd worried he'd hold it over my head."

"Was he like that? Where he'd be vindictive like that?"

"No. But I think I'd have always walked on eggshells in fear. And I couldn't live like that. I wanted Leo to choose me for me, not because he felt forced to."

"That makes sense," Whitley says with a yawn. When the bell above the door dings, she stands, stretching her arms above her head. "I'm going to make a latte. Do you want one?"

"Yes, please," I say, mimicking her yawn. They really are contagious. "Once the kids stopped puking, I was still up cleaning the apartment well past midnight. I'm working on fumes right now."

"You want your usual, or can I surprise you?" she asks.

"Oh, surprise me. I have yet to dislike one of your creations." Whitley loves running the attached café. With a few baked goods we get from Leo's sister, Isabella's, bakery, Whitley offers up one special sandwich per day, a soup during the winter months, and a salad during the summer. Coffee is her happy place, however, and she loves creating new and unique drinks to coincide with different holidays. For St. Patrick's Day last year, she created a rainbow latte that blew me away, and regularly uses herbs and spices that aren't considered normal for coffee.

"Hey, sorry I'm late. Belle got a late start this morning." I look up to find Ava, one of Isabella's employees at Bake, Batter, and Bowl, approaching me with a large plastic container full of baked goods.

"Isabella had a late start? Did hell freeze over?" I ask blandly. Isabella Santo Garcia is well-known for being scheduled, routine, and pragmatic to a fault.

"Well, she seemed to be a little flustered when she arrived at the bakery, and certainly looked well-fucked, so my guess is her hot husband is the reason for the delay," Ava remarks with a grin.

"I'd be fucking that man every chance I got if I were in her shoes, so I understand!" Whitley shouts from the café kitchen. I nod in agreement. Sebastian Garcia is absurdly attractive. He's the epitome of the tall, dark, and handsome vibe, but even more appealing is how desperately in love he is. Sebastian pined for Isabella for a decade, complete with secret tattoos, all kinds of adorable nicknames, and lustful gazes.

"All of the Santo kids are married now, right? Except for Leo?" Whitley asks.

"Yeah," Ava answers. "I tried to get Belle to set me up with Leo, but she refused. I also asked about Seb's hot friend Trace, but she said no to that as well."

"Girl, you're basically an infant," I blurt out. "You can't go after men that much older than you."

"Why not?" Ava asks flippantly. "I don't want a blubbering

doofus who comes in his pants because he's near a woman. I want a man who throws me around and tells me how much he wants to rearrange my organs. Once you've seen the sexual tension between Sebastian and Isabella, you realize that nothing less than that will ever be worth it."

I sigh. She's right, but I'm not going to tell her that. If she's expressed any interest in Leo, I don't want her knowing that he's exactly like she described. In person, Leo is controlled, subdued, and observant. In bed, he was wild, feral, and intense. He had an insanely dirty mouth, manhandled me like I weighed next to nothing, and followed through on every single one of his promises. If he said he'd make me come so many times I blacked out, that's exactly what would happen. If he commented he wanted to see if he could make me squirt, I would. Our sexual relationship was phenomenal. Well, I assume it was. I don't have anyone to compare it to. From what friends have told me about their experiences, I know Leo was an exception.

And I'm pissed that Ava wants that.

"Girl, you're kinda growling at me," Ava whispers, her eyes wide. "Which one of them is off limits?"

"What?" I stammer. "No, nothing. Sorry. Just thinking about something else."

"It's Leo," Whitley yells from the kitchen. "He's off limits."

Ava's eyes brighten. "Oh, good. I want Trace more anyway. Didn't you and Leo break up a billion years ago? You sure you're ready to start back up with him?"

"How did you know that?" I ask.

She gives me a sly grin. "My mom went to high school with one of the Santo boys. The oldest, I think. Plus I love reading *The Eagle Has Landed.* That family sure is featured a lot on there."

I hum noncommittally as I continue sorting the shipment of books I received this morning. "I don't really keep up with the town gossip. My life is a dumpster fire enough as it is."

I hear Whitley snort, but she doesn't call me out on my blatant lie. I read the town gossip website every day. I've done so for years. Even when Leo was thousands of miles away, there would usually be one article a week that would address his whereabouts. I was like a dog to a bone, inhaling any extra detail I could about his life without me. It became evident fairly quickly that I wasn't the only one kept in the dark about Leo's job, because nothing was ever breaking news in regard to him.

I bookmarked every damn article that featured a picture of him, though, and they became a lifeline for me when I finally found out he'd been injured and discharged.

"Ava, can I request a specific kind of muffin for next week? With the forecast calling for a winter storm, I want to bring in some hearty options for the menu," Whitley asks as she joins us again at my checkout counter.

"I'll run it by Belle, but she had already mentioned some thicker breads to have at Everlasting. I bet she'll be on board," Ava answers. Turning to me, she smiles. "You don't have to worry about me. I'll leave Leo alone."

"I wasn't worried," I say defensively. "Besides, you're acting like he'd fall all over himself if he knew you were interested. Maybe you're not his type."

Ava throws her head back with raucous laughter. "Girl, please. I'm twenty-two, I don't have a gag reflex, and my boobs are insanely perky. I'm every straight man's type."

"And obviously quite humble," Whitley mutters.

Ava shrugs nonchalantly. "I won't apologize for having confidence. And if I'm not a man's type? Fuck him. Billions of men on this planet. I'll find one who wants me exactly as I am. Eventually, I will wear Trace down, though. It's just a matter of time."

As if he were conjured out of thin air, Trace walks into the bookstore, but stops dead in his tracks when his eyes find Ava. I watch as Ava's gaze narrows, a smirk covering her porcelain skin, as she bites her lip. "Hi, Trace."

"Ava." He struggles to keep his eyes on her face, and she knows it. Crossing her arms under her breasts, his gaze immediately drops to them. He looks at me, then at Ava's chest, before back to me. It's like watching a tennis match.

"Trace, how old are you?" I ask innocently.

"Forty," he murmurs.

"Do you have any kids?"

"A daughter."

"How old is she?"

"Eighteen."

I muffle a giggle as Ava saunters up to him. He's a good seven or eight inches taller than her, and she uses it to her advantage. Stopping only inches from him, she peers up with a faux-innocent smile, then drags one fingernail up the length of his arm. "Oh? If you call me baby girl, I'll call you Daddy."

"Jesus Christ," Trace chokes out. He instinctively steps backward when someone simultaneously walks through the front door, shoving him forward. He's launched against Ava, who takes the opportunity to wrap her arms around his waist.

"Why the fuck are you standing right at the door, man?" A huff from behind Trace alerts me to the new arrival. Sebastian peers around Trace, and his eyes widen when he finds Ava cuddled up against his friend. "Well, this is an interesting development."

Ava giggles, lining her body up against Trace's, and he makes a strangled noise. They make quite a striking couple. She's tiny and blonde, all youth and innocence. Trace has speckles of gray peeking out in his hair and beard, with weathered lines on his face showing he's seasoned and experienced. But right now, it's clear Ava is holding all the cards. It makes me wonder how long he'll avoid the chemistry they have.

Trace grabs her hands, removing her arms from his waist, and steps to the side. "I, uh, wanted a sandwich, but I just remembered I have an appointment out of town. Seb, you good to get back to the Clubhouse?"

Sebastian studies Trace. "Yeah, I'm good."

Taking another step away from Ava, he nods at everyone. "Ladies."

As he hightails it out the front door, we all look to Ava. She gives us a huge smile. "This is going to be so much fun."

"What?" Whitley asks.

The smile turns wicked. "Breaking him."

Chapter 6

LEO

"Good to see you, man," Sebastian says with a smile, leaning forward to shake my hand. I nod as his grip engulfs mine.

"Thanks for the invite."

"Travis is here somewhere. Probably over by the food," he says with a laugh.

Brow furrowed in confusion, I say, "Trav doesn't ride."

"I told you it wasn't a requirement. This group is to give veterans a place to belong. Yes, the majority ride, but we have a ton of support for the rest of the veteran community. Go find Travis. Our guest speaker just pulled up, and now I see my wife is walking over. Actually, go see what your sister wants." Sebastian slaps me on the shoulder before striding toward the front of the Rocky Mountain Range Riders MC Clubhouse.

Turning, I take in the vast space. Sebastian has quite the setup on the outskirts of Eternity Springs. The Clubhouse is viewable from the road, but a few hundred yards behind it sits the home he shares with his daughter, Camila, and my sister, Isabella. The Clubhouse is open and inviting, with warm colors and comfortable looking leather seating. There's a wall with a variety of medals, commendations, and pictures, then a smaller display with a line of pictures and corresponding dog tags. I don't have to step closer to know it's an homage to the soldiers who've passed on.

Travis has a handful of tattoos for soldiers he lost on deployment, and Belle said Sebastian has his own ways to remember the fallen.

I hear a noise coming from the back of the Clubhouse, and see my sister walking in. She hasn't seen me, and I'm able to admire how confidently she walks. Isabella and I have always connected on a level quite different from the rest of our siblings. We're the quietest ones. The ones who don't have to star in the show, and we're happy to be on the outskirts of things. But watching how falling in love changed my sister was beautiful to see. Belle didn't lack confidence necessarily, but once she saw herself through Sebastian's eyes, she was unstoppable. She stepped into a new role in life, as well as becoming a mother to Sebastian's daughter, and it changed her for the better.

"Hey," Belle says, gracing me with a peaceful smile. "I'm so glad you decided to come."

"I'm not sure why I'm here," I admit, my voice low. "I don't know any of these guys except for Seb and Travis. It's weird."

She tilts her head to the side, studying me. "How is it weird?"

"I don't know. I don't ride. I don't know these guys. I'm doing fine. I don't need to be psychoanalyzed."

"You do understand that, in order to establish friendships, you have to actually meet people, right?" she asks sarcastically, but there's no heat in her tone. She's teasing me, in a way that only Isabella seems to be able to get away with. Even my brothers don't address the real issue at hand.

I chuckle lightly. "Is that how friendships work?"

"I know, it's a novel concept. But even if you eat some good food, and make one new friend tonight, it's a worthwhile evening. I don't think anyone will psychoanalyze you." She pauses, the corner of her lip quirking up. "Well, they won't do it anymore than your family does at dinner."

"I don't like answering questions about my time in the military," I blurt out.

Isabella nods, even though I'm sure she's shocked at my

honesty. I don't talk about my time overseas. Ever. No one knows the full details of how I almost died. "I hope you have never felt pressured by anyone in our family to share things. But, maybe being in a group like this, where there's bound to be someone who also experienced something at least remotely similar, will help you to feel more comfortable."

"Mom and Gianna are the only two who really pressure me about talking. They want me to talk to a therapist."

"Do you want to talk to a therapist?" Isabella asks pointedly.

"No."

"Let me rephrase the question. Do you think you need to talk to a therapist?" When I don't answer, she nods. "I'm not going to tell you what to do, Leo. I have absolutely no idea what you might have experienced. But I think you're hurting. Yes, I know physically, but also emotionally. I think you're angry, and sad, about how things went down. Maybe this group is a step in the right direction, where you can find some peace."

Peace.

Honestly, my concept of peace changed so significantly because of what I experienced in the Middle East. As a child, it's so easy to live in a blissfully ignorant way. We're taught early on that the United States of America is the greatest country in the world, and that we have the ability to bring peace to countries subjected to terrorist regimes, dictators, and awful living conditions. Even through my first few deployments, I still kept an optimistic mentality, thinking I was making a difference. It was only the last few missions where I began to see things for what they truly were.

People wanted me dead solely based on where I was born. They'd strap a bomb to themselves — or even worse, their child — and try to take me and my guys out. I lost track of how many services I attended for soldiers who were killed in the line of duty in Afghanistan. Seeing the boots, helmets, and rifles lined up, sometimes into double digits, for so many innocent people who were only trying to make a difference. It began to break me, and break my spirit.

That final mission, the one that took out half of our squad, was the time when I truly understood that there would never be peace in the Middle East. That thought was the last thing I remember as I faded into unconsciousness.

"Hey, man," I hear from behind me, and I turn to find my brother-in-law, Travis, smiling at me. He leans in to kiss Isabella's cheek, then slaps me on the shoulder. "Seb talked you into it too?"

"Honestly, I'm surprised none of you made Gia ask me to come," I answer dryly. "Guilting me into shit is very much in her wheelhouse."

"I don't think it's fair to say she guilts you into things," Travis says, defending his wife. It makes me love him even more. When I introduced the two of them, I never thought it would end up with a marriage and child, but I'm not unhappy about it. Most people don't stand up to me, but Travis does. I love that he'll fight for her. That's the kind of love my twin deserves.

"Asking you to attend a meeting where you might grow as a person shouldn't have to involve guilt, Leo. I fully support her guilting you into attending family events, but this group is for your benefit." Isabella speaks softly, but her chin is up. And that makes me love Sebastian even more.

"Range Riders!" I hear shouted.

"Hooah!"

"Jesus Christ," Travis mutters, rubbing his forehead. "I'll never get used to that."

I find myself smiling. "It's been a while since I've heard something like that. Makes me feel at home."

"Good," Isabella says as she shoves me toward one of the couches. "Go sit down, open your ears, and learn something."

I watch as all the men take seats around the room, with Sebastian and another man standing by a large whiteboard. A long column on the right side has a variety of numbers and dates, making me wonder what it all means. The left side lists a dozen names.

"The names are all prospects," Travis whispers, following my line of vision. "The right side is different routes we take for rides."

"We?" I ask, raising an eyebrow. "Since when have *you* ridden a motorcycle?"

His ears pinken with embarrassment. "I don't yet, but one of the guys has a sidecar, and I've gone out a couple of times. G doesn't want me to get my own wheels."

"Do you want to get a cycle?" I ask.

Travis shrugs. "I don't know. Maybe. I like the group mentality, and I think it's helped me find some friends. I didn't realize how much anger I had over the Army medically discharging me so many years ago. Being in these meetings has helped me deal with that."

"You really think you struggled?"

He nods. "I did. In all honesty, I've wanted to invite you to one of these for a while, but I was apprehensive you'd shut me down. You definitely got the worst part of the deal, and you lost more guys than I did. I didn't know how to approach you. Gianna asked Isabella to ask Sebastian about it. That's why the invite came from him."

"How many people know about me coming here?" I wonder aloud.

Travis snorts. "Knowing your family, I'm sure they all do. Knowing this *town*, I wouldn't be surprised if it makes *The Eagle Has Landed* website before morning."

I shake my head in mock disgust as Sebastian clears his throat. "Range Riders, I'd like to welcome Josh McKinnon to RMRRMC today. He was medically discharged from the Army after ten years of active duty, and has since gotten his master's in counseling. He's here to talk to us about his own experience when transitioning from active duty life back into the civilian world, as well as areas we can expect to find some difficulties."

I don't miss how Sebastian's gaze seems to drop on me as he says the word, "difficulties." Yeah, I know it hasn't been easy. Every other damn day I feel like I'm having more issues with my recovery. My body is seemingly falling apart around me, and no one really knows about it.

As Josh begins to speak, I don't realize I'm not paying attention. Instead, my mind drifts back to that mission, almost six years ago, when everything changed.

We'd been in the country for about three months. It was a boring deployment, where more time was spent shooting-the-shit than actually running missions. The one thing no one tells you about before signing up with a military branch is the concept of "hurry up and wait." Everything seems like it's rushed. Go, go, go! Then, once you get where you're supposed to go, now you have to wait. Minutes, hours, days. Weeks. You wait for new plans. Strategies. I never realized how much politics played into every fucking mission. Can't go there, that's where so-and-so is from, and he gives us intel and/or money. We have to wait until after this election, because someone somewhere ran on a no-war stance, so we can't jeopardize his campaign. That area of the country has too much oil, so avoid there. This path is too close to that country that really hates us, more than the country we're in that only mostly hates us. Great.

That day, we'd mostly been hanging out. There are only so many times you can go through your gear to ensure everything is in tip-top shape, and that day, we'd already done two workouts. We had to stay in good physical shape, but couldn't overextend ourselves, in case we got into a dogfight that required a lot of strength. And frankly, there are only so many hours in the day before it all gets incredibly boring.

So, we end up doing things like playing cards. Deployments taught me how to play poker, which still pisses my brother Dom off, because I almost always beat him on the rare occasion he hosts at his house. Some guys worked on crafty things. Others had

Kindles. One guy had a notebook where he'd write poems, then turn them into lyrics. After he got out, he sold a few country music songs.

I usually kept track of everyone, made sure our rucksacks were always organized and ready to go, and focused my energy into keeping calm. When the call came down that we needed to mobilize immediately, I remember thinking it was odd. Usually, we'd know exactly where we were going, and just needed to be given the green light to go. This time, however, we were given a completely different location and target. We scrambled, getting into our convoy in what seemed like seconds.

Less than an hour later, the world blew up.

There's something about bombs they don't fully show you in movies. I'd assumed an IED would be so astronomically loud that it would rob my vision and steal my hearing. I'd always thought it would feel like a wall of force hitting me straight in the face, but it's not like that at all.

I felt like the bomb came from inside my body when the vehicle lurched, metal shrieking, as it went airborne. One minute, the ground was there, and the next minute, it wasn't. I felt pressure pushing against me, and instead of a bright light taking away my vision, it was dull white, like all the color in the world had evaporated, or been sucked out through a giant straw. Once I could see properly again, it took every ounce of patience to focus, because everything looked like my worst nightmare. It took me seconds, or maybe minutes, before I registered the hollow ringing in my ears, because I saw my first sergeant's mouth moving, but couldn't hear a damn word he said.

The air was filled with dirt, dust, and debris. Parts of things — I hoped I never knew exactly what — had rained down on us. I tasted dirt and copper, only realizing much later that it was my own blood that filled my mouth. The scent of burned rubber and hot metal practically suffocated me.

How had I ended up outside the vehicle I was traveling in? I grabbed the helmet next to me, assuming it was mine, only then realizing it was still attached to the head of the corporal who'd only been with us for a month. I saw more unattached body parts in one minute than I'd ever expected to.

A quiet road, with no apparent life, now teemed with chaos. Sounds echoed around me as we all scrambled to protect our group. Radios blared, commands given, and urgent shouts as everyone seemed to sense the threat wasn't over. We had to take stock of ourselves, our injuries, and those who were lost.

I couldn't get up. My leg was full of shrapnel, a piece lodged in my side, and I couldn't stop staring at the helmet in my hand. Sounds reverberated around me, some controlled, and some panicked, as I looked up into the sky. The dust and dirt began to settle, leaving a muted brown haze, but I could see glimmers of blue sky. Was this the end of my life? Did I have everything settled for my family? I remember thinking I felt peace, knowing Gianna was happy with Travis, and Luca and Arianna had both found love. At least I'd gotten to see half of my siblings find happiness. I couldn't feel my leg. Cold began to seep into my bones, and I closed my eyes, slipping into emptiness.

The last thing I thought of was Ella.

Who would tell her? Would she be sad? I hope she knew how much I loved her. How I knew I'd never love anyone as much as her. How I wish I'd have one more chance to tell her, because she deserved to know.

A year later, after I'd been through countless surgeries at a military hospital in Germany, and more at Walter Reed Hospital in Washington DC, I'd run into Ella on the street. I'd only been home a few weeks, and had secretly devised a plan with Alex on approaching her. When I'd seen her wearing a baby, I'd lost it. I was ready to beg her to take me back, and she'd moved on. Helping her with her washer and dryer was the first time I'd spoken to her since.

"Dude," Travis whispers. "You okay?"

I'm jarred back to the present, and I realize my hands are gripping the fabric of my jeans so harshly my knuckles are white. Looking up, I find most of the room turned to stare at me.

"You good?" Seb asks.

"Uh, yeah," I mumble.

The speaker, Josh, cocks his head to the side, studying me. "No, you're not. What triggered you?"

"Nothing triggered me. I lost focus. What were you saying?" I stammer. My knee begins to ache, and I absentmindedly rub it.

"What's your name?" Josh asks.

"Leo."

"Rank?"

"Civilian," I snap, aggravated.

Sebastian speaks up. "He was medically discharged four or five years ago. I think he was Sergeant First Class."

"What happened?" Josh inquires.

"Convoy got hit by an IED," Travis supplies. "Half the squad didn't make it. He says he's fine, but he's not."

"And your name?"

"Travis Anderson. He's my best friend, and my brother-in-law. We were both Army Rangers, but I got out a couple of years before he did, also medically discharged. Mine wasn't the same, though. Just really fucked up my knee, and the Army didn't want me anymore."

"An injury doesn't have to be 'the same' to qualify as traumatizing, Travis," Josh says, using air quotes. "The Army medically discharging both of you over things neither of you controlled is still emotionally traumatizing."

"I know," Travis answers. "I've been in therapy. I can look back and realize it happened for a reason. I got to move here, meet his sister, and fall in love. I have no regrets."

"And you, Leo?" Josh asks, turning his gaze to me. "Do you have any regrets?"

I think for a moment. Does he mean regrets about my military career, how I handled that last mission, or how I was as a non-commissioned officer? Or is he talking about life in general? Ella's face flashes in my mind, causing me to rasp, "Too many to count."

"It's normal to have regrets. Are yours about your military career, or about your life at home?" he asks.

"Both," I say, hoarsely. The day of the mission, I'd pushed my guys to be faster as we packed up. Speed up. Let's go. What if I'd let them go at a slower pace? What if I'd taken the first truck, and had the others back a hundred yards? Would there have been less death? Fewer uniformed soldiers arriving at homes across the country to report on the death of their loved one? On behalf of the president of the United States, the Army, and a grateful nation … honorable and faithful service … deep sympathy … here, take this flag in his memory as we promise to honor his memory. It's all a bunch of bullshit.

In Germany, I had dreams of what it must have been like for my family to find out I was wounded. They never knew how bad it was. I'd waited to have anyone call them, forcing my first sergeant to promise he would only call if I didn't survive one of the surgeries. Weeks after the explosion, I finally called my parents. Even thinking it was only a busted calf and my mother was hysterical. My dad was especially quiet, which is when I knew he was struggling. He'd always cleared his throat a lot, but his complete silence was the sign that he couldn't handle what he heard.

Almost six years later, and I still wonder how Ella would have handled the news of my injury.

"Leo," Josh says quietly, and I find him kneeling next to me. I'd lost focus again, lost in memories. "I'd like to have you come into my office sometime this week. I think it's great you're here with RMRRMC, as they'll be a wonderful support for you. But you've been through an incredibly traumatic event that no one here truly empathizes with."

"Oh? And you do?" I retort.

He gives me a bitter smile and nod. "Unfortunately, I do."

Completely taken aback, I nod. Josh stands, heading back to where Sebastian sits, then turns to address the group. "It's simple to say that every veteran experiences the same things on deployment, or when they acclimate to civilian life again, but it's not the case. It doesn't matter the kind of support each of you have, how long you were active duty, or what job you have now. We all process things differently, and we can't predict how things might trigger us. Every day is a step, gentlemen. Slow and steady."

I watch as each man in attendance looks at me, most with varying expressions of sadness or pity. I don't know any of these guys. Until now, I'd have assumed I was doing okay. I have an amazing family who supports me wholeheartedly. I've been medically discharged for over four years. While doing odd jobs around the hotel isn't exactly what I had in mind for a lifetime career, at least it isn't behind a desk. I thought things were going fairly well.

And now, I'm so acutely aware of how wrong I was.

Chapter 7

ELLA

"Auntie! That man is at the door again!" Oliver shouts.

God dammit.

Jeremy will not leave me alone, and I'm two seconds away from screeching at him to read the room. I stomp to the door, throwing it open, and I find Jeremy with a smarmy grin. "Jeremy, what the hell do you want now?"

His eyes widen with surprise. "Oh, uh. Wanted to see if you could grab dinner, just the two of us."

I sigh in exasperation. "How many times have I told you that I'm not interested in dating you?"

He shifts awkwardly, and I grimace as I notice his too-tight tee shirt referencing some band I've never heard of, and a hole in his sneakers. I'd told Leo that Jeremy was mostly harmless, and I stand by that statement, but he aggravates the crap out of me. He's probably only thirty, never looks like he's showered recently, and plays loud music at all hours of the night. I'm very lucky that Oliver and Violet are deep sleepers, because the ruckus Jeremy makes certainly wakes me up.

"I mean, can't you get a sitter for the brats? It's not that big of a deal," Jeremy stammers, and my eyes narrow to slits. What the fuck did he just call them?

"You've got a lot of nerve —" I begin, but I'm stopped when a blur comes in front of me.

"Is he bothering you?" Leo snarls, his voice deep and menacing.

"Who the fuck are you?" Jeremy blurts out.

"None of your fucking business, that's who. El, is he bothering you?" Leo asks, turning his head to look down at me. I'm in shock, unable to form a coherent sentence. Why is Leo here? How did he get into the building? I catch a whiff of the same body wash he's used for as long as I've known him, and it brings back so many memories. My tongue feels sluggish as I try to respond, but all I can do is nod.

"I'm not bothering her, man. Calm down. You her brother or something?" Jeremy snaps, rolling his eyes, and I hear Leo growl in response. Tension emanates off Leo's body in waves, and I see his hands roll into fists. From what I remember Ember telling me, Jeremy moved into town about a year ago. He attempted to hit on her as well, but she put a stop to it very quickly. For some reason, nothing I say seems to hit its mark with him. Clearly he knows nothing about the Santo family, or my history with Leo, and I'm unsure how I should move forward.

Leo takes a menacing step toward Jeremy. "I am not her brother. It's apparent you don't know who I am, so let me enlighten you. I can be your worst nightmare. I have no problem making you disappear. You upset this woman, or you fuck with those kids, I will absolutely make it my mission to destroy you. Do you understand?"

"Jesus, all I did was ask her for dinner!" Jeremy exclaims, throwing his hands up in frustration.

"It seems you've asked more than once, and she's shut you down every time. This is your last hint, kid. Walk away." Leo continues to stand in front of me, watching as Jeremy slinks away, his head hung low as he mutters to himself.

"Did he just call you grandpa?" I finally ask, finding the ability to speak.

"He did," Leo says, his back still to me, but I can hear a smile in his tone. "Never been called grandpa before. Does he know you're the same age?"

"No clue. I've never given him the time of day. He only knows I'm raising Ember's kids, but she told me he'd hit on her as well, even when was she close to delivering Violet."

"Some men don't have boundaries." Leo turns to me, his eyes intense. "You tell me if he doesn't let up, okay?"

"You don't have to fight my battles for me, Leo. I'm perfectly capable of telling him no."

"If he continues, we'll go about this the legal way first," he says, disregarding me. "Alex can get you a restraining order. I'm not sure how that would impact his living arrangements, but that's not our problem. I'll look into it."

"I didn't ask for help. Why are you here?"

His gaze doesn't waiver. "I told Oliver I'd fix the lights."

"He probably forgot about it."

"I bet he didn't."

"Leo," I say exasperatedly.

"Ella," he mimics, a smile fighting to appear on his handsome face. There's more scruff on Leo than I'm used to seeing, but I notice a couple of spots where hair doesn't appear to grow. Scar tissue, perhaps? As my gaze lingers, Leo notices, raising a hand to scratch absentmindedly at his chin. I can't help but wonder how much of his body is damaged from the explosion.

"It's you! Are you gonna fix the light? And the screaming dishwasher?" Oliver shouts from behind me. Leo gives me a victorious grin, and I roll my eyes.

"I am. Are you going to be my assistant?" Leo asks, crouching down so he's eye level with Oliver. My nephew's eyes widen.

"I be your assistant?" he asks incredulously.

"Yup. You can hand me the tools. I don't think I can fix the lights without your help." He looks so earnestly at Oliver that my heart skips a beat. I'm watching Oliver, in real time, fall in love with a father figure. I just know it. He's never had a man consistently in his life, and I didn't notice until this very moment how much he must have wanted it.

"Come on!" Oliver shouts. As Leo attempts to shuffle past me, I reach out to grip his arm. He's wearing a navy long-sleeve shirt, and the tendons ripple underneath the fabric as my fingers surround his limb.

Leo inhales quite audibly, looking down at my hand, then carefully extracts himself from my touch. Suddenly embarrassed, I feel heat spread across my neck and jaw. "Oh, I'm sorry. But Leo, be careful. I don't know what you're doing here, and you certainly don't owe us anything. Don't make promises to Oliver you don't intend on keeping. He's too young to comprehend when you decide to leave again."

Leo's eyes widen as he steps away from me. "I didn't leave, Ladybug. You did. I was getting ready to propose, and you broke up with me. So don't you dare sit here and act like this was all my fault."

I gasp, flinging a hand over my mouth in surprise. Surely he's exaggerating. He couldn't have been "getting ready" to propose. I watch as he strides away, his gait off as one leg drags behind the other, following my nephew into the bedroom.

Closing the apartment door, I barely make it to the couch before I collapse. I'm transported back to our last few weeks together. Leo was home after a long deployment, and I remember him bringing up North Carolina often. My mom was struggling, feeling lost without my dad, and I couldn't fathom moving across the country. As much as I loved my brother and sister, I knew they weren't the rocks that our mom needed. Leo seemed different that visit, happier than I'd ever seen him. I'd chalked it up to him setting Gianna up with his friend, but now I wonder if he'd thought about proposing.

Leo and I broke up more than once during our twenties. I tried to understand where he was coming from. I tried to be patient. Looking back, I think I heard things I wanted to hear. I convinced myself he'd get out of the Army soon. That he'd want to be home. And maybe Leo had the opposite thought. That the only reason I wouldn't move to North Carolina was because he hadn't proposed.

In truth, I was a shell of myself every time he deployed. Each time, it was worse. I'd wake up screaming, convinced he was dead. I truly believed it would be even worse if we were married. If I moved to North Carolina, with absolutely no support system whatsoever. That when — *when* — he was killed, I wouldn't survive it. How could I be responsible for cleaning out his apartment, selling his car, and giving all the Army things back when I would be barely functioning? Could I have even gone on living, knowing the best part of me was gone? And how the hell do I explain what I thought back then to Leo today?

The more time I spent with Leo on that last visit, the more we argued. I pulled back, knowing I had to end it. Knowing if either one of us felt forced to move, it would end brutally. I needed to be in Eternity Springs, and he needed to be in North Carolina. An ultimatum would make both of us suffer. No matter how much I loved him, I couldn't keep him.

I never could have imagined how miserable I'd be afterward. I'd made peace with my decision, knowing I'd never love another man. Knowing no one could possibly compare to the one who cherished my heart for half of my life. But when I'd finally ended it, when he told me not to contact him again, part of my heart died as he walked away.

I was in the worst state of depression. I could barely eat, rarely showered, and only survived because of Ember forcing me to. Ember had double duty, taking care of me and our mom, because I couldn't do anything.

Three months after I ended things with Leo, I ended up in the emergency room. I'd lost a lot of weight, and Ember was freaked out. Consistent stomach cramps had her convinced I had an ulcer. I was miserable, truly thinking this was karma for breaking up with Leo. It wasn't an ulcer. It was much worse.

I was miscarrying our child.

In a moment of panic and heartbreak, I called Leo. He didn't pick up, and I didn't leave a voicemail. I figured he'd see my number and call me back. But he never did. I was all alone.

I hadn't known I was pregnant. I wasn't even sure I'd wanted children of my own. But the moment the doctor said he thought it was a miscarriage, I was devastated. It was a piece of Leo that I didn't know I still held, and losing that tiny piece destroyed me. What would they have been like? What traits of Leo's would have been genetically passed on? His beautiful brown eyes, his steadfast personality, or his stubbornness? What about the shape of his nose, or his loyalty? Would Leo's child want to join the military, too?

The miscarriage wrecked me, physically and emotionally. It felt like a penance. Like it was the universe serving me up a plate of reality for breaking Leo's heart. I didn't deserve to have a child. To bring life into the world, when all I was responsible for was breaking hearts. I didn't deserve to have anyone love me.

"Hey, El? Can you help me for a sec … are you okay?" Leo's voice reaches me, but it's hollow. I sense a shadow covering me as he kneels before me. "Ladybug. Look at me."

I can't. I'm lost to horrid memories.

Feeling the moment when I was no longer pregnant. The emptiness. The melancholy. Struggling to even breathe as I mourned the last connection to the only man I ever loved, and feeling like it was all my fault.

He doesn't even know about the baby. About the year that followed, when I was at my lowest. When I almost ended it all. No one would miss me. No one would notice.

"Baby," he whispers, the sound so full of sorrow that I clench my eyes tightly closed. I can't get out of the past. I feel the tears slide down my cheeks, and when he reaches up to gingerly wipe them away, I lunge to the side. *Don't touch me. You shouldn't show me compassion. I don't deserve it.*

"I need you to say goodbye to Oliver," I stammer. "I need you to go right now. Please."

"Ella. Tell me what's wrong."

I shake my head vehemently. "No. Please leave. I — you can't be here. I can't do this right now."

Leo hesitates. "I'm not leaving you alone like this. I don't even know why you're upset. Is it me? The kids? Something else?"

An odd ball of laughter bubbles up inside me as I push Leo away. "I'm fine. I'm always fine. I'll be fine. Please leave."

He falls backward onto his ass, staring up at me incredulously. "No."

"Leo, please. Just go."

"No! I'm not leaving." His voice rises considerably, and a cry comes from the baby's room. "Fuck. Was she asleep?"

"Yes, she was," I snap, trouncing around him. As I approach my bedroom door, where Violet's crib is, I whirl around to find Leo right on my heels. "Do *not* follow me in here!"

I barely make out his expression due to the tears, but he listens. I pull Violet from her crib, snuggling her into my arms, as I hear Leo murmur something to Oliver. When I don't hear the front door open and close, I know he'll stay until I come back out. He won't leave Oliver unattended. As much as that fact frustrates me, it allows me to relax for a moment, knowing my nephew is cared for.

As Violet slowly falls back asleep against my chest, I cry silently. I cry for the Ella of eight years ago, who thought she was making the best decision. I mourn for the Ella at her lowest, who knew she was unlovable. And I sob for the Ella of today, who feels lost and alone. I'm raising my niece and nephew, barely making ends meet, and I don't know how much more I can take.

*A*n hour later, I quietly open my bedroom door, not knowing what I might find. Leo and Oliver had been almost completely silent, and I'm shocked to find them playing with a container of Play-Doh toys on the floor of the living room. Not acknowledging them, I carry Violet into the kitchen to make her bottle, then pull out a frozen pizza to put in the oven for Oliver. After preheating the oven, I shuffle into the living room, quietly easing onto the well-worn leather couch.

Leo speaks first. "Are you okay?"

I sigh. "I'll be fine."

"That's not what I asked."

I sigh again, rolling my eyes. I push my hair out of my face, wondering how awful I look. "No, Leo. I'm not okay. But I'll be fine."

He carefully extricates himself from the Play-Doh toys to come sit beside me on the couch. "Would you like to talk about it?"

"No."

"The last thing I said was that you walked away."

I don't reply. We both know it triggered everything that just happened. Leo isn't dumb. Years of learning how my mind works tells me he can put two-and-two together.

"What happened after I left, El?" he finally asks.

It takes me a while to respond as I struggle to formulate the words. I could go with sarcasm. Tell him it was all death and despair. Or, I could be somewhat honest. I struggled more than I thought, and really went through a depressive period. I'm definitely not telling him the full truth.

I'm unprepared for what he says next. "Did you know my family kept tabs on you for me?"

"What?" I gasp, my head swiveling to gape at him.

He has the decency to look chagrined, rubbing his hand through his hair. "I didn't like how things ended. I knew something was eating at you, more than just moving. I was worried about you. It wasn't just about leaving your mom or Ember. Then I saw you a few years ago, with a baby on your chest, and I told them I never wanted to talk about you again."

"Oh," I whisper. "That was Oliver. I was babysitting."

"I realize that now." Leo pauses, clearing his throat. "When did your mom die?"

"About a year after we broke up." I close my eyes in pain. God, I forgot how easily he could see through me. "What does it matter now? That was years ago, Leo."

He's quiet for a moment. "It matters because you can barely look at me, and I want to know why. I need to know why you ended us. I felt like it came out of nowhere."

"And I felt like it was inevitable," I admit with a whisper. "I just couldn't do it anymore. I couldn't watch you deploy again. It destroyed me every time. If you'd convinced me to move with you, I'd have been in your home. Alone with your things. Praying you survived. Away from my entire family, with no one, and depending completely on you."

"Had the nightmares gotten worse?" he asks softly.

My head jerks to look at him. "I figured you'd have forgotten about them."

He smiles painfully. "I remember everything. I know you were really struggling with finding a balance between fear of the unknown and trusting nothing would happen to me. You'd said you dreamed about one of my brothers having to tell you I'd been killed, but I don't think I fully understood how you suffered."

"A lot of good that did, huh," I say bitterly. "I was still a basket case when I found out you were hurt."

Leo's quiet for a few minutes. "I told my parents not to tell you."

"Why?"

"Because I didn't want you to be upset."

"We'd been broken up for quite some time, Leo. That doesn't make any sense."

He leans back against the couch, placing his forearm behind his head. "I'd never wish ill will on you, Ella. Contrary to how we broke up, I still knew your heart. I knew you'd be upset, and I wanted to keep that pain away from you."

"Your parents didn't tell me," I confess. "I saw it on *The Eagle Has Landed*."

Leo growls. "That stupid fucking website. Did they at least get the facts correct?"

"I don't know." I look at him with my eyebrows cocked. "Does anyone actually know what happened to you over there? Full facts, Leo. Not whatever bullshit story you've told people, making it out to be less than it was."

Leo bites his lip as he struggles to hide a smirk. "It appears you may still know a little about *my* heart as well."

I know how he'd always chosen to protect his family. Lessening the details to make things seem safer.

When I read that he'd been injured, and that he'd had multiple surgeries at a military hospital in Germany, I knew it was worse than the article suggested. I knew that he was severely hurt, and part of me felt it was all my fault.

Chapter 8

LEO

"I knew it was worse than what the article stated," Ella says softly. Her hand twitches, only inches from mine, and I fight the urge to grab it tightly. I want this connection with her. Frankly, I need it. I know this conversation is long overdue, but it's making me feel stressed. Overwhelmed. Angry.

In an attempt to keep things light, I take on a laid-back tone. "Oh, yeah? What did you think happened?"

Ella's eyes narrow as she maneuvers Violet in her arms to rest on her shoulder, patting her back. "I know what happened, Leo."

"No, you don't," I chuckle.

"Yes, I do. I found out. Probably spent way too much time googling things. I know it was an IED. I know half the guys didn't make it. I know you were basically in a coma for quite some time before your parents even knew something had happened. Honestly, that didn't surprise me at all. You were always pretty secretive about what went on in your job."

"Most of it was top secret, El. It's not like I purposely hid stuff from you," I say, irritation evident in my tone. For the most part, Ella was always understanding about my lack of transparency about the Army. OPSEC — Operational Security — was drilled into our heads from the moment we got off the bus at basic training. Don't give out too much information. Never talk about where you're going, where you've been, or where anyone else may be. Protect the Army at all costs.

But there were times where I could hear the edge of hysteria in Ella's voice. When she knew I was going into a dangerous situation, and there was nothing I could say to give her any peace. And I hated it. I hated worrying about her. Not because it made my life harder, or it took my attention away from the mission. It broke my heart to cause her any pain. That was the only good thing that I could see about our breakup. I hoped no one told her anything, so she didn't worry. Blissful ignorance.

"Well? What happened, then?" Ella asks.

"Wrong place at the wrong time," I mumble, keeping my eyes trained on the floor. I don't want to get into this. I don't want to go back to that time.

"Seriously, Leo? That's how you're going to play this? Unbelievable," Ella huffs.

"I'm not talking about this. It's in the past. Over. No reason to discuss it."

"Well, that's an incredibly healthy outlook," she says with a bitter laugh.

"Ever heard the expression, 'no use crying over spilled milk'?" I ask.

She glares at me. "You're comparing a glass of milk to your friends *dying*, Leo. That's not a normal reaction."

I shrug, watching as Oliver smashes a bunch of Play-Doh pieces together. "Maybe if you walked a mile in my shoes, you'd see how my reaction is actually pretty normal."

"I'd love to walk a mile in your shoes, but you won't let me actually see anything," she retorts.

I sigh. "This conversation is pointless, Ella. God, how many times have we been over this through the years? You wouldn't like what you saw. You don't need to know every detail of my deployments. Yeah, they sucked. It's over. Move on."

I hear her audible intake of breath. "You know what? I think it's time you go. How much do I owe you for the light?"

My head pops up to stare at her in disbelief. "You can't be serious."

Ella stands, placing Violet in a jumping contraption next to the couch. "You did a service for me. Obviously you should expect to be paid for your time at the very least."

"El. That's bullshit, and you know it. We're friends. Friends do things for one another to help each other out."

Her eyes narrow. "We are not friends, Leo."

"Yes, we are. Pretty sure you know me better than anyone on the planet."

A flash of pain crosses her eyes before Ella schools her expression. I watch as she turns her neutral gaze to mine. "I don't think I know you at all, because the Leo that I fell in love with wouldn't gloss over what happened in Afghanistan. That man —"

I interrupt her as I rise to my feet. I take two steps until I'm toe-to-toe with Ella, my face only inches from hers, as I hiss, "Yeah, well the woman I fell in love with wouldn't have broken my heart for no fucking reason. So I guess we're both outta luck, huh, Ladybug?"

Color drains from her face, and I realize what I said. As I open my mouth to apologize, she shakes her head. "No. Get out."

"Ella …"

"Get out," she whispers. "I don't want, or need, your help. Don't come back here."

"I promised Oliver I'd fix the dishwasher," I stammer, humiliation vibrating throughout my body.

"I don't care. I'll figure it out."

"I know you don't like to get your hands dirty, El," I tease, but her expression only darkens.

"Things change. People change. I don't want to ask you again, Leo. Please leave."

Oliver looks up as I pause at the door, waving happily at me, and I wave back. Poor kid. I kinda liked hanging out with him. But it's clear Ella won't see things from my perspective, and I'll be damned if I'm going to hash through my final mission just to appease her.

Head held high, I stride out of Ella's apartment without a backward glance.

A few weeks later, on an unseasonably warm day, I'm relaxing in one of the large Adirondack chairs we have around multiple fire pits on the Everlasting property. I've been cleaning up the property this week. Lots of tree limbs, dead leaves, and various other debris are strewn throughout the acres my family owns. While it's not my most favorite task, it keeps me busy, so I do enjoy it.

But my leg is on fire.

I've lost track of how many surgeries I've been through on my leg. There was so much shrapnel that doctors worried they'd have to amputate. In some ways, I wish they had. Phantom limb pain is a thing, but there are some days where I'm in excruciating pain. It is exhausting trying to find the right medication, creams, and therapies to help me get even half of my leg strength back.

I'm at least thankful it's my left leg that's injured, because it means I can still drive without issue. This town is already too nosey, so if I had to be hand-delivered to every place I go, I'd hate it. I don't like being the center of attention on a normal day, so the thought of being the focus of the entire town because of my injury makes me want to curl up and die.

That's why I drive to Denver for physical therapy. And that's why the follow-up surgeries I've had have always been outside of Colorado. No one knows what I'm doing. Not even my parents. I keep to myself, and as long as I get the work done that they need from me, I don't feel like they have to know my everyday whereabouts.

As I reach down to rub along my scarred calf, a snowball hits me smack in the face. "What the fuck?"

"Oh, you deserved that one, jerk," Gianna retorts. Wiping the wetness off my face, I open my eyes to find my twin standing six feet away, fists on her hips in annoyance. "What the heck is wrong with you? Why did you start something with Ella?"

"I didn't start anything with her. Trust me. She about booted me out of her apartment, G," I retort.

I look down to swipe snow off my shirt, and miss the second snowball sailing at me. It slams into my chest. "Dammit, Gianna! Stop that!"

"I didn't mean you hooked up, asshole. I meant you just had to argue with her. I told you how much she's struggling, and you had to make it worse. Can you ever just think before you speak?"

"I think before I speak most of the time, actually. Just seems like the two of you bring out the worst in me," I answer, noting two more snowballs at her feet. "You prepped those before coming up to me? Cruel, Gianna. What a way to treat your injured brother."

Gianna growls as her eyes narrow. "I'm pretty sure the last time I let you play the 'woe is me' card was a good three years ago, Sergeant. If you think I'm falling for that shit now, you're incredibly mistaken."

I shrug, bending down to grab a handful of snow from behind the chair. Smashing it into a sphere, I toss it up and down a few times, while nonchalantly watching my sister. "So, you're here to bat for Ella? Protect her name or something?"

Gianna rolls her eyes. "Please. She's an adult. She can handle herself. She definitely doesn't need me fighting her battles for her. I'm here because you're my brother, and you were an absolute asshole. She didn't ask anything the rest of us haven't already asked of you. But I bet you bit her head off anyway."

I frown, thinking back. Some of the afternoon is a blur. I don't remember what the problem was with the two lights that sounded off, or how I got Oliver settled on playing with the Play-Doh. I know I shouted something, which is when Violet woke up, but I can't remember what. But I remember Ella saying she didn't know me at all, and I remember viciously responding by saying she broke my heart for no reason.

Ella and I rarely fought in high school. Even the first few years I was in the Army we did okay. Around the time we both turned twenty-two, things began to change. Maybe she saw that our paths seemed to be paralleling each other, rather than intersecting, or perhaps she knew, even then, that she didn't want to move away from Eternity Springs. Whatever the case, our fighting increased, and the number of breakups did as well.

"She wants details, G," I finally admit, looking up in the sky as I drop the snowball. Closing my eyes, I exhale deeply. "I can't go back to that time. I don't want to relive any of it."

"I don't think it's healthy for you to bottle all of this up," Gianna says quietly. I hear her boots smush through the snow as she approaches, and I feel her hand slip into mine. "I hate that I'm the only one who knows what you went through. You don't even keep in touch with any of the guys from your squad, even the ones who were allowed to stay on active duty."

"It was too painful," I confess, my voice harsh with emotion. "I didn't want to be discharged. I was forced out. I got the short end of the stick, and they were able to continue in active duty? It's bullshit."

"Leo," Gianna whispers. "It's not their fault that they weren't injured. Just like it's not your fault that you were. What about the guys who didn't make it? Was it their fault?"

"Obviously not," I retort, but my mind whirls with her first statement. It's not their fault that they weren't injured. I've honestly never thought of it that way. I guess I've been so wrapped up in what was taken from me, that I wasn't able to look at it from any other perspective.

"Belle said you had some kind of breakthrough at the RMRRMC meeting." The quick change of direction in Gianna's questioning has me chuckling.

"Definitely not a breakthrough. A mortifying moment that bordered on a panic attack? Yeah. Absolutely had that."

"Seb thought you vibed with the speaker."

I shrug. "Seb thinks everyone vibes. He's all hyped up on marital sex, and can't see anything beyond rainbows and orgasms."

Gianna smiles. "That's probably true. But Travis thought so as well. He told me he was proud of you for showing up, but that he really hoped you'd call the guy. He's worried about you."

Might as well kick me when I'm down, sis. "He has no reason to worry about me. I'm fine."

"You aren't, Leo. You haven't been since you were discharged. Every now and again, I see a little spark of the old Leo, and I wonder if you're coming back." She smiles wistfully. "But then I watch as you seem to collapse into yourself again. I'm worried, too."

I think for a minute. I don't want to go to a therapist. I don't see the point in talking about feelings and trauma. I can't change the past. Why dwell on it? I get by each day. That's really all that matters, right?

"I think you have survivor's guilt," Gianna blurts out. When my eyes meet hers, I see the sheen of tears. She sniffs hard, and I know she's trying to avoid crying. Gia is one of the strongest people I know, and she hates crying. "You're my best friend, Leo. You've been with me through everything. And I can tell you're struggling. I want you to get closure. I know you'll tell me it's in the past, and there's no sense in harping on it, but what happened in Afghanistan has dulled you. Out of the two of us, you were always the quieter one. But there was a palpable energy that rippled from you. That feeling is no longer there. It's like you're coasting along, just waiting for each day to pass. Not living, not dying. Just here."

"Wow. That's — uh, just wow," I breathe. She basically

described me exactly as I feel. Just here. I know I'm different today than I was years ago. Experiencing half of my squad dying impacted me more than I could have ever thought possible. I knew their names. Their wives and kids names. I knew what dreams each guy had for their future. Danielson wanted to open up a food truck with his dad. Brown intended to get a degree in education. Hepp was so excited about the birth of his first child, a daughter, and showed me ultrasound pictures almost every day.

Even if I'd been completely unharmed that day, I would have still come home a shell of my former self. In some ways, I was pissed that the Army dropped me as soon as it was clear I wouldn't have full use of my leg. But in others, I was relieved. I'm not sure I could have emotionally survived another deployment where we lost soldiers.

But, God, I'm angry. So fucking angry. Furious that my leg aches all the time, and sometimes my brain doesn't work like it should. Devastated that Hepp never met his daughter, and that she'll grow up never truly knowing what an amazing man he was. I'm pissed as hell that we got blown up for nothing to even happen over there. So many lives lost for no true reason, because Afghanistan remains the same today as it was when this war started over two decades ago.

"Maybe you're right," I finally rasp, my voice cracking as I clear my throat. I rub my forehead, aware of a general ache beginning, and know I'll have a full-blown migraine before long. "I'll call the guy."

"Do it right now," she commands. When I raise an eyebrow at her, she gives me a half smile. "I know you, Leo. You'll push it off until I bother you again about it. So do it now."

I sigh, pulling my wallet out of my pocket to retrieve the business card I'd stuffed in there when I left the RMRRMC meeting at Sebastian's. I'd thought about throwing it away, but couldn't bring myself to do it. Maybe I subconsciously recognized that I'd be calling the guy sooner rather than later.

Dialing the number, I practice what I'll say when his voicemail picks up. Hi, this is Leo Santo, I'm the weirdo you met at Sebastian Garcia's house the other day. The one you pegged as being full of trauma? Yeah, now my sister tells me I need therapy. So I guess we should meet.

Or maybe I'll say something even odder. Hi, I'm the dude that got triggered over nothing at RMRRMC. You think you can fix my broken noggin?

So when the guy answers the phone, saying, "This is Josh McKinnon," I overreact and blurt out the first thing that comes to mind.

"I need help with my brain."

Thankfully, Josh doesn't even make the slightest chuckle sound. "Alright. And who am I speaking with?"

"Leo Santo."

"Leo. From Sebastian's. I'm glad you called. I've actually been thinking about you."

"I bet you say that to all the broken veterans who call you."

"No one is broken, Leo. A little banged up, yes. But nothing that we can't work through. Have you ever heard of Kintsugi?"

"Sounds vaguely familiar," I answer.

"It's the Japanese art of taking something broken, and filling it with gold. It's used mostly on pottery. You can't bring the pottery back exactly as it was; instead, it's changed for the better. It's all about finding beauty in the flaws."

"I don't think any of my flaws are beautiful," I confess quietly. I feel Gianna's hand slide into mine, squeezing it gently. She lays her head on my arm, giving me her quiet strength, and I feel a wave of peace come over me.

"I think you're more resilient than you believe, Leo. Your story doesn't mean you're broken. It means you have an opportunity for renewal."

"How can you sound so sure?" I ask. "You don't even know me."

"I know enough," Josh says easily. "I know what deployments

are like, and I know the kind of man you are based on what Sebastian and Travis told me. And, to be honest, I researched the event that took out half your team. I know that had to be incredibly traumatizing. I saw that you lost five soldiers."

"Six," I whisper. "One died a few months afterward, due to injuries sustained from the IED." Six out of eleven on our squad. Half gone in a blink of an eye.

"I'd like to meet with you in person as we develop a rapport. Once we're more established in our therapist and patient relationship, we can move to telehealth appointments if you'd prefer that way."

"I'm fine with either way, as long as it isn't a group session." The thought of being forced to explain my feelings in front of a bunch of people I don't know makes my skin crawl.

"I don't do any group sessions, because I don't like them that much either," Josh says with a chuckle. "I prefer to have one-on-one appointments. I want to know the real you, not a mask you wear around others. And I know it's more comfortable to speak freely when no one else is around."

"Alright. So, when can we meet?" I ask.

"Let's talk availability."

Gia squeezes my hand, and I look down to find her beaming at me. She mouths, "I'm proud of you."

I'm kinda proud of myself too.

Chapter 9

It's been a few weeks since I've seen Leo, but it's as if he's watching me somehow. I feel him everywhere. Every memory we made seems to bubble up now. Thoughts I'd buried years ago. I'm frustrated, angry, and more confused than ever.

Gianna asked if I'd have dinner with her and her son tonight, and I almost canceled. The thought of facing Leo's twin is a little overwhelming. Our friendship has been strained since I broke things off with Leo, and I don't know how to talk to her now. Plus, while she and Leo are fraternal twins, their similarities are obvious. Same eyes, smile, and cock of the head. A ton of the same expressions. They both have the Santo drive that all the kids got, but Gia's a little more type-A than Leo.

Carson, Gianna and Travis's son, is only a year or two older than Oliver, and they've yet to meet. Ember didn't exactly run in the same circles as Gianna, and certainly would never step foot in Everlasting Inn and Spa, as she considered it enemy territory after my last breakup with Leo. Actually, she despised the place. While she liked Leo, she thought the rest of the family was stuck up. I never had that impression. I guessed she probably had the hots for one of Leo's older brothers, and when they weren't interested, she decided to hate them. It's an odd kind of girl math: I like you, but you don't like me, so I hate your family.

We're meeting at a small restaurant on the outskirts of Eternity

Springs because we know it will be quieter than the places in the center of town, and I'm thankful for that. Oliver has been off all day. Lots of meltdowns, and a refusal to have quiet time in his room. Occasionally I can convince him to nap, but those days are becoming fewer and fewer, so I transitioned to quiet time instead. It gives me a little time to breathe. On weekdays, when Oliver is out of school, he hangs with my nanny, Lauren. Since today is Saturday, he's grumpily trudging along beside me.

Entering the restaurant, I find Gianna and Carson already at a large booth. She waves energetically when she spots us, and I amble over with Violet's car seat on my arm, dragging Oliver behind me. He didn't want to come tonight. I'm hoping his sour mood improves once he sees Carson.

When I see Carson duck behind Gianna, I'm aware that tonight may not go according to plan. "Yours isn't happy either?"

"No," Gia sighs. Her tight curls bounce all around her face, giving her a youthful look, but I see the bags under her eyes. "I guess even older kids can have sleep regression periods. He's been waking up at three in the morning. I end up going to work by five because I can't sleep, then crashing in a spare room at the hotel after lunch."

"What if there aren't any vacancies?" I ask as I carefully place Violet's car seat against the wall, then slide into the booth. I grab Oliver's arm, dragging him in beside me, so I'm able to reach both of them whenever needed. Oliver glares at Carson, who buries his head in his mother's shoulder.

"I will sleep in my car. I have no issues with that. I'm too tired to care most days, and our house is too far away," she laughs, sliding an arm around her son, patting his back. "Carson, this is Oliver. He's four. How old are you?"

"No," Carson replies.

Gia looks at me with a lopsided smile. "Can't fault him for that answer. I don't want to tell anyone my age either."

"That's because we're old," I complain. "Honestly, I don't judge you one bit for sleeping in your car. My lunch break three times this week was a nap at my desk. Violet is getting up a lot right now as well."

"Is there something in the air? Mercury in retrograde? A sun spot? Leap year? Something?" Gia wonders aloud.

"Whatever it is, I'm tired, and I don't have the energy to research it."

Our server comes over to take our drink orders, and we resume chatting. Neither of us push the boys to interact. We wait until they're ready. Carson has the guts to speak first.

"I'm older than you," he says.

Oliver glares at him. "Well, I'm taller than you."

"No you're not!" Carson shouts, making Gia slap a hand over his mouth.

"No shouting!" she hisses, eyes darting from side to side as she watches to see if anyone is listening. Her face screws up in distaste as she removes her hand, wiping it on the front of Carter's shirt. "He licked me."

Gross. I stifle a laugh as I look down at Oliver. "Bud, Carson is probably taller than you, but mostly because he's older. When you're both adults, you might be taller. Or you could be the same height. And it really won't matter who is taller."

"Fine," he grumbles. "Do you like *Bluey*?"

Carter's eyes light up. "I do like *Bluey*!"

I pull out my phone, opening the *Bluey* app. Carson stands at the edge of the table, as both boys whisper about the game and show. Honestly, whoever came up with *Bluey* is a damn genius. It's the only surefire way to settle Oliver down when he's really over-stimulated.

After we order our food, Gia leans over the table, lowering her voice. "How are you doing? Are things better now?"

I shrug. "I guess. Nothing better, nothing worse. That's really all I can ask for at this point."

"Have you talked to Leo yet?"

I shake my head. "After I unceremoniously kicked him out, I'm not expecting an unplanned visit. We don't even have each other's phone numbers."

Her eyes widen. "You changed yours? Wait. You didn't. I've called you."

"No, mine is the same, but I assumed he'd have changed his by now."

"Nope. Still the same. He even kept it on for that entire last deployment, which I assume was for you to call if needed. Usually he turns it off, and only texts our family chat. He'd call occasionally, but it was pretty rare."

"I'm well aware of that," I mutter. The word "deployment" leaves such a sour taste in my mouth. Sometimes I'd go a few weeks without a word from him. I knew he wasn't doing it purposely. He was on a mission, or somewhere in the country where they didn't have communication set up. But it drained me, both emotionally and physically. I'd usually lose twenty or so pounds with every deployment, because I couldn't stomach food.

"Why didn't you tell either of us you were suffering so much?" Gianna asks quietly, reaching over to lay her hand over mine.

"What was I supposed to say? It wouldn't have changed anything. Leo couldn't come home, and it may have screwed up his mission if he wasn't completely focused."

"What about me?" she asks.

"You were newly in a relationship at the end. I wasn't going to butt in with my problems."

"But what about all the other deployments? El, he was gone half the time. I know you could have talked to me about it."

"I didn't know how," I confess, my eyes welling with tears. "I couldn't comprehend my own emotions a good majority of the time, so I didn't know how to express them to you. Plus, I figured you'd tell Leo anyway, and I didn't want him to worry. He also kept telling me he'd get out of the Army after that deployment, so I thought the end was coming. I wouldn't have to admit I was struggling, because he'd come home. And then he'd reenlist again."

"He told you he was going to get out?" Gia asks, her voice low. I should note the danger in her tone, but I'm too caught up in a memory. The final time, when I truly knew it was up, was when he'd taken me to dinner. We were in the center of the restaurant, a swanky place in Denver, and I'd hoped he was about to tell me he was moving home. How maybe the gossip website was wrong, and he'd propose on the spot. Instead, he announced he'd reenlisted for four more years. I'll never forget that feeling, knowing he'd told me in public so I couldn't react how I wanted.

"I knew I'd never be first in his life. And that's fine. Really, it is. I'm glad I found out when I did. Leo never made me feel like his job was better than mine, or it was more important than me, but what was I supposed to think? I certainly can't tell him not to go liberate a town that had been taken over by the Taliban, now could I? But I had to think about things. Because if we'd gotten married, and had kids, where would they fall on his priority list? How do you explain to a child that their father loves their job more than them?" I shake my head bitterly. "I just couldn't do it anymore. I wanted a partner, not a guy who swings into town a couple of times a year. What we had wasn't sustainable, no matter how much I'd hoped it would be."

"Should have made sure there was an icicle in that snowball," Gianna mutters. "Maybe it would knock some sense into the jackass."

"What?"

"Nothing. Oh, well, what do you know! Speak of the devil!" she grins wickedly as she waves to someone behind me. I turn to find Leo staring at us, the color draining from his face. My heart squeezes just seeing him. In a worn pair of jeans, a henley, and a red checkered flannel, he is the epitome of sex appeal. I know what he has under all of that, and I can only assume it's gotten better with age.

"Leo!" Oliver shouts, running to him, his arms outstretched. Leo quickly catches my nephew, hugging him tightly. "I missed you."

"I missed you too, buddy," Leo answers, his eyes on mine. The scene is too poetic, too poignant, and I turn away. What I wouldn't give to see Leo hug our child. The child I lost.

Leo looks over to where Carson is completely focused on the *Bluey* episode. and chuckles. "Good to know where I stand in Carson's heart."

"He never gets screen time, so he will pick it over anyone," Gianna answers, then turns to me as she lowers her voice. "You okay?"

"No," I answer truthfully, sliding out of the booth. "Can you watch the kids? I need to hit the restroom."

After Gianna nods, I keep my gaze averted as I rush past Leo, speed-walking around the restaurant to the other side. For once, I'm relieved at the setup of this place, because it puts me as far away from Leo as physically possible. I head into a stall, thankful this restaurant has actual toilets with lids, and I close it quietly. Sinking down to sit on the lid, I let out a pained breath.

Maybe I should move. I won't sell Purrfect Books. But moving out of Eternity Springs would at least give me a little more distance from Leo. The Santo family is basically royalty here, and right now, he's everywhere. So many years have gone by, and I'm still not over him. How can I move past the love of my life when I'm forced to be near him?

I sniff, feeling the telltale sign of a sob moving up my throat, and I struggle to hold it in. I don't know how thick these walls are, or when some other patron might come into the bathroom. If I'm caught crying while Leo is in the restaurant, it'll be on *The Eagle Has Landed* before bedtime. Hell, maybe within the hour. It'll be some ostentatious headline like "War Hero Refuses Rekindling with Disgraced Bookstore Owner" or "Leo and Ella, Part Six?" I really don't want to be on the front page of the website. Again.

When I hear the door open and close, but no detectable footsteps, I know he's followed me in here. The door locking reverberates across the tile floor.

"Ella."

I sharply inhale, his gravelly voice dragging across every inch of my skin. God, I hate how I respond to him. "What?"

"Come out here."

"No." The word comes out with a stubborn snap, making Leo chuckle.

"Yes."

"Why?"

"Because I need to see your face."

"No, you don't. I'm fine."

"Funny, that's what you said the last time, and you most certainly were not fine."

"Well, I lied that time."

"And you're lying now."

"No, I'm not." I pause, waiting for his rebuttal, but nothing comes. "Alright. I'm lying a little."

His loud laughter makes me jump. "Get out here, Ladybug."

Grumbling about how he's being an alpha male asshole and demanding shit, I slowly stand. Opening the door, I find Leo leaning back against the counter, arms crossed across his chest, and unlaced boots crossed against the floor. He's smirking, but it's not one of victory or control. It's one of peace and acceptance.

I stand at the entrance to the stall, not allowing myself to step even one foot closer to him. I have an overwhelming desire to jump him, latch my legs around his waist, and tell him to make me forget all of my problems, if only for tonight. I know I'd regret it tomorrow, but I'd certainly enjoy it right now.

"Why'd you run in here?" Leo asks quietly. "Tell me the truth, not some bullshit about you wanting to avoid me."

"I did want to avoid you," I answer haughtily. The corner of his mouth turns up, but he doesn't speak. God dammit. This man could always out-patience me. "Honestly? Gia said something, and it made me remember that time you took me to dinner in Denver so you could tell me how you'd reenlisted. I knew you did it there so I couldn't make a scene. Looking back, I knew at that moment our relationship was doomed. I'd never factor in your life decisions, and I didn't like that. I didn't want to be an afterthought in your world, Leo. I wanted us to make decisions together, and you constantly took that opportunity away from me."

His eyes widen with my admission. "You thought I didn't take you into consideration with decisions I made? Baby, you're the only person I ever thought of. Yeah, I could have handled things better. I didn't intend to blurt out about the reenlistment at that dinner. I was going to ask you to move in with me. Every month apart was slowly killing me. But I loved my job, and I truly thought I was making the world a better place, as cliché as that sounds. But I wanted you there. Always."

"Why didn't you tell me that, then?" I ask quietly, so quietly I wonder if Leo even hears me.

He gives me a weary smile, his shoulder slumping. "Maybe I knew you'd never move to North Carolina. Or maybe I feared you'd break up with me. It was easier to keep the status quo than rock the boat."

I look down at his boots, at the familiar pattern of stitching on the sides. "Did I get you those?"

He nods with a chuckle. "Yeah. Finally got them broken in."

"Leo, I gave those to you ten years ago."

Leo winks. "Took longer than I thought it would."

I sigh with an exaggerated huff. "You know, for someone with years of military experience, it's shocking that you've got them unlaced. You're bound to trip and break your neck one of these days."

His smile drops slightly. "It's hard for my leg to bend at the knee sometimes. So it's easiest if my shoes are all basically slip-ons."

My heart jumps to my throat. "You can't bend it?"

"Not really, no. My calf is all fucked up, and I've had so many surgeries on my leg that I've got a lot of scar tissue built up. It's not the prettiest."

"How have I never heard about this? Did everyone hide it from me or something?" I ask, hurt evident in my tone.

Leo's eyes meet mine solemnly. "Besides Gia and my parents, you're the first person I've told any specific details."

I gasp, hands coming to my mouth in shock. As tears fill my eyes, I do what I wanted to do only minutes ago. I rush to him, throwing my arms around his neck, and he lifts me so my legs can wrap around his waist. Burying my face in his neck, the familiar scent of his cologne filling my senses, I'm overcome with emotion. His arms tighten around me as he rests his head against mine.

It's been ages since I've been in Leo's arms. One of the only places I ever felt was completely safe, and irrevocably mine. I can't remember the last time I'd even received a hug from a man. Possibly with my brother at my sister's funeral. Before that … well, probably the last time I was privileged enough to be held by the man holding me now.

I never truly understood how perfectly Leo's embrace was until I couldn't experience it anymore. Even when he was deployed, I knew he'd come home. There was a stopwatch counting down, letting me know I'd experience it again. And now, as I feel a tremor rack through Leo's body, I wonder if he's feeling the same way.

How has he gone this long without telling anyone about his injuries? Why did he keep it bottled in for so long? And why the hell did his family let him get away with it? Anyone can see he's hurt. Leo has always held emotions in, and he's not one to admit when he's hurt. Surely I can't be the only one to see the pain in his eyes or the limp as he drags his leg. Tears fall as I think about this poor man, feeling lost and alone, finally admitting to me that he's been in pain for years.

"Why?" I finally rasp, squeezing my arms around his neck tighter, then shivering when his hot breath hits my neck.

"Who would I tell?"

"Your siblings."

I feel him shake his head against me, sending another shiver when his lips brush against my skin. "They wouldn't have handled it well. Too much chaos at home. Hannah and Arianna were new moms. Dom's ex-wife was causing trouble. Alex was struggling. Knowing the extent of my injuries would have been salt to the wound. All they knew was my calf was messed up."

I raise my head, pulling back to look in his eyes. I used to get lost in his irises, mostly dark brown but with golden specks toward the outside edge. I could always see love there. Now it's mostly pain, confusion, and sadness. "Why haven't you told them that you're still struggling?"

His mouth opens and closes once, then his eyes dart to the side as he forces out a loud breath. "Because they'd look at me with pity, and I can't stand that. I hate feeling like I've let them down. I'm supposed to be the strong one."

"Is that why no one knows? Because you think they'd feel sorry for you?" I ask quietly, and he nods. "They'd hurt *for* you, Leo. That's what loved ones do. They'd want to take away the pain from you if they could."

His gaze snaps back to mine. "I don't want that either. I just want to feel normal."

"Then why did you tell me?" I utter.

"Because you're the only person who has ever accepted me as I am."

This poor man. "Leo, that's not true at all. Everyone in your family loves you so much. You could have been honest with them. They have to know something is going on."

"They never ask, so I don't tell them."

"You're holding it against them that they're respecting your boundaries?" I ask incredulously. I try to unwrap my legs from

Leo's waist, but he clamps his hands down on my thighs, holding me in place. His fingers flex against me, and I struggle to keep my breathing normal. "You've always held things in. Everyone knows this. So they're waiting for you to come to them. They don't want to push you away."

His forehead drops to mine, and I wait for him to respond. It's been years, but I know how his brain works. He's working out every available answer before he'll choose what he thinks is the best one. "Everyone has enough on their plate, Ladybug. I don't want to add to the stress. I've got sixteen nieces and nephews now. Sixteen! I honestly don't know how my parents keep track of them all. Shit is constantly falling apart at Everlasting, and I'm the one that has to put it back together. Alex and I were talking about getting a woodworking business together —"

"Oh my God," I interrupt, delighted at that last detail, "you'd be so perfect at that! You always loved messing around with wood-carving. What would you guys focus on?"

A tiny sparkle comes back in his eyes as he lifts his head to look at me, a peaceful smile popping onto his face. "Cabinets and furniture, mostly. But I think we'd be open to some custom projects, depending on the customer."

"I still have that jewelry box you made me for my twentieth birthday," I tell him, grinning. "It's been locked for a few years, because I can't remember how to open it anymore."

Leo chuckles. "That doesn't surprise me in the slightest. Your ability to follow directions leaves a lot to be desired."

I gasp in mock surprise. "I'll have you know, I singlehandedly put three of the bookshelves together in Purrfect Books."

"Aren't there around fifteen or twenty bookshelves?" he asks.

"That's beside the point. I did three by myself. I deserve accolades, dammit."

His grin widens. "Alright. Well done, El. You're doing an exceptional job at adulting."

"You know what? I fucking am!" I shout gleefully, getting a bark of laughter from Leo. "I'm keeping two children alive, I haven't burned any food this week, and I haven't had to sell my business. I'm peak adulting right now."

"Burning food?" he asks, letting go of my thighs, and I reluctantly slide my legs from around his waist. The fact that this entire conversation has happened nose-to-nose is surreal, but I've always felt more comfortable doing just about anything with Leo than I ever wanted to feel away from him.

"Okay. I'm honestly not the best cook, but my oven is also a bit temperamental." I look up to find his grin gone, and the intense Leo back in place.

"Define 'temperamental,'" he says, with air quotes.

"Well, half will be burned, and half will be uncooked." It's aggravating to cook something that may work out or may not. I'm thankful Violet is still on mostly formula, and Oliver is in a phase where the only acceptable foods are dinosaur chicken nuggets, macaroni and cheese, and fresh fruit, so I've basically stopped using the oven. If it can't be cooked on the stovetop or in the microwave, I'm not making it.

"The heating element probably went out, or is going out, but it's an easy fix. If you tell me the model, I can get a new one for you," Leo offers.

"Oh, is that it? I can probably handle that. Does it just plug in somewhere in the oven?" I ask, frowning when he bursts into laughter.

"No, Ladybug. It doesn't plug in. I'll handle it. Just text me the model number."

I stare at him in disbelief. I assumed Gianna was mistaken. "Do you still have the same number?"

He nods. "Kept it in case you ever tried to reach me."

Chapter 10

I can see the wheels turning in her head. She's confused.

I'm surprised she thought I'd change my number. I'll admit, I thought about it. It was easy to think about how it might hurt her, if she ever did reach out, to know she couldn't contact me. But hurting her wouldn't change a damn thing. So I kept the number. Occasionally, I'd change my voicemail message to be something ridiculous that only she'd understand, like that Blake Shelton song. After a ridiculously drunk night two years after Ella broke up with me, I left a message that said, "leave a message if you love ladybugs."

The one fucking time Luca decided to actually call me, he hears that, and he's never let me live it down. Pretty sure he still has me nicknamed as Ladybug in his phone.

In any case, I'm surprised to receive a text from Ella later that night. I left not too long after telling her to text me, even though Gia asked if I wanted to stay for dinner. While Ella didn't look opposed to that idea, and Oliver was certainly on board, I didn't want to crash their dinner. I was only there to pick up a takeout order and head back to my house.

Today was nuts. While Dom is the CEO of Everlasting, my dad still likes to go around and tinker with shit when he's bored. When I received a frantic call from my mother that Dad had messed with the reservations system, I knew I was in for a rough day. Honestly, the system is outdated, and Dad barely understood it when it was installed years ago. It needs to be updated, and he should be locked out of the computer system altogether. Technology and my father do not mix, but I'm certainly not allowed to tell him that.

The problem with fixing the reservation system is I had to do it at the concierge desk. That meant every guest who came in interacted with me. I'm introverted to a fault, but when I'm forced to make small talk with people I don't know, I get awkward and over-stimulated really quick. It was a very uncomfortable day, which culminated in me having to deal with draining and treating one of the indoor hot tubs because someone thought it would be a good idea to take a diaper-wearing child into it. Regular diapers fill up, then sort of explode. Swim diapers are different. Not only was this a regular diaper, but the child had an accident as well. It was not my idea of a fun time, but the guy who usually maintains the hot tubs and hot springs had already gone home. I'm basically the jack-of-all-trades for Everlasting, so I had to get it cleaned up.

I don't mind the work. It's better than doing something monotonous behind a desk. But I certainly never thought I'd be part IT, janitor, groundskeeper, and front desk attendant all in one. This isn't the future I envisioned for myself when I became an adult. But, frankly, nothing I thought about at eighteen ended up coming true.

As I'm cleaning up my dinner after watching a rerun of *Criminal Minds*, my phone chimes with a text.

Ladybug: Hi.

Me: Hi.

Ladybug: How are you?

Me: Okay. How are you?

Ladybug: Alright. Just got the kids down for the night. I'm hoping Violet only wakes up once.

Me: When do infants usually sleep through the night?

Ladybug: According to all the research I did, it varies. But she's usually up two or three times during the night. My sister never talked about it, so I don't know if she's always been this way.

Me: I can ask my siblings, but I have to assume there's a spectrum where they'll say every answer under the sun.

Ladybug: Gia said Carter had waves where he struggled, so hopefully this will go away. I've learned to live with five hours of sleep a night.

Me: That's not healthy.

Ladybug: I'm aware. It is what it is. I don't have much of a choice. Certainly can't let her scream, or she'll wake the entire building up.

Me: That dipshit from upstairs give you any more trouble?

Ladybug: No. He glared at me the other day, though. I think you scared him.

Me: Good.

Ladybug: Anyway, the stove is a Frigidaire, and the model number is FEB556CESH.

Me: Jesus. It's from 2008.

Ladybug: I knew it was old. It basically snarls at me when I turn it on.

Me: Are there any appliances in there that DON'T make an odd noise?

Ladybug: I plead the fifth, in fear that anything currently working might hear me and decide to break down in solidarity with its comrades.

Me: May the odds be ever in your favor.

Ladybug: LEO! Did you just make a Hunger Games reference?

Me: I have been known to have a sense of humor from time to time.

Ladybug: I didn't think you paid attention when we saw it in the theater. You were definitely not looking at the screen at all.

Me: Yes, I believe I focused on you the entire time. It's your fault you wore that cute, pleated skirt with the cherries on it.

Ladybug: I can't believe you remember the exact skirt.

Me: Hard to forget. I'm pretty sure I dreamed about that skirt for quite a few years after that. And I remember a lot about that movie, because you made me come in my pants right at the end.

Ladybug: (blushing)

Me: You blushed that night too.

Me: When I licked you off my fingers.

Ladybug: Holy shit, Leo.

Me: I'd apologize, but I'm not sorry. You were wrapped around me a few hours ago, baby. It got me reminiscing.

Ladybug: It made me think about things too.

Me: Like what?

Ladybug: Shit. Oliver is up. I have to go.

I lean back against the couch as I adjust myself in my jeans. Memories are flooding in, and I'm the most turned on I've been in years. Every first time has been with Ella. My first kiss. First time seeing breasts in real life. Feeling a woman's pussy, and experiencing a blow job. As cliché as it sounds, we had sex for the first time at our junior prom. It was enlightening to say the least.

Sex with Ella was unreal. Yeah, I don't have anything to compare it to, but I can't fathom anyone being better. The connection we have — had — was untouchable. Even after being apart this long, I haven't been able to sleep with another woman. We were broken up, but the thought made me feel like I'd be cheating on her. She was always the one for me, and I know she'll always be the one.

Our conversation tonight went off the rails pretty quickly. I had no idea a *Hunger Games* reference would bring up that memory, but it did. I was home on leave for a month, and Ella dared me to get her off in public. Our small town doesn't have a movie theater, thankfully, so we drove into Denver. I figured we'd make out a little, I'd get her off, and then we'd focus on the movie. Honestly, I'm not sure how I remember a damn thing about the film, least of all an actual quote. As soon as I felt Ella clench around my fingers, whispering my name against my lips as she came, I became feral. I couldn't stop touching her. I lost track of how many times she came, including once on my tongue as I kneeled on the floor, desperate to drink every bit of her up. At the end, all she had to do was squeeze my dick through my jeans, whisper in my ear that she wanted to give me a blow job on the way home, and I came in my pants for the first time since I was a teenager.

Closing my eyes, I let my mind drift back to that theater. How Ella looked. The scent of the vanilla lotion she always used, and how her hair felt against my skin when she rested her head against my arm. The sweet mewls and moans she'd make as she came, each time with a look of wonder, like she couldn't fully understand how I'd played her body like a fiddle. I knew every inch of her perfectly, and I bet I could still find each perfect erogenous zone that got her off the fastest.

Groaning, I palm my dick again. Jesus, I'm harder than I've ever been. Unbuttoning my jeans, I slide my hand inside, hissing when I hit the tender tip. A drop of pre-cum has already dripped out, and I drag it down my length, gripping it tightly. I envision it's Ella, riding me, her perfect tits bouncing in front of my face. I drop my phone on my chest as I imagine gripping her hips, adjusting her so she rides me harder. Deeper. "Fuck, Ella, yes. Like that."

If she were here, I'd reach up to grab a handful of her hair, wrapping it around my fist, dragging her down to kiss me. God, I've dreamed about her mouth. Those exquisite dusty rose lips, perfectly pouting and best when wrapped around my cock. I'd kiss her deeply, reveling in the feeling of her tongue circling mine. "Missed kissing you, baby. Get on your knees and swallow."

She'd scramble to her knees, sucking me down to the base. We'd worked up to it, until she could take all of me in her mouth. Every guy I'd ever talked to about sex had whined about his woman never giving him head, but Ella loved it. She'd be mad at me if I didn't let her. The vision of her on her knees, tears in her eyes, was one that got me through too many deployments. That look was imprinted in my memory, and it still has the power to unfurl me.

"Fuck, yes," I groan, coming harder than I've come in ages. I let out one last moan as I exhale, feeling sated for the first time in years. Until I hear a faraway voice say, "Leo?"

My eyes pop open, and I look down to find my phone, face up, with a connected call. To Ella.

It shows the call has been connected for two minutes, which means she heard the whole thing.

"Leo, I know you can hear me," she snaps, irritation evident in her tone. I reach to the side, grabbing a takeout napkin to wipe myself off, then pick up the phone.

"Ella."

"Did you seriously call me to jack off?"

"Not intentionally, no," I murmur, feeling embarrassment heat my face.

"Well, what were you thinking about?" Ella asks, her voice much quieter. Wait. Did it turn her on to hear me come? Did I say something out loud? "You told me to swallow. Were you still thinking about that night in the movie theater?"

"Yes. But you didn't go down on me that night. I went down on you," I answer, my voice husky. I'm already getting hard again.

"Do you remember how many times I came that night?" she asks breathlessly.

"Not the exact number. Are you touching yourself, Ladybug?"

"Yes."

"Did it turn you on to hear me come?"

"God, yes," she moans.

"How are you touching yourself?"

"Touching my clit," she murmurs.

"How many times did you come that night, baby? At the movie, and then afterward. In my car."

"Eleven."

Shit. I didn't think it was that many. "Guess I've got a number to beat. Think I can make you come twelve times?"

"I'd settle for one, if I'm being honest," she blurts out.

"Oh, my needy girl. You know what I'd do if I were there right now?" I ask, gripping my throbbing cock tightly.

"Please tell me. Please, Leo."

"I do love it when you beg," I murmur. "Such a good girl."

Ella moans incoherently, making me remember how much of a praise kink she's always had. "I know what you need, sweet girl. You need my tongue. You want me lashing that clit. Sucking it, maybe nibbling on it a little. You like a teeny bit of pain with your pleasure, don't you?"

"Oh, God, Leo, yes! I'm coming! I'm coming!" she cries out, and when she lets out a guttural moan that I feel down to my soul, I come again, groaning as my release coats my abdomen. We're both silent for a few minutes as we come down from our respective highs, and then Ella lets out a tiny giggle. "I should be embarrassed about that, but I'm oddly not. I really needed that."

I chuckle in response. "Guess I did, too."

"Should it feel weird?" Ella asks softly. "It's … us, and we have so many things that we should talk about."

I sigh. "I don't know. It's not like we can ignore the chemistry we've always had. I don't regret what just happened, and I hope you don't either."

"I don't regret it. But I should probably get going. Night, Leo."

"Night, Ladybug."

Rendezvous a la the public bathroom

Imagine my surprise when I received a picture of Leo Santo following Ella Langley into the women's restroom at Dixie's Cafe. My source says they were locked in the bathroom for at least twenty minutes, and when they emerged, Ms. Langley's lipstick was smudged, and Mr. Santo escaped into the men's restroom immediately.

In other news, we have another marmot theft to report. Mason absconded with Marybeth Nix's decorative rug she leaves by her front door. He was seen dragging it into the forest behind Everlasting. If anyone sees it, please let Marybeth know.

Me: If I ask you a question, do you promise not to give me shit about it for the rest of your life?

Luca: Why MY life? Why not the rest of YOUR life?

Me: Because if you give me shit for anything longer than a day about this, I'm murdering you and making it look like an accident. So think wisely, dickhead.

Luca: Fine. What can I help you with, Ladybug?

Me: I'll let that pass, because I need some help.

Luca: You've come to the right place!

Me: You don't even know what I need help with.

Luca: If it involved moving a body, you'd ask Alex. If it was business related, you'd go to Dom. Anything about food would be Belle, and anything else you'd ask Gia about. Since you're coming to me, I know it has to do with sex.

Me: How'd you get to that conclusion?

Luca: Everyone referred to me as a man slut for years, man. I know how this family thinks. I may be a happily married man, but I was once a ho. So go ahead, ask your question.

Me: You ever accidentally call someone while you were jerking off, and they heard you? Then basically asked you to help them finish, too?

Luca: I …

Luca: How the fuck …

Luca: WHY IS THIS NOT IN THE GROUP CHAT, LEO?

Me: Don't you dare put this in there! I hate that fucking chat, Luca. You know that.

Me: God dammit.

Me: Why aren't you answering?

Luca: Sorry. I forgot you took yourself out of there the last time I pissed you off. Adding you back in now.

Me: NO!!

LUCA SANTO HAS ADDED LEO SANTO TO THE CHAT.

Me: God dammit.

Dom: Oh, how the mighty have fallen!

Dom: This may be the best day of my life.

Alex: I thought that was when you married Kate.

Dom: She'll understand.

Me: What did he tell you?

Luca: I didn't TELL them anything.

Alex: Screenshots are forever, my guy.

Sebastian: I haven't been married into this family for that long, but this seems like a really unhealthy relationship between all of you.

Travis: You get used to it.

Stone: No, you don't.

Stone: I've tried to leave, but short of blocking every last one of these assholes, Luca keeps putting me back in here.

Me: You guys can get a divorce. I'm forced into this by blood.

Dom: Well, we can't get to helping you with advice until you tell us who the lucky lady is. Someone we might know?

Me: Does that detail really matter?

Alex: It does if it's who we think it is.

Travis: IT'S ELLA! Gianna confirmed.

Me: What the fuck?

Me: She went to my sister to gab about this? Fucking hell.

Me: Couldn't she have gone to anyone else? Now I can't look G in the eye. Hell, I can't look any of you in the eyes.

Luca: Trav, did Ella complain about anything?

Travis: According to G, it was "hot as hell" and she was "unprepared for it," whatever that means.

Me: It means I literally started jerking off, talked out loud like it was Ella, she heard, and then I came.

Dom: Seriously. Best day of my life.

Luca: I feel awful for your wife and children, Dom. Like … really awful.

Alex: And then she asked you to reciprocate?

Me: For the most part, yeah.

Stone: And you did.

Me: Fairly certain the screenshot explained that.

Sebastian: Did you ever call that therapist from the RMRRMC meeting?

Sebastian: I'd say he'll have a lot to unpack about this.

Me: It's nice to know you hate me, Seb.

Sebastian: What? No, I don't!

Luca: YOU'RE GOING TO A THERAPIST?

Dom: Oh, that tracks. You could use one.

Alex: I don't want to shit on you right now, and I also don't want to make you uncomfortable, but I'm proud of you. It takes a lot of guts to admit you need someone to talk to.

Luca: This might be the best day of my life.

Sebastian: Now I understand.

Sebastian: My bad.

Me: I really hate you all.

Me: Except Stone. He stayed quiet.

Stone: Appreciated. Next haircut is on me.

LEO SANTO HAS LEFT THE CHAT.

Chapter 11

I don't hear from Leo for a week, and I welcome the reprieve. I can't wrap my head around everything that has happened between us recently. Memories I buried long ago are resurfacing, mixing with the Leo of today, and it's confusing the hell out of me.

"Auntie Ella, when can Leo come over again?" Oliver asks from his perch on the couch. I'm making his favorite dinner, boxed macaroni and cheese, while cooking a sweet potato for Violet to try. The pediatrician suggested I try solids with her again, but we're taking it slowly. Ember saved this high chair that fits onto a kitchen chair, and it's perfect for Violet. She looks quite confused as she watches me at the stove, her bottom lip stuck out in an adorable pout. Whitley got her a set of six-to-nine-month sleepers, each featuring a different fruit, and today's sleeper is covered with raspberries. No one can convince me that sleepers, especially the fleece ones, aren't one of the most brilliant inventions for parents. It's horridly cold today, with a fierce wind that sucked the breath from my lungs when we came home from Oliver's preschool earlier.

"I don't know when Leo will come over again. He was helping us out before. Right now we don't need any help," I finally answer.

"We could make stuff up. I like playing with him. He lets me have all the good Play-Doh. And he doesn't tell me to be quiet."

"That is very nice of him," I comment. "Has someone told you to be quiet?"

Oliver nods. "Teacher gets mad at me cuz I talk a lot. And that man who Mommy brought home a bunch did too."

This is the first I'm hearing about Ember bringing a man home in front of Oliver. I wish she were here, because I'd rip her a new one for that fact. "Oh? Did Mommy bring him here a lot?"

"No. I didn't like him."

"And what about your teacher? Do you like her?"

"I do!" he shouts. "She's the best. She gives me smelly stickers on my hands every day."

I open the fridge, pulling out the half gallon of milk, and measure enough for the mac and cheese. "Where are these smelly stickers? I've never seen them."

"They're on my hand, silly!" Oliver holds up his hand, and I can see a discoloration. Walking to him, I peer down, noticing a circle mark. I pull his hand to my nose and sniff.

"Huh. Blueberries."

"It's my favorite one. She has a whole set. They look like lip ticks."

"Lipsticks?"

"Uh-huh. Lip ticks." Whipping out my phone, I google scented lip products, and a line of lip balms come up. I show Oliver the image, and he squeals with excitement. "That's them! They're my favorite."

"Good to know," I say with a smile. The mind of a four-year-old. Always intrigued with unique things and easily amused. How nice it must be to get smelly stickers, have a personal chef, and never have to drive anywhere.

As I'm plating up the mac and cheese, the power goes out.

"Shit," I gasp.

"Shit! Shit! Shit!" Oliver chants gleefully.

"Shoot. Oliver, don't say that." It's already dark outside, and the only flashlight I own is in the other room. I feel along the room until I reach the couch, finding Oliver's head. "I'm going to go grab the flashlight, okay? It's by my bed. You stay right here."

"Okay!" he exclaims. The darkness doesn't faze him. Even Violet is cooing and shrieking in the highchair, oblivious to the distress I'm feeling.

As I feel my way down the hallway, I'm running through my options. What if the power doesn't come back on quickly? I live in an older building. The windows aren't the best at keeping outside temperatures where they should be. I can certainly keep the kids huddled up with me in one room, but we're bound to get cold. How much of the town is out?

I'm in my room when my cell phone rings, sitting on my night-stand. The flashlight on the phone sure would have been nice moments ago. I look at the screen to find Gia calling.

"Hey," I answer.

"You okay?" she asks immediately.

"Uh, yeah? Why?"

"The whole town is without power. A transformer blew. They're not sure when power will be restored."

My stomach sinks. "Damn. I'm glad I just finished cooking dinner so I can at least feed the kids."

"Nuggets or mac and cheese tonight?" Gianna muses.

I snort. "Mac and cheese."

"We're headed up to Everlasting for the night. There are a bunch of open rooms. Do you want to come?" she asks.

"I can't afford that," I confess. We're living paycheck to paycheck right now. I love Everlasting, and I've stayed there a couple of times, but right now, I can't drop that much money on a hotel room. "How do they still have power?"

"Bunch of generators. Besides, I'm sure you could get the friends and family discount," she teases. "Especially after what happened with you guys on the phone last week. Did I tell you that Leo reached out to Luca for advice, and Luca threw him in a group chat with all the guys? Even Travis. The thread was hysterical."

"I don't think I want to know what anyone said," I say hurriedly, grabbing the flashlight on my dresser. Turning it on, I walk back to where Oliver and Violet wait patiently. "I'm going to act like it never happened, so you should too. Everyone should. Besides, it's not like your family is hoping we start back up. I broke up with him last time. Anytime I've seen your mom, she's crossed the dang street."

I grab Oliver's mac and cheese, place it on the table, then motion for him to follow the flashlight into the kitchen. Once he's situated, I make Violet's bottle. My goal for her tonight is to try five bites of the sweet potato puree, but I know the majority of her meal is the bottle.

"My mom said she's done that because she didn't want to make you feel uncomfortable. Not to avoid you." Gianna's voice is hesitant, like she wants to tell me more. I hear murmuring in the background, recognizing Travis's deep timbre. "We're heading out. You should come to Everlasting, El. Get out of the apartment for the night. You know the buffet always has nuggets and mac and cheese anyway."

"Thanks, but we'll be okay." Putting a small dollop of sweet potato on the tiny baby spoon, I push it through Violet's pursed lips, then wait for her reaction.

"Are you sure? Snow is supposed to start tonight. I don't want you to be stuck, especially with that creepy neighbor of yours." Violet's face is screwed up in confusion as the puree hits her taste buds, and I wish I wasn't on the phone so I could take a video.

"We'll be fine." God, I've really used the word "fine" way too many times over the past few weeks. I'm not sure I even know what it means anymore to be "fine." When Violet pushes my hand away after the fifth bite, I set the container down victoriously. She ate solids!

"I'll check in with you in the morning, okay? If it gets too cold, come find me!"

"Alright," I say with a laugh as I settle Violet into my lap.

Ending the call, I watch as Oliver inhales his mac and cheese, and Violet happily drinks her bottle. We'll be fine. Whatever that means.

e are most definitely *not* fine.

"Auntie Ella, I'm scared," Oliver whispers, his body suctioned to mine in my bed.

"I know, buddy. It sure is loud," I answer. Loud doesn't even begin to describe the sounds coming from all around us. Without the normal noises in our apartment when the furnace kicks on, or Oliver's sound machine, we hear every creak and moan of the apartment building. The wind whips around from every direction, howling fiercely.

What's worse, however, is how quickly the temperature plummeted in our apartment. My concern for the windows was valid. I can see the curtains moving because of drafts coming through the window seams. With every blanket I own piled onto my bed, and the three of us wearing winter coats, it's still freezing.

Checking the screen on my phone, I find it's just after ten o'clock. My battery is under ten percent, and I silently curse myself for not buying a portable charger when I saw it on sale for Black Friday a few months ago. I'm completely unprepared for this, and it makes me feel absolutely awful that my niece and nephew are suffering because of me.

"When will it stop?" Oliver whines.

"I don't know. I wish I had an answer."

A sudden banging makes me scream in fright, and it takes a repeat of the sound for me to realize someone is beating on the front door.

"Ella!"

"Leo?" I ask incredulously, ripping the blankets off the bed. Grabbing Violet, wrapped up in three sleepers, I run to the door.

Throwing it open, I find Leo with his hands braced on either side of the door. Wearing a thick camo coat, a black and tan trapper hat, and massive boots, he looks like some kind of soldier lumberjack here to sweep me off my feet. "What are you doing here?"

He steps toward me, making me instinctively step backward. When he feels the air temperature in the room, he winces. "Saving you from yourself, woman. Why aren't you at Everlasting with the rest of my family?"

My gaze locks on his boots. They're tied today. It must mean his leg is feeling okay. "I'd be too uncomfortable, and I really can't afford the price of a room there."

"They wouldn't have made you pay, El. You should know that," he says quietly.

"Why? I'm nobody. I'm nothing to any of them. That's just dumb," I snap.

Leo steps toward me, his hand coming up to grip my chin. He pushes upward until my eyes meet his. "That's not true, and you know it. You've always been mine. Put some shoes on. You're all coming with me. Oliver, you want to go on an adventure?"

"Yeah!" Oliver shouts.

I don't move, staring in shock at Leo.

"You good?" he asks, smirking, and that gets me out of my stupor.

"You can't just come in here and demand that I stay at your family's hotel!" I sputter.

Leo shrugs. "I'm not. I'm taking you to my place."

"Wait. What?"

He cocks an eyebrow at me. "Did you think I still live with my parents, Ladybug?"

"No, not necessarily," I answer warily. "But I've never heard of you having your own place."

"Turns out some things actually do stay off the gossip website. I've got a house on the edge of the Everlasting property. Got generators too. It's nice and toasty in there, but if you'd like to cuddle, I can be amenable to that," he says, winking at me. My mouth drops open incredulously. Leo Santo just winked at me. That's at least the second time he's winked at me.

Before I know it, he takes Violet out of my arms. "What about you, pretty girl? You ready to go on an adventure?"

My sweet niece, who hasn't smiled once in the past five months, looks right at Leo, and grins.

*A*s we pull up to a rustic looking log home, my mouth drops open in surprise. A wraparound porch graces the front, and I see two rocking chairs on the sides of a bay window. With the street lights out, and no lights from within Leo's home, I can't tell how large the home is. "Are you sure you have a generator? Did you just bring us out here to murder us?"

"Dang, you've foiled my dastardly plan," he says dryly. He pulls his truck next to a large garage. "I turned the generator off just in case I ended up staying in town. Since it's off, I can't open the garage. I'll come around to help you out."

"Leo, I'm not broken. I have a flashlight on my phone. I'm perfectly capable of getting out of a car," I snap. Throwing open the door, I step onto the driveway right as Leo reaches me.

"You know, it could have meant that I wanted to get you out of the car myself, Ladybug. Just because you're capable of doing something doesn't mean you should be forced to do it all the time," he says, clearly chagrined.

I give him a grin. "I'm a single, independent woman."

He raises a brow as he opens the door where Violet is cuddled in her car seat. "You still deathly afraid of spiders?"

I still, my eyes widening. "Why? What did you see? It's too cold, right? Are there cold weather spiders out there? I thought the whole point of frost was to kill off all the creepy-crawlies. Is something crawling on me? Leo!"

The grin Leo gives me is absolutely beautiful. So wide it shows his mostly hidden dimples, that I always secretly loved, but kids made fun of him for. Even in the dark, I can see his eyes twinkling. "Totally kidding, Ladybug. No spiders. I promise."

Tilting my head back, I look up at the night sky. The wind has calmed for a moment, but I know it's only a matter of time before it picks back up.

"How many nights do you think we stayed up to look at the stars?" I ask quietly. In my periphery, I see Leo tilt his head to look at the sky.

"Over the years? Hundreds probably. You were always fascinated with the stars and constellations." I know he's undoubtedly right. Especially in high school, when he'd drop me off at home after a date, and we'd count the stars because neither of us wanted to say goodnight.

"What was the wish you always made?" I ask. "Did it come true?"

Leo sighs, his gaze dropping to the concrete driveway. "No. It didn't come true."

We'd made a pact to only tell the other when our wishes came true. "I'm sorry. Mine didn't either."

I'd wished to marry Leo. If we'd decided to have a family, that was fine, but I'd just wanted him to be my husband. I wonder what his wish was, but I know he won't tell me. I'd begged and pleaded all through high school for him to tell me, and he never would. That man guards information like it's a matter of national security.

While I get Oliver out of his car seat, Leo carefully carries Violet's bucket seat into the house, setting it just inside the door. He sprints back outside to help me with Oliver, while I grab our bags from the trunk.

"Stay here. Let me turn the generator back on so we can have some lights," he says, once we're all inside. He steps into what I'm assuming is the garage, and soon thereafter, I hear a hum of electricity. As Leo returns, he flips a switch, lighting up the hallway we're standing in. As I take in my surroundings, I gasp in awe.

The log cabin Leo calls home is quite possibly the most beautiful home I've ever seen. The great room is a massive A-frame, with a wall of windows facing the northwest, giving Leo perfect mountain views, and what I can only imagine as spectacular sunset pictures. One wall is covered with a stone fireplace. A spiral staircase sits in the corner, and I look up to find a lofted area above us.

"That's the library," Leo comments, watching me carefully. His gaze is loaded with attention as he waits for my response. "The main bedroom is behind the fireplace, and the three guest bedrooms are on the other side of the house. Then, on either side of the loft, there are two more bedrooms."

My mind immediately goes to an inappropriate place, thinking about how loud I could be when I sneak into Leo's room.

If. If I sneak into Leo's room.

Leo sets Violet's seat down, then unbuckles her. She squeals when he picks her up, settling her into the crook of his arm. God, he looks so unbelievably perfect with a baby. It's unfair, really.

I kick off my shoes, then bend to remove Oliver's. As I unzip my jacket, and then Oliver's, I peek into the gourmet kitchen. A wall of cabinets on one side, then a bar on the other. I frown, looking for counter space. There's hardly any. How does he cook?

Leo snorts. "There's a butler's pantry behind one of the cabinet panels."

I whip my eyes to him. "How did you — are you reading my mind?"

"I know the way your brain thinks, El. It may have been a few years since I've seen it in action, but you haven't changed. You're analytical. You probably saw all of the cabinets, thinking how everything would be hidden nicely in its place, and then you realized there isn't a lot of counter space. Honestly, I don't cook that often. My mom sends me home with food all the time. But the butler's pantry has a ton of counter space."

He motions for me to follow him to a doorway on the edge of the kitchen. When he slides the pocket door open, I see a long hallway, empty counters, a wine fridge, and boxes of coconut water. My face screws up in distaste. That stuff is so gross.

Leo snorts. "Good to know your opinion of the water I drink hasn't changed at all either."

"Honestly, I'd hoped you would have gotten sick of it by now. Like maybe you'd suddenly realize how bad it tastes."

"Sorry, Ladybug. I'm still drinking it," he replies cheerfully. "Let me show you where you'll be staying."

We follow Leo down a hallway, and he opens a door on the right. "This is the room my nephews stay in when they come to visit."

Oliver squeals in delight. "This is the best!"

The room screams boy. Orange and blue paint covers the walls, along with a set of blue bunk beds and a loft bed. The loft bed features a blue ladder and tent, giving an outdoorsy vibe. A checkered rug covers the floor, along with shelves full of Legos, cars, and books. Oliver yammers on about how neat the room is, how he'd love to sleep in the loft bed, and already asks when he can stay at Leo's again.

Leo chuckles good-naturedly and replies, "We'll see. Come on, let me show you the girls' room."

We exit the room, continuing down the hallway. Leo stops at the next door. As he opens it, I'm expecting to be hit with an explosion of pink, but that isn't the case. The room has the same general setup, with bunk beds and a loft, but this room features all white furniture. A mural on the main wall is of a pastel rainbow. The bedding is all different colors of the rainbow. A corner chair includes a canopy, and the shelves are full of dolls, stuffed animals, art materials, and books.

"I would have loved to have this room when I was younger," I comment. When Violet claps her hands together, I look over to find her gaze latched on a string of pastel pom-poms, hung along the edge of the bunk bed. "She's too young for this room. I forgot her travel crib thing."

"I got one of those pack-and-play contraptions a couple of years ago. I keep it in the closet of the third room, since that's where any parent stays anyway. Violet will be contained and comfortable."

I breathe a sigh of relief. The thought of co-sleeping always freaked me out. It's probably why I struggled to bond with Violet initially, because she was used to co-sleeping with Ember. Every study I read was vehemently opposed to it, and I was paranoid about all the bad things that could happen. Maybe that's why she refuses to smile at me. She's still pissed I essentially sleep-trained her at two months old.

"Leo? Can I have a snack?" Oliver asks, looking up hopefully at Leo.

"The power went out right as I was finishing dinner. He finished his, but I think with all the excitement, his body hasn't calmed down," I explain, looking at Violet, who is currently sticking four fingers into her mouth. "She needs something too."

"Alright. Back to the kitchen, then." I open my bag to remove my slippers, sighing in bliss as my feet sink into the plushness. I then pad down the hallway, into the kitchen, and find Leo pulling out a box of mac and cheese.

"Since when do you eat mac and cheese?" I ask incredulously. Leo was always acutely aware of healthy foods, how to appropriately fuel his body, and what ingredients were an absolute no-no in his diet.

He gives me a lopsided smile. "I allow more cheat days in my old age now."

Not able to curb my interest, I open his fridge. Tons of vegetables, many fruits ... and then the same coffee creamer I've used since high school. Shocked, I grab it, then turn to Leo. "What the heck?"

He stifles a laugh. "That may be the most lasting impact you had on my life. I drink coffee now."

"You didn't the last time we were toge—" I stop myself from finishing the sentence. His smile drops as he looks away.

"Yeah, well, lots of things have changed since then."

I hate that he's putting the shutters up again, but I know I'm the one to blame for it. I broke both of our hearts, but I know, at the time, I thought it was the best thing for us. What I wouldn't give to pull him into my arms and soothe his pain away.

Thankful I grabbed some premade jars of baby food as we left the apartment, I pull Violet out of Leo's arms, and walk to the table beside the kitchen. Maybe I can get her to try seven bites of sweet potato with her evening bottle. Looking down, I notice the table, with an ivy pattern along the edge. "Why is this familiar?"

"It was at my parents' house," Leo replies gruffly. My eyes widen as I remember. Stooping down, I look at the base of the table, and sure enough, I find our initials engraved there.

L + E

"Did they ever find out we did that?" I ask.

"They did."

"God, I would have thought they'd get rid of it then," I muse.

"I told them not to."

What? I turn to Leo, watching as he pours the macaroni into the now boiling water. "Why did you tell them not to?"

"Because I wanted the table."

"Why?"

His eyes find mine, his gaze intense. "Because I'm not done with you yet."

Chapter 12

LEO

I'm not done with her. I'll never be done with Ella. She's always been the one, and she'll always be it for me.

I knew the moment I stepped into her apartment that I was completely screwed.

But I'm fucked up, her life is chaotic, and I'm not sure I'll ever be ready to trust her with my heart again. Every single time we've broken up, it was her call. I've never wanted to end things. To start anything with Ella again means I'm opening myself up to the chance of heartbreak yet again, and I'm not sure that I'm strong enough to handle that right now.

"You're not done with me?" Ella asks softly, her eyes wide. Panic is in her gaze. I'm not dumb, I know I shouldn't have said that.

"I didn't say that correctly," I reply hastily. "I meant that I didn't want to throw away the memories we had. Regardless of where we are now, you were my first love. I spent half of my life loving you. I'm not going to ignore that."

"Oh," she whispers, dropping her gaze to Violet. When Violet refuses the canned goo Ella attempts to feed her, she grabs the bottle, and walks to sit on the couch. I turn away, choosing to focus on the boiling pasta. I have so many things I could talk to her about, but I can't find the words. There's so much she doesn't know.

How she was the last thing I thought of before I assumed I'd die.

That I built this house with her in mind.

How I have an entire closet full of gifts I've bought for her over the years, because I never stopped thinking about her.

And most importantly, how I know about the baby she lost. Our baby.

Arianna called me in tears. My baby sister has struggled with her health since she contracted Hemolytic Uremic Syndrome as a kid, requiring two kidney transplants before she turned twenty-five. At a routine checkup, she saw Ella at the hospital, and overheard Ella's friend Whitley talking about the miscarriage.

I was two days out from a deployment, desperate to come home, with no alternative but to push forward with my guys. It's the main reason I kept my phone and number the same. I missed one call from her, but she didn't leave a message. We were overseas at that point, and I was on a mission for a month. By the time I got back, I couldn't find the courage to return her call.

If you ask anyone in Eternity Springs, I'm sure they'll tell you I'm the bravest guy they know. Sure, I'm brave when it comes to protecting people from dictators, providing aide to those who need it, and taking out the bad guy. But in matters of the heart, I'm a complete pansy. Hell, I watched Ella for months before I could even say hello to her. The thought of calling her an entire month after she first called me made my heart rate skyrocket, and I broke out in hives. I was terrified of what she might say. Would she tell me about the baby? Maybe tell me she'd changed her mind, and didn't want to break up? What if the baby wasn't even mine? We'd been broken up for a few months. She could have slept with someone else. That thought alone is what kept me from calling her back.

Instead, I went into denial. I did anything that could take my mind off Ella. Doubled my workouts. Read self-help books. I rarely spoke to my family, because thinking about them in

Colorado meant I'd inevitably begin thinking about Ella. Frankly, I wasn't strong enough to do that.

And now she's here, in my house, where just about every inch of the space was created with her in mind. I pretended she didn't exist, then built a fucking shrine for her.

Now I'm here, feeling like this is as close to a family as I'll ever get, and I want to demand she never leave, then take her into the bedroom so I can put a baby in her belly.

I have seriously lost my damn mind.

"Did you eat anything at your place?" I ask gruffly, stirring the macaroni. Grabbing the colander, I place it in the sink, then drain the pasta.

"No, I usually just munch on whatever Oliver doesn't eat."

"That's not a meal, Ella. That's table scraps."

"Well, sometimes it's all I can handle," she replies, a bite to her tone.

"I'm going to make myself a sandwich. Do you want one?" I ask, ignoring her comment.

"Sure."

I prepare the mac and cheese according to the box directions, then dump the contents into a bowl for Oliver. He happily tells me thanks as he shovels the first spoonful into his mouth, and I chuckle as I pull out lunch meat and vegetables for sandwiches. Almost without realizing I'm doing it, I begin to make Ella's favorite sandwich. White bread, toasted. Mayo on one piece, with a one large piece of lettuce. Mesquite turkey and two pieces of salami, with American cheese. Simple. Standard. And so Ella.

Sliding it in front of her, I notice her stare at the sandwich, then subtly shake her head. I grab Violet out of Ella's arms while I wait for the inevitable.

"Can I have a —" she begins to ask, then stops when I slide a knife in front of her. She's going to cut the sandwich in half. In the past, I never knew if she'd cut it across or diagonally, which is why I give her the knife. I stifle a laugh as I watch her out of the corner of my eye. First, she positions the knife across. Biting her lip, I hear her mumble, "no," before repositioning it diagonally. She gives a satisfied nod after slicing through the sandwich, then picks up one half. She struggles to hide her smile as her gaze meets mine, and I throw my head back in loud laughter. I can't remember the last time I laughed this much. Even with how off the rails my family gets, they've never made me as joyous as Ella does without even trying.

"So," I say, once my sandwich is complete, "tell me about the bookstore. When did you add the café?"

"About five years ago. Whitley came up with the idea. She's always loved the bookstore, and thought a little café would be a great addition. People love getting a cup of coffee, and whatever sandwich of the day Whitley comes up with, and then perusing the bookstore. In the summer, she sells out of almost everything before noon."

"How do you keep the cats out of there?" I ask. I sit Violet on the counter, with her back against my chest, keeping my sandwich well out of her reach. She happily slaps the quartz as El and I eat. "Surely that has to be a health code violation."

"Next time you're in, you'll see that we have a half-wall separating the café and bookstore, then netting hangs down to contain the cats. We have a door that goes between, and Whitley also has an outside entrance to get people straight off the street. It's worked really well. Plus, the cats love the netting. Makes it look like they're dangling in midair," Ella explains with a giggle. I can imagine that's quite the sight.

"Leo," Oliver says suddenly, and I turn to him. "What do you do all day?"

What a question. Pondering it for a moment, I respond, "Well, I do a lot of things. My family owns a hotel. Do you know what a hotel is?"

Oliver shakes his head. "No."

"It's a place where people can sleep when they're on vacation, or traveling, or maybe even when they just want to spend a night away from their homes."

Oliver turns to Ella. "Can we stay at a hotel?"

Ella smooths a hand over Oliver's hair. "Maybe someday. But hotels cost money, sweetheart. I'll try and save up for a special night at Leo's hotel, okay?"

Oliver claps his hands in delight. "Yay! So what do you do at the hotel?"

"Whatever needs doing."

Ella's eyes narrow. "You need to be more specific than that, Leo."

I grin, giving her a wink. I've never winked this much in my life, but each time I do, Ella blushes. "I know. I do lots of things. Sometimes I fix appliances, like what I did for your dryer. I work outside, making sure everything works all around the hotel. And I'm in charge of keeping the internet working. You know how you watch videos on Ella's phone?"

Oliver nods. "I like *Bluey*."

I smother a laugh. "I know. Well, that's on the internet. I keep the internet going at the hotel so everyone can watch whatever they want. Even *Bluey*."

"So you're busy a lot?" Oliver asks.

I nod. "I like to stay busy."

"What else do you do besides work?"

"I exercise a lot. Hiking, running, lifting weights." Jesus. My life literally consists of work and exercise. I'm leading such an exciting existence.

Oliver's face drops. "Oh."

"What's that face for?" I ask, taking a big bite of my sandwich.

"I thought maybe you could be my daddy. But you're too busy."

Inhaling quickly, part of the sandwich gets lodged in my throat, making me cough harshly. Ella stands, rushing to me, hitting me on the back a few times. Tears fill my eyes as I frantically grab my water, choking some down to clear my throat.

"Are you okay?" Ella asks, her eyes full of worry.

I nod, but I'm honestly not sure. "That's not what I thought he'd say."

She rubs my back briefly before returning to her seat. Turning to Oliver, she quietly says, "That's not how it works, sweetheart."

"I don't have a dad, and he doesn't have a kid, so I thought it *could* work." Oliver's expression is so earnest, so innocent, that it breaks my heart. Poor kid doesn't have a father, he lost his mother, and he's here asking me to step in.

"Listen, Oliver," I state, standing to approach him. Kneeling down, I continue. "What you said is true. I don't have a kid. And you're a pretty special kid. I may not be able to fill the daddy role, but I can be your very special friend Leo. I don't have any friends that are kids, so it would be new for both of us. How does that sound?"

He looks skeptically at me. "Could we have sleepovers? I'm gonna want to sleep in that cool room again."

"I'll see what I can do," I say with a chuckle.

I look at the clock, willing it to be further along than the last time I looked. Shit. Three-fifteen. Literally only five minutes have passed since I looked. I can't will my mind to calm down.

I've always been incredibly lucky in the sleep department. It's like there's a switch in my brain, and when it's time to sleep, I simply turn it off. Not tonight, however. Ella is in my house. All I can think about is wondering what she's wearing. How I'll probably creepily smell the sheets when she's gone to see if they have her vanilla scent.

Sighing, I flip so I'm on my stomach, staring at the clock on my nightstand. Only three-sixteen now. Christ almighty. Should I count sheep? Sing *Ninety-Nine Bottles of Beer on the Wall*? Hum the *Jeopardy* tune for Final Jeopardy? I bet none of it works, because a room across the house holds the most beautiful woman I've ever seen, and she may or may not be wearing next to nothing.

Occasionally, Ella would break out lingerie. It would be a sexy nightgown, or a matching bra and panties set. Never anything out of her comfort zone, which I loved about her. I don't need bondage or things that make no sense. I always wanted her to feel confident. But, in all honesty, what I liked best was when she wore one of my tee shirts to bed. It was, without a doubt, the sexiest thing I've ever seen.

I have a feeling, though, had that phone call we just had been a video call, it would have been sexier than anything I could ever imagine.

"Shit," I groan, feeling my dick come to attention. Just the thought of her in my tee shirt, and it's trying to force its way through the mattress. Rolling over, I palm it through my comforter, willing it to calm down.

Sitting up, I sigh in frustration. This is never going to work. I'm too keyed up. The best bet for me tonight is to make a glass of tea and try to calm down. Grabbing a pair of sweats, I slide them on, then make my way out of my bedroom.

Quietly ambling into my kitchen, I come to an abrupt stop when I find Ella at the stove, waiting for my tea kettle to heat up. Fucking hell. She's wearing an oversized shirt that hangs down to just above her knees, and it looks somewhat familiar. "Is that my shirt?"

Ella shrieks, jumping as she whirls around, her eyes wide. When I see the front of the shirt is almost completely faded, where I can barely make out the Denver Wolves logo, I know it's mine. "Jesus, Leo! You scared me half to death!"

I ignore that. "You still sleep in that? When did I give that to you?"

Her face flames in embarrassment. "I'm not sure you gave it to me. I think I may have liberated it from your closet when we were in high school."

I take a step toward her. "How often do you wear it? Looks pretty worn out."

"I don't know," she murmurs, her eyes wide as I take another step.

"Do you still have all of the clothes you've liberated from my closets over the years? There must be a couple of hoodies in there too."

Ella bites her lip as she nods. "Three hoodies."

I take another step, my heart beating erratically, sensing a change in the air. It's heavy, primed with anticipation. "Do you wear them often?"

She nods again. "They're comfortable. And they ..."

"They what?" I ask when she trails off, and I step even closer. So close our toes almost touch.

Ella sighs. "They've always made me feel closer to you."

God dammit.

I'm not sure who moves first. All I know is one moment Ella is looking at me, and the next she's in my arms, her lips plastered to mine.

It's my first kiss since we broke up. Years I've gone without this connection, because I couldn't kiss anyone unless it was her. Kissing is one of the most intimate things we do in life. I wasn't about to give that to someone else.

Ella sighs against me, and I pick her up, her legs automatically wrapping around me. I feel the heat of her core hitting my rapidly growing cock, and I revel in it. Fuck, I've missed this. I've missed the sex, sure. But this moment, where we're caught up in the feel of each other, is perfection.

Sliding a hand up her spine and into her hair, I grip her head, moving it to the side so I can deepen the kiss. Her tongue tentatively skirts out to touch mine, and I groan. Her taste explodes on my tongue, and I suck it deeper into my mouth. I take a step to the right, away from the stove, and set her down on the counter. I need my hands to be available, because I can't wait another moment. I have to touch her, right fucking now.

Breaking off the kiss, I drag my lips along her chin and onto her neck, enjoying the tiny moans and whimpers of pleasure Ella lets out quietly. I nibble on her collarbone as my hands slide up and down her thighs, goosebumps erupting in their wake. I'm remembering every curve of her body like I just touched her yesterday. The curve of her hips, the divot above her ass, the spot on the back of her knee that is remarkably ticklish. I've explored every inch of her, and God, I didn't know how much I missed it. How desperately I've craved her.

As I begin to slide my fingers up the inside of her thighs, feeling heat the closer I get to her pussy, the tea kettle screams, making both of us jolt. Ella pushes me away, jumping down from the counter. Her eyes are wild, but I can't get over how deliciously swollen her lips are. Ella takes the kettle off the burner, then looks at me.

"That shouldn't have happened," she stammers, crossing her arms over her chest, not knowing it pushes her tits out more. I'm bummed I didn't get a handful before the kettle was done.

"Agree to disagree," I respond easily, stepping back so I'm leaning on the opposite counter. Her mouth drops open. "What?"

"You think that *should* have happened?" she asks incredulously.

I shrug. "Yeah. I'd like it to happen again. Often, actually. With less clothing."

"Who are you and what have you done with my Leo?"

I smile wolfishly. "*Your* Leo?"

"You know I didn't mean that literally," Ella snaps.

"You may not think so, but it's my opinion that your subconscious is working here. I think even your body knows what it needs."

Ella shakes her head vehemently. "No. We're not doing this. I'm not — I'm not in a place where I can do this, Leo. I'm just not. That kiss never should have happened."

She rushes past me, but I grab her wrist. "You can deny all you want, Ladybug. But this is happening, whether you want to admit it or not."

Ripping her wrist out of my hand, she flounces down the hallway. Expecting her to slam the door, I'm surprised when I hear it close quietly, then remember the presence of two children in the home. Even when she's mad at me, she thinks about them, choosing to quietly stew in private instead of making a loud ruckus. Chuckling, I open the cabinet behind me, pulling out my favorite sleepy time tea.

wake completely disoriented at the amount of light in my room. It's never this light at seven in the morning. I'm almost always awake around sunrise, which means during the summer months, I'm awake at an ungodly early hour.

Shit. I overslept.

I roll over, my feet slipping over the edge of the mattress. Raising my head, I find that I'm across the bed. How the hell did that happen? Wait? Why is it so quiet? There's no way Oliver is still asleep. I squint at the clock, noting it's after nine. Holy shit! I can't remember the last time I slept this late.

Grabbing a shirt, I pull it on as I open my bedroom door. The house is way too quiet for a four-year-old and an infant. "Ella? Ladybug?"

As I stride toward the other side of the house, I see a piece of paper on the kitchen counter. Fuck. Walking over, I grab it with a huff of frustration. I already know what it'll say without even reading it, but I still take in Ella's words.

Leo,

Thank you for coming to get us last night. Sleeping comfortably was much appreciated, as was the extra dinner. Power has been restored to the town, and I called an Uber to come get us so it wouldn't impact your sleep. I removed the car seats from your car.

What happened between us cannot happen again. As nice as it was to revisit the past, I don't have the luxury of doing that. My priority is parenting Oliver and Violet. You deserve someone who can give their all to you, and I simply can't do that. You need to forget about me.

- Ella

I laugh as I read her words again. Fat fucking chance. No way in hell am I forgetting about her. This woman is engrained in my soul. She's tattooed on my heart. No one could ever take her place.

I guess I'll just have to patiently remind her how wonderful we are together. And since I'm arguably the most patient man in the world, I fully expect her to capitulate before I would ever give up.

Game on, Ella Langley.

Chapter 13

ONE MONTH LATER

"You think Leo's stopping by today?" Whitley asks as we unload a box of supplies for the café.

"I don't know," I murmur.

"Do you want him to stop by?"

I look at her, contemplating my answer. Whitley is my best friend, and she sometimes knows me better than I know myself. With the smile that spreads on her face, I can tell she's waiting for the answer she already recognizes. "I honestly don't know if I want him to, but if he doesn't, I'll probably be sad."

"He's stopped by every day for the last month, El. You have to at least admire his persistence," she comments, turning to place bulk orders of plastic utensils on the back counter. She's not lying. He's been here every day I work. He walks in with a huge smile, peruses the shelves, nonchalantly asks me a few questions, then leaves. Often he'll tell me I look beautiful, or bring up a past memory. He's brought me flowers twice, telling me he saw them, and couldn't pass them up.

He's not once asked me out, or brought up the kiss.

Fucking asshole.

"He's pissing me off," I snap, suddenly acutely angry at him.

"He's doing this on purpose. He's out-patiencing me. Who the hell does that? I said we couldn't talk about the kiss, so he's just staying in the outside part of my brain. I can't forget about it because he won't let me."

"Pretty smart if you ask me," Whitley says with a laugh. "He's abiding by your wishes, but not letting you forget about the kiss. Remind me: how good was the kiss?"

My eyes close as I'm taken back to that night. "The best."

Whitley snorts as my mind reminisces. I couldn't sleep. I have tons of nights where I struggle to fall asleep, but I knew exactly what the problem was that night. I was in Leo's house. How could I sleep, knowing he was mostly naked in his bed? And when he was suddenly there, in the kitchen with me, all shirtless and manly, and I struggled to form coherent sentences. I tried not to look at the various marks along his torso, undoubtedly from shrapnel, but I still thought he looked so insanely phenomenal. I'd hugged him, had my legs wrapped around him, and I knew what was beneath his clothes. Every rippling muscle, that delicious V below his hips, the perfect pecs.

But the kiss … our kisses had always been great. But this kiss was out of this world. Beyond comprehension. It took my breath away. Feeling his lips trail along my skin sent zings of pleasure throughout my body. When the hiss of the kettle broke our kiss, I had a moment of clarity. No matter how good, *how right*, it felt, anything with Leo wasn't in the cards.

I'm barely keeping my head above water. I'm working or dealing with the kids. I don't have time in my schedule, or my mind, to take on potentially dating someone. Even Leo. And what pisses me off is the fact that Leo realized it immediately, and he's using it against me now. The jackass.

Instead of asking me questions, or texting me nonstop, the asshole is patiently inserting himself into my life by showing up during hours I can't do anything but work.

"Does he ask you anything revolutionary? Your views on world politics or the state of our country?" Whitley asks.

"No," I murmur. "Usually they're just simple questions, and many confirm what he already knows. He asked if I still prefer chocolate ice cream over vanilla, and if I still enjoyed reading romance books."

"Does he know about your chocolate habit?" Whitley asks with a laugh.

"Oh, I'm well-versed in the chocolate habit. I'm the one who started it," comes from behind us, and I look over my shoulder to find Leo smiling at us. Wearing a thick jacket and jeans, with his hands tucked into his pockets, he looks disarmingly handsome.

"Oh? Is he the cause of the chocolate jar under the register?" Whitley asks.

I nod. "One hundred percent his fault."

"What prompted it?" Whitley inquires.

Leo looks at me, one eyebrow cocked. God, he looks so undeniably sexy. "I believe it started with a chocolate cake."

I giggle. "Oh my God, I forgot about that! It was chocolate cake!"

"I find it hard to believe that a cake is what changed El's life forever," Whitley says.

I nod. "It seriously did. It was the best cake I've ever had. This tiny little bakery in Golden had these individual cakes, and Leo took me there for a date in tenth grade."

"How'd you get there? I thought you were the same age. Who drove?"

I look at Leo, and he shrugs, so I answer. "Leo's mom. She had to run an errand, so we tagged along. I wasn't really allowed to date yet, but since Leo's mom was going, my parents allowed it. I think it helped that it was with Leo. The Santo family has a reputation for being good people, so my parents naturally assumed Leo would treat me well."

"Which I did," Leo interjects. "I didn't even try to hold your hand. You grabbed mine on the car ride back to Eternity Springs."

I laugh. "I did. I forgot I did that. Wasn't I the one who instigated the first kiss as well?"

Leo nods, his smile growing. "You were. Put the moves on me."

"What a little hussy!" Whitley teases. "I had no idea I was in the company of the town ho."

"I'd had a crush on him for so long, I guess I couldn't wait a moment longer," I explain, feeling a blush heat my cheeks. I know Leo didn't intend for this conversation to go the way it has, seeing as how he walked into it innocently, but it's definitely affecting me more than it should. We were so young, without a care in the world. Not knowing how we'd be twenty years later, with scars and trauma locked into our hearts.

"I'd had a crush on her for longer," Leo boasts.

"How much longer?" Whitley asks.

Leo glances at me. "I first noticed you in eighth grade. When did you notice me?"

My mouth drops open. "Ninth grade."

He smiles victoriously. "I win."

I shake my head in confusion. "No. There's no way. You couldn't have seen me. I'd just moved here, and I barely knew anyone."

He shrugs. "I saw you. It was probably your first day. I notice things, you know that. I'd sit in the cafeteria and watch people. You walked in with a paper sack, so unsure of yourself. You got pulled into a table with all the cheerleaders, and you smiled at something someone said. The minute you smiled, I knew I was a goner."

I'm stunned. I had no idea. We'd never spoken about the first year I lived in Eternity Springs. I'd hated it here, missing Silver Mist Falls so badly. While Leo may have seen me sitting with a group of strangers, I certainly wasn't participating in the conversation. I barely made it through each day, desperate to get out of this part of my life.

Until Leo. When I finally saw him the following year, our eyes met, and I felt like I'd been zapped with electricity. His dark brown eyes seemed to see directly into my soul, and when I finally approached him, I felt a warmth seep over me. He gave me peace, and I craved it. While I wasn't technically allowed to date him, as my parents had a strict rule of no dating before the age of sixteen, Leo had my heart well before that.

If I'm being honest, he still does.

"Why didn't you come up to me?" I blurt out, suddenly angry. "I hated that year. I hated middle school, and the fact that I'd been forced to move. Those snotty cheerleaders were awful. If I'd met you then, it would have given me a sliver of hope. I'd have liked life a little bit more, Leo. I wish you'd come up to me."

His smile fades, but I see the understanding in his eyes. "I wish I had. You know I'd have done it, just to take away your pain, Ladybug. I thought you were out of my league, and if you hadn't come up to me the following year, I don't know if I'd ever have gotten the nerve. I still think you're out of my league."

I can't respond. I'm tongue-tied. He's a decorated war vet with all kinds of life experiences I couldn't even dream about. He comes from an amazing family, with tons of nieces and nephews, whereas I have one dead sibling and one live one that I barely speak to. My parents are both dead, and the only "family" I have is my chosen one of Whitley. I'm raising my niece and nephew and can barely make it out of Eternity Springs to eat at a new fast food restaurant. If anything, he's *way* out of my league.

The bell chiming to signal a new customer walking into the bookstore makes me tear my gaze from Leo's. "I have to go."

I glide past Leo, catching a whiff of his cologne, which only makes me think of our kiss in his kitchen, with his bare chest pressed up against his old shirt that I refuse to throw away.

The shirt that hasn't been washed since that night, because it still smells like him.

*L*ater that day, Leo texts me.

Leo: Did I ever tell you about the time we were coming home from Afghanistan, and we had a layover in Dublin?

Me: I don't think so.

Leo: We got into a drinking game with a couple of locals.

Me: Oh, I definitely didn't hear about this. I'd have remembered that. How plastered were you?

Leo: Evidently, I lost the ability to move my right foot.

Me: Just your right one? So did you hobble around?

Leo: There's a video somewhere of me sort of dragging my right leg behind me, and hanging on Sergeant Baker.

Me: Was Baker the one who used to send videos to his kids where he'd sung lullabies?

Leo: No, that was Stitchum. Baker had the two German shepherds that he considered to be his children.

Me: Oh, I remember him! Where he'd watch them on the camera that dispensed treats.

Leo: Yeah, until one of the shepherds actually ate the camera.

Me: Oh no! Did it survive?

Leo: The camera? No. The dog? Yes.

Me: Are Baker and Stitchum still active duty?

Leo: No. Baker was injured the same time as me. Stitchum didn't make it.

Me: Oh, no. How many children did he have?

Leo: Three.

Leo: They're doing okay. I keep in touch with their mom. She's getting married in the summer, actually. Seems like the dude is a good guy. Kids really like him.

Me: That's good at least. You keep in touch with her? Do you do that with anyone else?

Leo: All of them. I keep in touch with all the wives. It's my duty as the first sergeant of the squad. I didn't keep their husbands alive, so I make sure they're doing okay now.

Me: Is that how you really think of it? Like it's your fault your convoy hit an IED?

Leo: It doesn't matter about the semantics, El. They died on my watch.

Me: How would you make things different, if you could?

Leo: Well, they wouldn't be dead, for one.

Me: I mean anything else. Would you plan your route differently, or move a day later? Would you ask for more insight into the area?

Leo: It wouldn't have mattered what time we left, or if it was a day earlier or later. The IED was already there.

Me: So your convoy would have hit it regardless, or another convoy would have hit it.

Leo: Yes.

Me: Was there any way of you knowing ahead of time about the IED? Like a local who could have told you?

Leo: Highly unlikely. They may have been able to tell us that there were IEDs in the field, but not the exact coordinates. Technology is getting better where soldiers will have equipment that can detect IEDs, but we didn't have that when we hit one.

Me: So there would be no way of you knowing.

Leo: I guess not.

Me: So it's not your fault.

Me: It's not your fault, Leo.

Me: You can ignore me all you want, but you need to hear those words. It. Is. Not. Your. Fault.

Leo: Thanks, Ladybug.

*D*ays later, I'm still not sure why Leo texted me to ask if I remembered that story or not. I'm tempted to text him to ask, but don't feel comfortable enough. Sure, we had an amazing kiss, but I'm still rattled from it. The conversation in Purrfect Books didn't help ease my nerves either.

So, while I'm out on a Saturday afternoon running errands with Oliver and Violet, I'm unprepared to run into Leo and his mom.

"Leo!" Oliver screams, ripping his hand out of mine to run for Leo. Thankfully, Leo catches him as I chase after him with Violet's stroller. As I catch up, I notice Mrs. Santo's eyes on me, not the kids.

"Ella," she says impassively. While certainly not pleasant, or warm, I know immediately how she feels about me. Frankly, it's warranted, and I try not to let it hurt me.

"Mrs. Santo," I reply. Looking at Oliver, who has his arms wrapped tightly around Leo's neck, I add, "Oliver, you can't run away from me like that. That wasn't a safe choice."

"She's right, buddy," Leo says. "You don't have to run. I promise I'll always say hello."

"I missed you, Leo," Oliver says with an exaggerated pout, bottom lip quivering. I can't help the major eye roll. Good Lord, he's really laying it on thick.

"I missed you too, but I don't want you to get hurt. Auntie Ella would be so sad if that happened," Leo says, looking over at me, lips tipped in a small smile. When he catches me watching, he winks. Good lord. What is it with this man and winking?

Mrs. Santo doesn't take her eyes off me. "I was sorry to hear about your sister, Ella. How are you handling things?"

"Doing the best I can, I guess." I hate that so many people ask me this. What do they expect me to say? Well, it sucks. Sometimes I don't want to get out of bed. I eat ramen a lot because I can barely pay the rent, but at least I kept the heat on this month. People don't want to hear honesty.

"She's doing better than she thinks, Mom. They're lucky to have her," Leo says warmly, and Mrs. Santo's eyebrows raise almost to her hairline.

"Oh?" she asks, and Leo nods.

"Absolutely. I know Ember would be incredibly proud of her."

A wave of emotion overtakes me. I've often wondered how my sister might feel about my parenting skills. I'd never felt especially maternal, and certainly didn't feel like having children was a must for me. I'd enjoyed being an aunt, and after the last breakup with Leo, I didn't expect I'd ever have a family of my own. I love Oliver and Violet like an aunt, but they've become so important to me since my sister died. They're the family I didn't know I needed. I hate that their mom died. I'd give anything to get my sister back. But I'm so thankful I'm here to step in.

"Don't cry, Ladybug," Leo whispers, sweeping a tear off my cheek.

I let out a bubble of tearful laughter. "I've wondered how Ember would rate my parenting, but never thought she'd be proud of me. Thank you for saying that. It means a lot."

Leo cocks his head to the side. "Why do you think she wouldn't be proud of you?"

I shrug. "I don't know. We were very different. I was never exactly maternal, so her trusting me with her children was a leap of good faith."

Oliver kicks his legs, and Leo sets him down. He comes to me, pulling my hand until I crouch so we're eye-to-eye. "Mommy told me you'd be good."

"When did she tell you that?" I ask, curiosity taking over. He's four. She's been gone for four months. How much could he remember from before that?

"She visited me last week, Auntie Ella," he says matter-of-factly. "In my dream. Said you're doing a good job."

"In your dream," I repeat.

He nods emphatically. "Uh-huh. She also told me to tell you that the sink eater was her fault."

"The sink eater ..." I trail off, trying to track what he is saying, then my eyes widen. "The garbage disposal?"

Oliver grins. "That's the sink eater!"

"That was her fault? All this time I thought it was me!" I say with a laugh, shaking my head. That little snot. I thought for sure I broke it while I was washing bottles the week Violet was born. Ember vehemently denied being to blame. "I wonder what broke it."

"A penny," Oliver chirps.

"One penny?"

He nods. "Yup. A penny. She said it jammed in there."

"Ladybug, why haven't you gotten it fixed yet?" Leo asks.

"Honestly, I forgot. It's been broken for so long, and I've gotten used to cleaning scraps off in the trash. I didn't even think to call a plumber once I moved in, then it became commonplace."

"You should have told me about it when I fixed the oven."

"I'm not kidding when I say that I forgot. I'm too used to it now."

Leo sighs dramatically. "I *guess* I can fix it for you."

I look at him warily. "Isn't that a job for a licensed plumber?"

His eyes narrow. "Do you really think I can tackle a broken washing machine but not install a disposal? Ladybug, I'm *hurt*."

"Oh, don't be so dramatic. You are not." I roll my eyes, but not before I notice his grin. "How expensive are disposals? I can probably afford it next week, but I have to see how much formula Vi goes through before then."

"She still fighting switching to solids?" Leo asks.

"Yes," I say with a sigh. "I even started with the sweeter ones, like pureed blueberries. She's just not on board with any of it."

"She may not be fully ready yet," Mrs. Santo pipes up. Leo and I both turn to her, and she smiles, warmer this time. "Leo didn't like solids either. Gianna took to them like a champ, but it was a good month before he followed suit. Try a little infant cereal mixed with formula first, then try pureed avocado. All of my kids loved avocado. What have you tried so far?"

"Sweet potato, apples, and green beans," I answer, slightly

confused. "The pediatrician told me not to bother with infant cereal."

"Do you see Doctor Suggs?" she asks, and I nod. She scoffs. "That man is older than dirt and needs to retire. He said that with all seven of my children. Violet may like it, so try it. If she doesn't, it's fine. Mix a little of her formula in there, and it'll be an easier transition."

"Okay," I murmur, slightly terrified at the change in her demeanor. "We need to get going before the post office closes."

"Good to see you, Ella. Goodbye, Oliver and Violet," Mrs. Santo says, waving at the three of us.

I walk away, slightly confused. Mrs. Santo began the interaction standoffishly, but ended it nicely. Does she hate me? And as Leo turned to head off with his mom, he didn't look at me. What the hell is that about?

I walk away in confusion, annoyance, and a little bit of warmth.

Mrs. Santo Has Entered the Villa

Take a look at these lovely pictures from moments ago, captured by yours truly! While on my way to get my weekly shampoo with Stone Dixon, I happened upon Ella Langley, Leo Santo, and matriarch Sofia Santo. While both women appeared tense at first, they relaxed as the focused swiveled to the always adorable Violet and Oliver Langley. I'm sure their mother Ember — God rest her soul — is looking down from Heaven with keen interest on whatever is developing between her sister and Leo Santo.

Will there be another Santo wedding in the near future? Only time will tell.

Chapter 14

LEO

"Jesus, Mom," I say exasperatedly, watching Ella walk away. "Whiplash much?"

"What?" she asks innocently. We begin walking in the opposite direction, toward Isabella's bakery, Bake, Batter, and Bowl.

"Don't pull that. You know exactly what I'm talking about." I look over at my mother to find her grinning at me. "What?"

"You like her. Them. All of them." She's smiling from ear to ear. "I was ready to be a bitch. Read her the riot act. Blast her for treating you poorly."

"Mom, you don't have it in you to be a bitch," I say with a chuckle.

She scoffs. "The hell I don't! You were miserable for years, Leo. There aren't many things I wouldn't do for my children. Treating an ex-girlfriend like trash is definitely something I can handle accomplishing."

"I wouldn't say I've been miserable for years," I lie. I hate that she saw right through the mask I wore, but I never could hide things very well from my mom.

Cocking her head to the side, she studies me with a sympathetic look covering her face. At sixty-six, my mother is beautiful. Only recently deciding to forgo hair dye, silver strands are now scattered throughout her dark brown locks, but the curls match

Gianna's perfectly. Eyes the same chocolate brown as mine, sparkle with love and compassion. "Leo. Not many can see your hurt like I can. They think you protect your heart, when in reality, you wear it on your sleeve. Or at least, you did. But I think you gave it to Ella when you were still a boy, and you never took it back."

Clearing my throat, I reply, "I didn't. But she says she can't be with me."

"What a choice of words," Mom says with a laugh. "She can't be with you. Not that she won't. Can't."

"I know. I'm trying to play the long game here. Not pushing anything. I stop by and say hello when she's working. Text her occasionally. Offer help when I can."

"Gia said she's the reason why you're back in Ella's life. Is that true?" she asks.

"Yes, but don't tell Gia that. It'll go to her head," I joke, and Mom laughs. "Ella's had a rough go of it since her sister died. I don't think anyone would have known if Gia hadn't randomly decided to call Ella one night. Caught her at a bad moment, and she unloaded on Gia. Gia called me and asked me to help, and I didn't know who I'd be helping. Honestly, if G had told me, I doubt I would have gone. I thought El had moved on. Thought the kids were hers."

"Leo," Mom gasps. "How did you not know?"

I shrug. "No one talks about El, and I certainly don't ask. Saw her with a baby the one time I was out with you four years ago, and after that, I avoided town altogether. I didn't want to be reminded of what could have been. I was struggling enough as it was without thinking about Ella all the time."

Mom slips her arm through mine, squeezing my forearm gently. "That's the thing about love. Just because we avoid something doesn't mean we forget."

Ain't that the truth.

"Alright, Leo," Josh says, snapping his notebook closed. "Did you do the homework I sent you?"

I sigh. "Yes, but it was weird."

Josh chuckles. "You're not the first person to tell me that, and I doubt you'll be the last."

I'm in my third session with Josh. The first two were basically meet-and-greets where we got to know one another. While our active duty times did overlap, I was never in the sandbox with Josh. He was in a completely different career field, and we didn't even have any of the same superiors. But it's still somewhat promising to know he understands the life of a soldier in a war zone, even if he can't empathize with being traumatically injured.

Josh approached me with a couple of different ideas for therapy. We decided upon Cognitive Processing Therapy, which will be talk-based. Basically, Josh and I will talk through my experiences in the military, during which time Josh will help me to retrain my brain to challenge the misbeliefs I think about my time in the military. We'll tackle the IED explosion head on, looking at all the details that have shaped my life. His goal is to modify and conceptualize the unhelpful beliefs I've lived on for so long.

I like talking with Josh. He has a sarcastic nature, and I don't feel emotionally drained after our sessions like I did with the doctors through the VA. Even through telehealth, a session would leave me borderline catatonic. I couldn't talk to people for days, choosing to escape into my own bubble. Even my parents didn't know how depressed I was, how triggered I became while reflecting on my injuries.

I've yet to admit to anyone, even Josh, that I debated on ending it all. What good was I when I couldn't even stomach looking at myself in the mirror? I was convinced I was unlovable, a stain on the world, and would be better off dead.

I'll never forget sitting in my room at a hotel near Walter Reed

National Military Medical Center, staring at two full bottles of opioids. I'd managed to survive the next to last surgery using only over-the-counter medications, and for the most recent surgery, the doctors didn't think twice about prescribing more opioids. Why bother asking the patient if they needed more? Just prescribe it. No problem. Didn't matter that the previous surgery was only a couple of months before this one. Just divvy out the drugs.

Pouring them out, I counted forty-five tablets. Earlier that day, I'd received the call letting me know the Army was done with me. I was finished. Medical discharge. I wasn't any good to them with a bum leg. The Army was the only career I'd ever wanted to do, and it was over without my approval or input. I had no other skills.

I'd separated the tablets into three piles, figuring I could swallow fifteen at a time. As I'd filled my palm with the first pile, my phone rang with a call from Gianna.

I'd answered it, because I wanted to hear my twin sister's voice one last time, and to tell her I loved her.

"Hey, sis," I'd said.

"I love you, Leo. You know that, right?" G had said, and her voice trembled with fear.

"I know. I love you too."

"No, I don't think you really understand. I'm so incredibly thankful you're my brother, and that you're still with me. It could have been different. I don't know what I would have done. You're my best friend, and you needed to hear that."

She knew. Twin intuition or something, but she knew. I felt the tablets drop onto the table as I closed my eyes in anguish.

"G," I'd whispered. "It's too hard."

"I know, big brother," she'd answered. Gianna only pulled out the "big brother" card when she knew I really needed it. "I know you're struggling. You lean on me, okay? I don't care what time of day it is. Whenever you're thinking these things again, you call me. I'm here for you always. You are so much more than the Army."

"I don't think I am," I'd confessed.

"Leo. You're an amazing big brother. You're like the baby whisperer, you've always managed to get the kids to sleep faster than anyone else. I don't know how you got a green thumb when mine is very clearly black. Everyone goes to you for advice. You've always taken to technology, whereas I would be totally fine going back to an old flip phone. And, while I definitely will deny this if you admit it to anyone, you're Nonna's favorite. You always were, and you always will be. Honestly, I think she'll leave all of her recipes to you when she dies, because she doesn't trust anyone else with them." She'd hiccuped then, like she couldn't get the words out. "You're such an integral part of this family, and I wish you could see it through our eyes. Please don't leave me."

"I don't know how I'm supposed to move forward."

Gianna cleared her throat. "It's simple. Get up. Pack your stuff. Come home. We'll take care of the rest."

So I did what she'd asked. The unspoken command, which I felt was loud and clear from my twin, was to flush the drugs. I did that, feeling a tiny bit relieved to watch them disappear in the swirl of water. I was back in Eternity Springs a week later, under the watchful eye of Gianna and our mom, slowly recovering. We never spoke again about that phone conversation, and I never asked if my mom knew about it.

I think of that phone call almost every day.

As I hand the worksheets over to Josh, I think about what he'd had me work on this week. The first piece of homework was to write a list of self-soothing techniques that work for me. He'd given me a list to try, which made me feel like a complete tool. Listening to different kinds of music, taking a walk, drinking different kinds of tea. Which tea was more soothing, chamomile or peppermint? Did I relax while listening to country, jazz, or classical? Was a hike more soothing, or a walk by a lake? One technique he wanted me to try was taking a bath. I'm six-three. The large soaking tub I have in my bathroom probably wouldn't be comfortable for that, and I doubt I could pretzel myself enough to fit everything under the water. Honestly, I haven't tried to fit in there, but didn't want to try now. I filed that under "no" for soothing.

The second item I worked on was a letter of self-compassion. He had me write one for every day of the last week, describing an event where I'd felt like my emotions were out of control, or a time that I'd felt I'd been too negative on myself. I had to write the letter about me, but also *to* me. It was bizarre, and I disliked every moment of it.

"How many of the letters are about how much you hated writing them?" Josh asks, flipping through the pages.

"More than half," I answer honestly.

Josh chuckles. "Fair. I had you pegged as five to six letters, if I'm being honest."

"One day I got a splinter in my thumb, and another day I burned my dinner." I pause. "Oh, then there was the day I got a card in the mail from a gold star wife."

Josh's gaze whips to mine. "One of yours from the IED in Afghanistan?"

I nod. A gold star wife is the widow of a soldier killed in the line of duty. I wasn't lying when I told Ella that I keep in contact with the families of every soldier I'd lost that day. What I'd left out is that I do that so it's on my terms. I'm emotionally prepared for it. I put on my mental armor, ready to go into battle. When a spouse contacts me, and I'm not expecting it, I go into a spiral.

"What did she say?" Josh asks.

"She wants me to come to her wedding this summer. I knew she was getting remarried. I'm happy for her. Really, I am. But she asked that I give her away, because she doesn't have anyone else to do it. She said that she thought Stitchum would have wanted me to."

"How do you feel about that?"

"Honestly? I don't want to. I feel like I'll be thinking of him the whole fucking time, and it'll bring up too many memories. I held his hand as he fucking died, Josh. Now I'm supposed to smile and give his wife away to someone else? He loved her so much. Had her picture sewn into his hat. Talked about her all the time. I know he'd want her to be happy, and he'd never stand in the way of her getting married again. But, fuck. I don't want to be there to watch it." I rub a hand across my forehead, willing the tears to stay away. I miss him. I miss all the guys. Lives cut short, for what? Absolutely no fucking reason.

"You're allowed to feel how you feel, Leo. You're entitled to say no to this request. You don't owe her anything."

"My decision is what cost her her husband," I snap.

"Not your decision."

"I pushed us to leave when we did. I could have chosen another route, or asked for more scouts, maybe find whoever planted the IED. So many things I could have done differently."

"Leo, you could have changed all of those things, and the result may have still been the same. Or, it might have been worse. We can't play the 'what if' game with the events from that day." Josh's voice is calm, pleasant even, but it feels like fingernails on a blackboard.

"Or it could have meant everyone survived. Everyone. Do you even know what it's like to live with that on your conscience? To know you're responsible for six guys dying?" I shout, looking down at Josh. I don't remember standing up, but my chest heaves as I'm taken back to that day. "It *is* my fault. It'll always be my fault. Nothing you say will ever change that."

In the worst timing ever, the timer sounds on Josh's desk, signaling the end of the session. Tilting my head back, I close my eyes, uttering a deep "Fuck."

"I absolutely despise ending a session like this, Leo. I never want to send someone away when they're angry. I want you to go home, thinking about your emotions right now. Name them. Write down exactly how you feel. When you're this angry, how does your body feel? Does your pulse race or your breathing increase? Do you feel like you could snap at anyone for just about anything, even if it really isn't their fault? Then I want you to write down the opposite emotion. So if you're angry, you write jovial. If you're sad, write down happy. We're teaching your brain to rewire itself, Leo. Every time you feel a new emotion, write it down in your notebook, and we'll discuss it all next week."

After shaking Josh's hand, thankful he doesn't comment on how my hand trembles in his, I leave his clinic a bundle of taut nerves. God, I'm so fucking pissed. I stop by my car, reaching up to grab handfuls of hair. I pull it hard, hoping the pain helps to ease some of the aching in my heart, but all it seems to do is exacerbate it. I hate this.

I hate that my brain is fucked up.

I hate how my friends are dead.

I hate that my parents walk on eggshells around me.

I hate that the love of my life broke my heart.

I hate that she moved on and got the family I wanted.

I hate her.

But I don't actually hate her at all. Quite the opposite, which makes me furious. Nodding my head, I unlock my car, jump in, and decide I'm telling Ella exactly what I think.

Thirty minutes later, I'm beating on Ella's apartment door, consequences be damned. It's only as I hear her unlocking the door that I realize the kids may be asleep, and I'm momentarily chagrined. As Ella opens the door, I find her wearing another one of my old shirts. It's an old Eternity Springs High School wrestling shirt, and she probably stole it back then too. It only heightens my fervor.

"Where are the kids?" I blurt out, my breathing ragged and audible. The hallway is hot. Why is it so fucking hot? I whip off my coat, attempting to cool off, and catch the quick glance Ella does as her eyes track down and back up.

"Whitley has them tonight. She said I deserved a break. Are you okay, Leo? Your face is red," Ella says quietly, studying me in that edifying way she's always done where I could never tell a lie because she'd home in on it immediately.

Fuck this.

Reaching out, I step into Ella's apartment, my hand simultaneously cupping her neck, my thumb over her throat, and I feel her swallow harshly. I feel her quick intake of breath as she steps backward, but I track her. Slamming the apartment door, I follow her across the room until she's backed against the wall. Her pulse beats wildly under my thumb, and her eyes are wide as she waits for me to speak. "I'm so fucking mad at you, Ella. So mad. You broke me. I'm fucking broken because of you, God dammit!"

I watch as her eyes fill with tears, but it doesn't satisfy me to see her pain or guilt. It just fuels me even more. "You could have talked to me about things. Why didn't you trust me enough to be honest? We'd been together for that long, and you couldn't even tell me the truth about what you were feeling. You waited until you broke up with me to admit you'd been struggling. How can I fix something I don't know is broken? How fucked up is that?"

"You would have heard what you wanted to hear, Leo," she states, her voice remarkably clear and strong. I'm momentarily struck by how proud I am of the woman Ella has become. She doesn't get rattled by every little thing, and she holds her head high. "If you can honestly stand here and tell me that our breakup was out of the blue, and that you had no idea I was struggling, then you're completely full of it."

"I would have done anything for you," I say passionately. "I would have come home. I swear."

Ella shakes her head as the tears fall. "And I would have felt awful about that. I wanted you to come home because you wanted to. Not because of me. If I'd asked, and you came home, I knew the guilt I'd feel would be insurmountable. I couldn't do that."

"Then why couldn't you move to be with me? Why? I'd have

dropped everything for you. It would have been amazing, El. But you wouldn't even give it a chance," I say quietly, my own vision blurring. Leaning my forehead against hers, I align my body so as much of me as possible touches her. Breathing her in, I whisper, "I don't know how to un-break me. I don't know how to move on from you. And worst of all, I know I don't want to."

Chapter 15

The anguish in Leo's voice is almost my undoing.

I could tell by his knock that he was keyed up. I didn't expect to be backed into a wall as soon as I opened the door, but here we are.

Every inch of him vibrates with energy. Leo always had this enigmatic aura around him that seemed to swirl through the air, but tonight, he's even more intense than usual. As tense as he appears, his hand still cups my neck tenderly, his thumb absentmindedly stroking my skin.

"I want to hate you, Ella," he says, his voice growly as his hot breath dances across my skin. "But I can't. How am I supposed to move on when all I can think about is consuming you?"

Holy hell.

My hands find purchase on his waist, gripping his shirt tightly. He drops his jacket at our feet, and his hand slides over my hip to the top of my ass. His fingers flex, and I let out a tiny moan. "I forgot how you taste, Ladybug. I can't remember the sounds you make when you come on my tongue, or how it feels to have you clench around me. As much as I think I should walk away, because this won't end well, I fucking can't, because I might die tonight if I don't fuck you."

"Please," I rasp, my body shaking with adrenaline. It's been so long since I've been touched by a man. Well, since Leo. He's the only man I've ever been with. The only kiss, caress, and lovemaking. Every first of mine has been his. "Leo, *please.*"

"Fuck," he croaks, crashing our lips together in a passionate kiss. Letting go of my neck, he grabs both of my thighs, boosting me to wrap my legs around his waist. My hands drift into his hair, noting how much thicker it is, loving how he groans into my mouth as my nails scratch against his scalp. He's ravenous for me, and I for him, as my hips begin moving on their own accord, pressing down against his bulge to find the best friction. But he's wearing a belt, and it's poking against me.

Sensing what I need, Leo jams a hand between us, undoing his belt. He shimmies his jeans down slightly, just enough for his cock to bounce out, and it hits my clit perfectly. I'm wearing very thin panties under Leo's old wrestling shirt, and I recognize the exact second he notices. "God *damn*, baby."

God damn is right. I need him. Right now. Right here. I know how perfect it feels to be filled by him, and I have to have him. "Leo, *I need you.* Right fucking now."

He doesn't answer, but slides a finger under the hem of my panties, pulling them to the side. Then the head of his cock is pushing against me, sliding inside, and I let out a guttural moan as he fills me. It's perfect. The burn from years without sex is just a smidgeon outside of painful, but I love it. I'd almost forgotten how spectacular this feeling is. Or maybe in a method of self-preservation, I'd blocked it out. Because this? There is no way anything could ever top how extraordinary it feels to be fucked by Leo Santo.

"Jesus, El," he grunts. "God, you feel so fucking good. This is gonna be quick. I need you to get there with me."

I murmur incoherently, aware that my orgasm is barreling toward us at breakneck speed. Leo barely has time to pull all the way out before I've clamped down on him, my back bowing off the wall. A kaleidoscope of color explodes behind my eyelids as I cry out. Leo only manages a couple more pumps before he comes, resting his head against my neck.

"That was quicker than I intended," he mutters sheepishly, chuckling against my skin. The sensation makes me shiver, and I feel him smile. "It's, uh, been a while for me."

"Me too," I admit, suddenly shy. It's like our first time all over again, but we're middle-aged and sex-starved. I let my legs slide off his waist, and he slowly lowers me to the ground. As soon as his cock slips out of me, I feel empty. That familiar ache is there, but it feels wrong all of a sudden. Like Leo is meant to always be inside of me.

The familiar feeling of his release slipping out of me makes me grimace, and Leo's eyes widen. "Shit. I didn't use a condom."

"It's okay. Pretty sure it's the wrong time of the month," I tell him as I walk into the bathroom.

"You aren't on birth control?" he asks.

"No. Not dating, so no need for birth control. Plus, that costs money, and I'd rather my funds go to food and utilities," I call out as I clean myself up. I hear a knock on the door, and as I walk back into the living room, Leo is opening it to a frazzled Whitley. "What happened?"

"She's got a fever, and she literally won't stop crying. I tried everything, El." Whitley looks exhausted, with a handful of hair out of her messy bun. As she walks toward me with Oliver trailing behind her, Violet lunges out of Whitley's arms and into Leo's.

"Hey, baby girl," he coos, settling her against his shoulder. He absentmindedly kisses her forehead, then looks at me. "She's really warm."

"Let me grab the thermometer and infant Tylenol," I say, dashing into my bedroom. Whitley follows me in, cornering me by my en suite bathroom.

"Did I interrupt something?" she hisses. "Crap. I'm so sorry. You look deliciously fucked, my friend."

"You technically didn't interrupt anything, but you would have if you were five minutes sooner," I admit with a grin. Whitley squeals, jumping up and down as she claps her hands.

"I knew it was only a matter of time! Good for you, girl. Get back on that horse!"

I shake my head as I stride past her, items in hand. Violet's cheeks are red, and she looks miserable as she rests her head on Leo's shoulder. I run the temporal thermometer across her forehead, finding it well over one-oh-two.

"Is the butt temperature only for really new babies?" Whitley asks, and Leo chuckles.

"The butt temperature," he deadpans.

Whitley throws her hands up in frustration. "I don't know what it's called! You stick it up their butt."

"It's a rectal thermometer, and yes, it's usually more accurate at this age. But," I say, rubbing my hand down Violet's back, "I don't want to aggravate her any more right now. She clearly feels like crap. We'll see if Tylenol helps."

"What if it doesn't?" Whitley asks.

I shrug. "Then I call the pediatrician in the morning."

"You're pretty blasé about this," she says.

"My sister used to say, 'treat the child, not the fever.' So I'll give her some meds, then see if she improves. If she gets worse, we'll go to the emergency room."

"Auntie Ella?" Oliver asks.

"What, buddy?"

"Can I get a snack?"

"How about some string cheese?" I ask, and he nods. After getting him the snack, I turn on the television for him, then walk Whitley to the door. "Thanks for watching them for a little bit."

"I'm sorry I ruined your evening," she says quietly.

I smile with a one-shoulder shrug. "It was probably over anyway."

Whitley gives me a quick hug, waves over her shoulder to Leo, then escapes out the door. I turn to look at Leo, as he's slowly sitting on the couch. "What are you doing? I can take her."

"I think we both know she's going to scream her head off if you try," he says calmly. I watch as he kicks off his shoes, then settles back into a lounging position. Violet lifts her head to look at Leo, then turns to look at me. Once she sees me, she sighs, then lays her head back down. "Get the Tylenol, Ladybug. Let's get this little lady feeling better."

I quietly measure out the age appropriate dosage for Violet, then approach them. Sitting beside Leo, I'm just about to push the syringe into Violet's mouth when she vomits all over him. "Oh no!"

When I go to grab her, he stops me. "It's alright. Let her finish."

"Let her finish puking on you?" I ask incredulously.

"I'm already a mess. Besides, it's not like she did it on purpose. This way you don't have to clean anything." Leo carefully pats her back as she throws up again. As soon as she's done, she lets out a pained yowl. "Okay. She's done."

"How do you know?"

"Baby, I have a billion nieces and nephews, plus three younger siblings. Four if you count Gia. I know things about kids. Can I use your shower?" he asks as I pull Violet from him. Grabbing the baby wipes container, I clean her face and hands, noticing not one drop of puke got on her.

"Yeah," I murmur, watching as he carefully stands up, moving his shirt to contain all the puke. "I can wash your clothes if you'd like."

"I'd prefer clean clothes over sitting in this," he calls out as he strides into the kitchen. I watch as he dumps the liquid into the trash can, then peels off his shirt, placing it in the sink. He unzips his jeans, and I realize he never buckled his belt after we had sex. Stripping his jeans off, he places them next to the shirt. "I'll, uh, go shower now."

My mouth drops open as Leo confidently walks past me.

Scores of tattoos cover his pecs, and I almost step forward to get a closer look. I bet there's a story for every one of them. Then my eyes dance south, stopping to ogle his butt. God, he has an amazing ass, and his boxer briefs make it look even better. But then my eyes drift lower, and I see his mangled legs. Scars from shrapnel dot along both legs, from ankle to thigh, but one leg looks significantly smaller than the other. Multiple long scars travel the length of his calf, and his knee is misshapen. Tears fill my eyes as I think about all the trauma he's been through. Trauma he handled alone, because he didn't have me, and he didn't want to burden his family.

God, what a selfish bitch I am.

"Auntie Ella, why are you crying?" Oliver asks softly. I look over at my sweet nephew, innocently chewing on his string cheese, and wipe the tears from my face.

"Just sad for a second, bud. I'm okay." Standing, I walk into the kitchen to grab Leo's clothes. As I grab them, his wallet falls out. "Shit. Glad I didn't wash this —"

I bend down to grab the wallet, but a group of papers falls out of the pocket. I'm shocked to find my own picture staring back at me. What the hell? It's an old photo, one he took when we were in our early twenties. I'm smiling gaily at him, and I remember him kissing me right after. He was home after one of his first deployments, and so happy about his decision to join the Army. I was blissfully ignorant of how much anxiety his deployments would cause me, and still thought he'd only be active duty for a tour or two.

I drag my finger along the worn edges of the photo. I can remember every detail about that day. How we daydreamed about the future, and the promises we made. Most of those were broken within a few years. I thought he'd be back home, we'd be married, well on our way to a kid or two. He promised to always be truthful, never make any big decisions without my input, and be the kind of partner we'd both witnessed with our parents.

How many times has he pulled this out of his wallet? Has he

pined for me all this time? Did he have any regrets about that period in our lives? We were so different, yet somehow the same.

"Ella," Leo says quietly, standing before me wrapped only in a towel. I raise my head, letting the tears fall. Violet sighs against me, and I realize she's fallen asleep. Crap. I should fully bathe her, but I know it'll throw off her mood even more, and decide I'll bathe her in the morning.

"Please tell me you just put this back in your wallet, and that you haven't had it in here the entire time," I blurt out tearfully. "Please, Leo. I don't know if I can take it if you tell me you've kept this in there, and you looked at it often."

He approaches me slowly, reaching up to push an errant piece of hair behind my ear. "There was a time when I promised you I wouldn't lie to you."

Scrunching my eyes closed tightly, I drop my chin to rest on the top of Violet's head. "Shit."

"It's not that bad, Ladybug," Leo says with a light laugh. "I'll admit I've taken the picture out occasionally. But honestly, there were many times I forgot it was in there."

"Then why didn't you throw it away when you did realize?" I ask. "I can't even imagine what other girls thought about you having my picture in your wallet, Leo. That had to have led to some really uncomfortable conversations."

He shakes his head. "First of all, I haven't dated. No woman has seen the inside of my wallet. Second —"

I interrupt him. "What do you mean you haven't dated?"

He blatantly points to his leg. "Kinda been busy. May I continue?"

I slam my mouth shut, and nod.

"Alright. I left the picture in there for a variety of reasons. Regardless of what status we were, you'll always be my first love. You've inspired me, and challenged me, and I don't ever want to forget that. And I figured if I ever even thought about dating, I needed to be reminded that you set the bar incredibly high. So if I didn't think a woman would come close, it wasn't worth my time."

"Leo," I whisper, overcome with emotion.

"And last ..." he trails off, his eyes darting down to look at Violet. When he finally meets my gaze again, he gives me a lopsided smile. "There were a number of times over the past decade when I thought things couldn't get any worse than they were. Times when I wondered if I'd make it through. Your picture reminded me that there's always darkness before the dawn. There might be a storm, but the beauty after the rain is worth it. When I passed out after the IED blew up the convoy, your face was the last thing I saw. For a moment, I was pissed that our time was over, and that you'd be finding out from someone that I'd died. But then I was so fucking thankful, because I got to experience *you*. I was loved by you. And no matter what life brings me, I'm so fucking grateful I had that privilege."

I'm speechless.

I don't think. I step forward, plastering myself against his bare chest, careful not to jostle Violet. Sliding an arm around his waist, I hug him as tightly as I can. He doesn't speak as he loops his arms around me, and rests his chin on my head. Closing my eyes, I listen to the steady beat of his heart. I'd forgotten how eloquent and poetic Leo can be. Quiet, introspective, and focused, but also romantic and thoughtful. I was the lucky one who'd had the privilege of being loved by him.

"Auntie Ella," Oliver calls out from the living room. "I tired."

Regretfully pulling away from Leo, I keep my gaze cast downward. "I need to get him into bed."

"Do you want me to take Violet?" Leo asks.

"No, I'll put her in her bassinet, then put your clothes in the washer."

"Any chance you have any more of my shirts in your closet?" Leo jokes, making me blush.

"There's a chance you might find a few more in the bottom

righthand drawer of the dresser," I confess. Looking through my lashes, I watch as Leo grins. I follow him into the living room, watching as he gives Oliver a fist bump. Motioning for Oliver to walk ahead of us, I stare at Leo's back. More shrapnel scars. This sweet man. I'm heartbroken for what he went through, and how my absence may have played a part in his recovery.

We have a lot of trauma to dig through if — or when — we think about a possible redo of our relationship.

Chapter 16

LEO

It's been more than a few weeks since that night at Ella's. At the time, I'd wondered if it would be a turning point in our relationship. I hadn't intended on fucking her against a wall, but once I saw her in my shirt, I felt like I didn't have control over my body.

After getting the kids to bed, we'd watched a movie while my clothes dried, and I woke up with her snuggled in my arms. It felt perfect. Kismet. Karma. Me, her, and the kids. Like we were meant to be.

But once Ella woke up, it was clear she was uncomfortable. She barely made eye contact and ushered me out of there as fast as she could. I'd intended to ask if I could cook her breakfast, but she made up some bullshit story about work that I knew was a lie. Violet had woken up fever-free, but I knew Ella wouldn't be out and about with Violet that fast after a fever. She just wanted me out of her space, so I left.

And I haven't spoken to her since.

I continued to occasionally stop in at Purrfect Books, but she was always conveniently tied up. Lots of imaginary phone calls happened right as I walked in, or she'd tell me a delivery was at the back door. It was all crap, but it's not like I could call her out on it. I know the way Ella's mind works. While I've always been the kind of person who sees most things in black and white, Ella walks through life in the gray areas. She needs time to work through things.

So, I took a step back. Figured I would touch base with her at some point.

But then life got in the way.

One of the water heaters went out at Everlasting. Then two ovens stopped heating. I had a checkup at the VA in Denver, which ended up lasting two full days because of issues with their computers. We had two spring storms that dumped close to a foot of snow each time, and both times, it forced me to stay at Everlasting so I could keep track of all the mechanical systems.

I kept thinking I'd contact Ella the next day, but something would end up throwing a kink in my plans. But every night, as I laid awake in bed, I wondered if she was thinking about me.

Once life seemed to finally calm down, it was almost two months after the night at her apartment, and I figured there was no way I could possibly contact Ella without coming off like a complete tool, or like I was trying to get a repeat performance. I allowed myself one week of melancholy, holed up in my shrine of a home to her, and then I chose to keep moving.

Fortunately, my dipshit brothers and brothers-in-law kept things mildly interesting with a group chat of sheer chaos. I was added back against my will again.

> Stone: Alright. Which one of you numb nuts hid a pickle in my house?

> Luca: Oh, is THAT what we're calling it these days, Stone? Gross. That's my sister you're talking about.

> Stone: Suspect #1.

> Alex: Are we talking about an actual pickle? Or like that weird ornament you're supposed to find on the Christmas tree?

Dom: Katharine tried to start that tradition last year. I hid the damn thing in one of the gutters. It's bad enough she makes us do that stupid elf.

Sebastian: Elf on the Shelf is big in our house too. Isabella is amazing at creating all these phenomenal scenarios for it. On the rare occasion I'm expected to do it, I just TP the tree.

Stone: I hate that I can't tell if any of you are trying to redirect the conversation so I don't realize you're the asshole that hid a very large and real pickle in one of my floor vents.

Dom: How large?

Stone: The size of my forearm.

Alex: Jammed in the vent?

Stone: Yup.

Luca: If I say it wasn't me, will you believe me?

Stone: Nope.

Luca: Asshole.

Me: Why assume it was someone in this chat?

Stone: Who else would it be?

Me: You're assuming the women you all married aren't capable of pulling a prank. Frankly, didn't Isabella shove all kinds of shit into the vents of her ex's apartment?

Sebastian: DUDE I INVITED YOU OVER TO MY HOUSE!

Me: So?

Sebastian: This is how you repay me? By going after my wife?

Me: She's been my sister for much longer than she's been your wife. And technically, you invited me to your clubhouse. Not your house.

Dom: Leave it to Leo to home in on a technicality.

Alex: Seb, he's got a point. Your wife does have quite the little mean streak.

Luca: Do you remember when she set me up to take the fall for that stupid vase that she broke?

Stone: God, even I remember that. Me and Alex couldn't believe your parents bought it.

Travis: Late to the convo, and happy to say I didn't jam a pickle into your floor vent, Stone. Definitely not a sentence I ever thought I'd say.

Stone: Noted.

Stone: It is interesting that Leo didn't deny anything, but turned the blame onto his sister. And he's the most likely to be able to sneak in and out of someone's house without being detected.

Dom: That is true. Leo, what do you have to say for yourself?

Me: I'd have no reason to hide a pickle anywhere.

Me: Why a pickle?

Me: How long did it take you to find it?

Me: Was it beginning to mold or decompose?

Me: Couldn't you smell it?

Me: Why am I the only one asking actual questions?

Stone: Okay, it's definitely not Leo.

Me: Thank you.

Travis: Leo, Gianna wanted me to tell you that you're dead to her. Again.

Alex: Uh-oh. Trouble in twin paradise?

Me: What for this time?

Travis: That you still haven't reached out to Ella since you banged her.

Luca: LEO DID WHAT NOW???

Dom: Holy shit.

Alex: You fucked Ella? Really?

Me: Travis, please tell my sister that YOU are now dead to me.

Travis: Totally worth it, honestly.

Dom: Leo, we need answers. Are you guys back together?

Me: No.

Alex: Was it a one-time thing, or will you be hitting it again?

Me: I don't know. Probably a one-time thing.

Luca: Why?

Me: It happened weeks ago, and I haven't reached out since, and she's obviously pissed if Gianna is now pissed, so I can't see her willingly giving me another chance.

Stone: How long ago?

Me: Like six or seven weeks ago. Maybe eight.

Alex: I know it's not the same thing, but Natalie gave me multiple chances when I kept fucking it up. Don't count yourself out just yet.

Dom: Dude, she was pregnant with your baby. Not the same.

Luca: Leo and Ella have decades of history though. It may not be a bun in the oven, but it has to count for something. We need to coach him on how to court Ella. He's bound to be a dipshit if we don't.

Dom: With all due respect, Luca, the only one here who didn't truly fuck things up with their wife at least once was Sebastian. Mostly. Although you did forget to tell her you owned her building until you'd moved her into your house.

Sebastian: Are we pointing out dumbass ways? Alright. You didn't ask your wife to marry you, Dom. You fucking TOLD HER TO.

Alex: Did you really expect anything less from Mr. Control Freak?

Dom: I don't think you want me taking a trip down memory lane with all of your transgressions, Alessio.

Me: If it helps, Stone, I saw Luca on your street three days ago carrying a grocery bag.

Luca: YOU MOTHERFUCKER

Stone: Payback is a bitch, Luca.

Luca: You had it coming after you switched my protein powder with all-purpose flour. You try dry-scooping a mouthful of flour and see how fast you retaliate.

Travis: How do I unsubscribe from this chat?

Alex: You married into it. Most of us are forced by blood.

Knowing Gianna is pissed at me makes me nervous. Usually I can tell when she's upset, and we'll talk it out. But right now I don't feel a connection to her. After texting Travis to find out what times G will be at home, I take a page out of her playbook, and show up out of the blue one evening bearing one of her favorites: mint chocolate chip ice cream.

When she answers the door with a narrow glare, I hold up the bag of ice cream pints. "I come with a gift. An offering."

Propping her shoulder against the door, she crosses her arms over her chest to look at me with a cocked eyebrow. "Oh? And do you feel you deserve to be forgiven?"

I tilt my head to look at her. "I never said it was about forgiveness."

Gia rolls her eyes. "It should be. You're an asshole, you know that?"

"Yes," I sigh. "I'm aware."

Her eyes soften slightly as she moves out of the doorway.

"Come on. Carson will be excited to have some ice cream before bed."

As I step into her house, I bend down to kiss the top of her head, then poke her side right where I know she's ticklish. She responds by sticking her fingers into my armpit, and I throw an arm over her shoulders so her face is jammed against me. "What's that? Oh, you love me, too? That's so nice, Gianna. So sweet."

"Uncle Leo!" Carson shouts, bounding toward me. He's an eclectic mix of my sister and Travis. He's type-A like Gianna, but outgoing like Travis. He has our eyes, but Travis's hair color and complexion. It never ceases to amaze me how genetics work. "Is that ice cream?"

"It is," I tell him as I bend down to scoop him into my arms. The movement makes my leg cramp, but it's worth it when Carson squeals in excitement. I place him on a kitchen chair, standing, while Gianna grabs spoons and bowls. "No bowls needed. I got us each our own pint."

"My own pint!" Carson shouts gleefully, jumping up and down. He's wearing Spiderman pajamas, with a hole in one knee, and his chaotic energy makes me grin.

"You will be having a small portion, sir," Gianna chides. She looks at me in disapproval. "He has school tomorrow, Leo. I'd like him to go to bed before midnight if possible."

I wince as I realize the error in my ways. "Whoops. Sorry, kiddo. Mom rules this house, not me."

"Aw, man," Carson says with a pout as he drops his butt to the chair. "No fair."

Gianna crouches next to the chair. "I guess you can go to bed with no ice cream, then. Would that be better?"

"No!" he shouts.

"Okay, I'll give you a little bit, then."

"Yes, Mommy." Carson beams up at his mom, and my heart cracks a little. I'd never really planned on or expected to have a family. It wasn't something I considered to be definite. If it happened, great. If it didn't, I was happy being an uncle. But every moment with Ella, Oliver, and Violet has made me want more. For the first time, I'm jealous of my sister because she's a mom.

Travis gets home as Carson is finishing his ice cream, and dutifully takes him up to bed for the night, leaving me with my sister. She doesn't speak, only raises her eyebrows at me. "Why are you looking at me like that?"

"Like what?" she asks.

"Like you're waiting for me to drop a bomb on you."

"You showed up here unannounced, Leo. Clearly you have something you want to talk about. You've never appeared here for no reason, so spill it." Shit. She's right.

I blow out a breath, scrubbing a hand over my face, then sliding it around to grip the back of my neck. "I think I accidentally fucked up, and I don't know what I should do next."

"Accidentally."

"Yes."

"How does one accidentally fuck up, Leo?" she asks, her voice deceptively calm. This is when Gia is the scariest, if I'm being honest.

"I need to know how much you know before I continue," I stammer. "I'm not sure where to start."

Her eyes narrow. "How about you start with the weeks after you banged my best friend against her apartment wall, then didn't call her once?"

My hackles rise as I feel myself go on the defensive. "I showed up a couple of times a week at the bookstore for a bit, but she wouldn't see me. I assumed she wouldn't answer my call either."

"But you didn't try."

"No," I admit. "And before you ask, I didn't text either. I wanted to see her. I knew she was freaked about what had happened, and I knew anything on the phone wouldn't help matters. So I kept going into the bookstore, but she was never available. I figured if she could see me, she'd see that I wasn't going anywhere. That I wanted to keep seeing her. And then life happened, and all hell broke loose at Everlasting. I basically lived there for two straight weeks, and stupid shit kept breaking, and I never had time to make it back to Purrfect Books. So now it's been like two months since we were together, and I don't know what I should do."

Closing my eyes, I tilt my head back to rest against the top of the chair. I wait patiently as Gianna processes my info dump, and she finally says, "Have you actively been seeing that therapist this entire time?"

I nod. "I have. We did telehealth the weeks I was at Everlasting."

"Does he know about Ella and the kids?" she asks.

"He does."

"What does he say?"

"He doesn't say anything specific about Ella, but he's helped me work through some of the anger I have with her over our breakup."

"So you can understand where she was coming from all those years ago?"

I sigh. "Yeah. She commented once that she thought we may have both been hearing what we wanted to hear for the final year or two of our relationship, and I can see that now. I kept thinking if I could just get her to North Carolina, everything would be fine. She'd be there, I'd come home to her. We'd get married, and everything would turn out as it was supposed to. But I wasn't factoring in how abundantly clear she'd been about moving. I wasn't taking into consideration how I'd told her I wouldn't reenlist, and then pulled the rug out from under her when I did it anyway. I was being a selfish prick, and expected her to come to me. For her to make all of the changes to make our relationship work."

Gianna nods. "It took me quite some time to see it from her eyes as well. I was so hurt for you, but she pulled away from me too. I didn't realize how painful it would be for her to be surrounded by our family. Pulling away from everyone was the easiest thing for her. I can't imagine how it must have felt at the time."

"I really want to talk to her, G. I want to tell her that I'm here. I want to be with her. But now it's been so long that I don't know how to move forward."

"What if she doesn't want to get involved with you again?" Gianna asks quietly.

"Then I'll have to be okay with that. All I know is I've been in love with her since I was fourteen. Even when we've been apart, no woman has ever caught my eye. I have to at least try, right?"

Gia gives me a small smile. "I'm rooting for you, big brother."

Chapter 17

ELLA

I think I'm dying.

Okay, I'm being overly dramatic. But between the fact that I can't catch my breath, and my heart rate currently has my watch sending me alerts, maybe I'm actually dying? I don't know.

"Girl, I need you to take a deep breath," Whitley says quietly, rubbing my back. "In and out of the paper bag. Slow breaths."

I inhale slowly, a shaky breath that barely takes the edge off my hysteria. How can I do this? What do I say? What if it happens again? I don't know how to handle this right now. I'm barely getting by, and now everything is up in the air.

"Are you sure?" Whitley asks, her voice soft and soothing.

"N — no, not completely sure."

"So there's a chance you're wrong?"

"I know my body, Whit. I've only felt this way one other time."

"And you're late?"

I nod, a fresh set of tears filling my eyes. Yeah, I'm that kind of late. The kind where periods don't show back up for almost a year. Where the body either changes as it grows a human being, or decides to stage a battle with the uterus by ending a pregnancy.

"Do you want to take a test?"

I nod again. I'm about ninety percent sure I'm pregnant, but I need to know for certain. Figures that I have sex once — ONE TIME — in years, and get knocked up. "I can't waltz into a drugstore to buy a test. I'll have to drive out of town to get one. Too many nosey people here."

"I have one at home," Whitley says. "Would you like me to go get it? That's easier than you dragging the kids out of town."

"Why do you have a pregnancy test?" I ask.

"Long story that I don't feel like explaining right now," she replies. "I'll go grab the test. Sit here, keep breathing slowly, and don't spiral."

Thankful Whitley lives only a few minutes from the bookstore, I stay behind the register, focusing on my breathing. When the bell over the door jingles, I assume it's Whitley returning, then jolt in surprise when I find Jeremy smiling at me.

"Hey, Ella," he says smoothly.

"Hello. What can I help you with, Jeremy?" I reply, keeping my voice even-keeled.

"Can I take you out to lunch?" he asks bluntly.

"No."

"Why not?"

"Because I don't want to go," I answer. I've tried to be nice to this kid, but he's not taking the hint. It's time to be as specific as possible. "I've made it clear I have no interest in you, Jeremy. I think it's time you hear what I'm saying."

He has the audacity to pop his lower lip out in a childish pout. "Oh, come on. You're no fun."

Before I can respond, a deep voice from the door snaps, "The lady answered you."

A shiver skirts down my spine as Leo approaches, his eyes dark and dangerous as he crowds Jeremy against the counter. Jeremy immediately recognizes the expression, throwing his hands up in submission. "Dude, I was just asking. Chill."

"No, I won't fucking chill," Leo answers. "You can't seem to take no for an answer. If this happens again, rest assured you'll be answering to me, and the outcome will only be beneficial to one of us."

Jeremy looks at me, his eyes pleading. "A little help here?"

"Don't look at her. Look at me," Leo growls out. "If I hear that you're bothering her in any way, you will not get off easily. Do you understand me?"

Jeremy nods quickly, then slides out from between Leo and the counter. "Understood."

As I watch Jeremy's quickly retreating back, I don't notice Leo rounding the corner until he has my face in his hands. Before I know it, his lips are on mine, and I reflexively relax into the kiss. I'm backed into the wall as his tongue skirts along my lips, and I sigh into his mouth. I thought I'd forgotten how wonderful Leo's kisses were. I went years without them, though I honestly don't know how. I've been craving his kisses for the past two months like an addict needing another hit.

"Alright, I've got the goods — oh, shit," Whitley blurts out as she bursts through the door. But Leo doesn't jump away from me. He ends the kiss slowly, sensually, then pecks my lips a couple of times before stepping back.

"Hi," he whispers, a smile twitching on his lips.

"Hi?" I reply, confusion evident in my tone. He's wearing joggers, a tee shirt, and a Denver Wolves hat, looking sinfully rugged and manly. A hysterical giggle escapes my throat when I think about the fact that I fucked this man against a wall.

And he probably got me pregnant.

And then I remember the jackass hasn't called me since then, and I'm suddenly pissed off. Placing my hands on his pecs, I push him back a few feet. "What the hell was that? Playing a game of 'I licked it, so it's mine'? Pretty childish, even for you, Leo."

He smiles sheepishly, reaching up to scratch absentmindedly at his beard. "Would you believe me if I said that wasn't my intention at all? I was only going to check on you, because you look a little pale, so I wasn't sure if that jackass said something to upset you. But then you bit your lip, and that's always been my kryptonite."

I'd forgotten about that. I teased him mercilessly in high school about it, because I could basically tell him anything, and he'd forget all about it if I bit my lip. "Why are you here, Leo?"

His smile falters. "Can I come over tonight?"

My mouth drops open in shock. Seriously? Did he just ask me for a booty call?

Leo's eyes widen. "Shit. Not like that! I meant dinner. Or after dinner. I never did check on your dishwasher, and I'd like to see the kids too. And you, of course. But I'd like to talk. To explain some things, if that's alright with you."

I should say no. Tell him tonight isn't a good time. Come up with any excuse: Violet has a cold, or Oliver has something scheduled with a friend. Anything. But instead, while looking at Leo's earnest expression, I nod. He sighs in relief. "Good. Great. I'll bring a pizza. Will that work?"

I nod again, unable to speak. Leo leans in to kiss me quickly, then turns to stride away. He says hello to Whitley, who subtly hides the pregnancy test box against her chest, and then walks out the door. Whitley immediately giggles. "What the hell did I just walk in on?"

"I don't even know," I reply shakily, dropping onto a stool by the register. Laying my head on the counter, I groan. "Jeremy came in and asked me out again. All of a sudden, Leo was in here, threatening Jeremy, and then we were kissing. I don't know how it happened."

"Leo threatened Jeremy?" Whitley asks as she hands me the pregnancy test, and I nod. She hums in approval. "Those Santo boys do enjoy the potential for violence."

I snort. "They really do. An ex of one of their sisters showed up at the police station quite a bit worse for wear back in the day, but Leo and his brothers claimed they weren't involved. I bet they still maintain their innocence."

"Having a sexy man willing to go to bat for you isn't the worst thing."

"I guess not."

"Alright," Whitley says, clapping her hands. "Do you want to do the test here, or wait until you get home?"

"Here, I think. I need to know now, especially if Leo will be over later. So I can plan how I tell him."

"How late are you?" Whitley asks.

"I don't even know," I moan.

"Are you late often?"

"My cycles are pretty irregular. It never occurred to me to track anything because I wasn't having sex." I rip open the box, removing the stick. "God, I haven't taken one of these in years. Should I read the directions?"

"For fuck's sake. No, El. They haven't changed the test. Pee on the stick, wait a few minutes, then hyperventilate. Pretty standard."

I turn the box over to look. "Oh, good, a digital test," I say, relieved. "I don't like looking for lines. I want a 'yes' or 'no' response."

"Agreed. I tend to think I see a line when there isn't one, so I prefer the digital tests too. Now get in the bathroom, ma'am. You know we'll get that afternoon rush right before we close."

I head into the employee bathroom at the back of the store. In the quiet space, I feel like crying again. I can't believe I'm in this situation. I'd have never thought this kind of history would repeat itself, and certainly never with Leo as a participant. I was almost positive that night wasn't near the middle of my cycle.

After peeing on the test, I stick it back into the wrapper, wash my hands, then make my way back out to the register. When I see Whitley speaking with someone, I carefully place the test in my pocket, then jolt when I see the customer Whitley is helping is Gianna. Her face lights up when she sees me. "Hey! I came to see if you wanted to do dinner tonight."

"Oh. I can't tonight. Are you available tomorrow or Saturday?" I ask, choosing not to tell her that Leo is coming over tonight. I'm not ready to tell anyone about — well, I'm not ready to tell anyone about anything.

Her face falls. "Oh, bummer. I can't tomorrow, but I can on Saturday. Better yet, want to meet at the park with the kids? It's supposed to be really nice. We can bring a picnic."

"That sounds wonderful. Noon okay?"

"Perfect. See you then! Bye, Whit," Gianna says with a wave, then walks out.

"Did you ever notice she and Leo have the same walk?" Whitley blurts out, and I burst out laughing. "What? They really do!"

"I'd never thought about it, but you're right," I tell her, rubbing my eyes.

"I wonder if your kid will walk like that," she muses, then slaps a hand over her mouth. "Jesus. I should think before I speak. If you're pregnant, do you plan on keeping it? I mean, you don't have to answer if you don't want to. It's honestly none of my business. I won't judge you whatever you decide. I'm here for whatever you need."

"I don't know yet," I confess. "I don't even know if I can carry a pregnancy. There was no real reason why I miscarried before, but I didn't look into it further. I don't think I could have an abortion, though."

"Miscarriages can happen for all kinds of reasons, El," Whitley says quietly, placing her hand on my shoulder. "I hate that you've struggled with what happened to you, but it doesn't necessarily mean it'll happen again."

"But what if it does?" I whisper tearfully. "What if I tell Leo, and he gets all excited, and then I miscarry? He might never forgive me. I'll have to move, because I won't be able to live here and get hateful looks from his entire family. I'll lose Gianna again, and have to pull Oliver and Violet from the only home they've ever known …"

"Woah, woah, woah," Whitley says, squeezing my shoulder. "Don't spiral. We're not there yet."

Oh, I'm spiraling. "I'll have two under two! Do you know how expensive diapers are? And what if I can't breastfeed, so I'll need the expensive formula Violet drinks? God, what if she never takes to solids, and she's still drinking that formula then? Oliver will probably regress, and then I'll have three drinking formula and pooping in diapers and I'll never be able to see adult humans again because I'll just be covered in puke and poop and pee and —"

Whitley slaps a hand over my mouth, effectively stopping my psychotic outburst. "I highly doubt Oliver regresses all the way back to drinking formula. Yes, diapers are expensive, but we can research cloth diapering. It's gross, but cost-effective. If you can't breastfeed, we'll cross that bridge when we come to it. All formula isn't as expensive the crap Violet needs to have, and at some point, she'll wean off of that too. You're taking every molehill and making it into a mountain, El. You might not even be pregnant. And furthermore, you know Leo is going to be one hell of a hands-on dad."

My face screws up as emotion overtakes me, and I wail, "Yeah, but I'm going to be an awful mom!"

"Fucking hell, maybe you are pregnant," Whitley mutters. "While I know you don't consider yourself a mother because you didn't birth Oliver and Violet, you are, in fact, the only mother figure they have. That makes you a mother. And you're doing a great job with them. I know at times you think it's going horribly, but I have to assume all moms feel that way. Pull the test out, El. Let's cross this bridge now, and we'll figure out all the other steps in the future."

Sniffing hard, I wipe the tears from my face as I nod. Guess I have to rip off the Band-Aid. Here goes nothing.

Yanking the wrapped test out of my pocket, I slowly turn it over.

We're quiet as we stare at the digital display.

"Now what?" I ask numbly.

Whitley sighs. "Now we figure out a way to tell Leo he's going to be a dad."

Chapter **18**

LEO

I'm happily whistling as I walk up the stairs to Ella's apartment. I'm sure if any of my siblings saw me, they'd be concerned I'd cracked my head open, because I'm absurdly happy. I'm so close to getting what I want, what I need, and I can't help but feel so damn optimistic about the future.

I didn't intend to go into Purrfect Books today. I'm not entirely sure how I ended up there in the first place, as I was a couple of blocks away, then suddenly seemed to almost materialize in front of the bookstore. All I remember was seeing red when I looked in to find Ella's neighbor bugging her. I could tell by her expression that she didn't invite the interaction, and I was all too eager to assert some dominance over the jerk. Again.

How I ended up behind the counter and kissing Ella is a bit of a mystery, but I'm not mad about it. That lip bite, and I was a goner. And then, she fucking melted into me. It wasn't an especially sexy kiss, and it definitely wasn't an "I licked her, so she's mine" kiss, but it was perfect for us. There's nothing quite like feeling the world disappear around you, knowing your woman is fully invested in your kiss, and getting to make her feel how much she means to you. I don't think I'll ever forget that kiss.

Shifting the six-pack of beer so I can balance the pizza on top of it, I knock loudly on Ella's door. I hear Oliver excitedly shout, "Leo's here! Hurry, Auntie Ella! Let my Leo in!"

I can't help the wide grin that breaks across my face. My Leo. Wow.

When the door opens, I barely glance at Ella before Oliver tackles my legs. "Leo! Can we play with my Play-Doh again? Will you have a sleepover? I don't think you can fit on my bed, but we could build a tent and sleep on the floor. Oh, pizza! I'm so hungry. Hurry up, come inside!"

"Wow," I blurt out, chuckling.

"He's a little energetic tonight," El says quietly. Looking up, I find her paler than she was at the bookstore, her face somber.

"Are you okay?" I ask. "You look like you don't feel well."

"Upset stomach," she murmurs, then motions for me to walk inside. I hear a squeal, and find Violet jumping in some kind of contraption that I've seen my nieces and nephews have.

"Hi, baby girl," I coo, walking over to Violet. After placing the beer and pizza on the table, I gently scoop her up from the bouncer. "What is that thing called?"

"A Jumperoo. I'm glad my sister saved it from when Oliver was a baby, because Violet loves it even more than he did." Ella watches me with a faint smile as Violet grabs onto my beard hairs, making me wince. "If you put her in her high chair, I'll get plates for everyone."

"Is she doing better with food?" I ask as I place Violet into the high chair. As soon as I attach the table part, she slaps her hands against it gleefully.

"She's done a little better, but she still prefers a bottle. I've gotten her to eat a bit of solids though. Your mom was right, as Violet does really like avocado," Ella says over her shoulder as she pulls three plates from a cabinet. As she walks back to the table, she grabs a container of baby food, and a spoon, then calls for Oliver to come eat.

"Do you want me to feed her?" I ask, sitting beside Violet.

"I can do it," Ella says with a yawn.

"I know you can, Ladybug. I'm offering. You look dead on your feet. I got this. You can go take a nap, if you want," I tell her. Our talk can wait. El looks like she could fall asleep sitting up.

"Normally, I wouldn't, but honestly, I'm just so tired, Leo. I could really use an hour," she admits.

"Go, baby. We'll be fine." I give Ella a smile as she stands up, but as she walks past me, I wrap an arm around her waist, pulling her into my side. "We're gonna talk later, okay?"

"Okay," she whispers. I watch as she pads down the hall into her bedroom, closing the door quietly behind her. I turn back to Oliver and Violet, who both smile at me.

"You ready to eat?" I ask.

"Did you get cheese? I like cheese," Oliver replies as he sits beside me.

Opening the pizza box, I pull out a slice of cheese, placing it on one of the plates. "It's your lucky day, my man. I got extra cheese."

"More cheese," Oliver whispers reverently, his eyes wide as he takes in the slice. "Are you gonna cut it?"

"Uh, no?" I pull out a slice for myself, then open the container of pureed bananas Ella set out for Violet. "Just pick it up and eat it."

"Auntie Ella always cuts mine into little bites," Oliver states.

"Auntie Ella is asleep. Eat it like me," I tell him. I pick up the piece, then wait for Oliver to mimic me. Once he does, I take a small bite. "See? We don't need knives for pizza."

"No knives!" he shouts, making me chuckle.

"A little quieter. Let's not have Auntie Ella figuring out we're rebelling, okay?" When he nods, I turn back to Violet. "Alright, baby girl. Let's see how much banana we can get on your face."

Three hours and two baths later, Oliver is sound asleep in his bed, and Violet is sleeping on my shoulder, when a very confused Ella stumbles out of her bedroom. "What time is it? Where's Oliver?"

"It's nine. Oliver is in bed. He ate two pieces of pizza, somehow got sauce in his hair, got a bath and brushed his teeth while in the tub, then convinced me to read him three books. He fell asleep during the second one, but he made me promise to read all three even if he was asleep. I don't break promises."

"Good to know," she says with a yawn. "Did Violet eat?"

"Finished the whole container, but it's been a while since I've fed an infant, so I'm not sure how much actually made it into her mouth. She also got a bath, then a bottle, and she's been asleep for about thirty minutes."

"You made a bottle?" Ella asks incredulously.

I nod. "You know there are directions on the container, right? It's not like I solved world hunger."

"How many ounces did you make?"

"Six. Since she did eat some of the bananas, I figured she wouldn't drink as much formula. In all honesty, googled that part to confirm my suspicions."

Ella's lips twitch as she tries to hide a smile. "I appreciate the honesty. Let me put her in her crib."

As Ella gingerly scoops Violet off my shoulder, I tell her, "I didn't want to wake you, so I didn't bring her in."

"Oh, she's not in my room anymore. She's in her crib in her room. The bassinet was only until she was sleeping through the night. Once she did that, and she started trying to sit up during the night, it wasn't safe in the bassinet anymore. And I wasn't about to disassemble and reassemble the crib to put it in my room. Frankly, she needed to be in her own space anyway, and I'm relieved to have my room back."

"Damn, I wish I'd known that. I'd have put her in her crib already," I reply. Not wanting to be away from Ella, I follow her down the hall and into the small room meant for Violet. "Jeez, this room is tiny."

"It's fine for her right now. She really only sleeps in here," Ella whispers as she bends over the side of the crib to place Violet on the mattress. "Eventually I'll clean out the other room and move her in there. I need to go through my sister's things and get rid of stuff anyway."

She motions for me to follow her back into the hallway, stopping momentarily to turn on a sound machine. She leaves the bedroom door ajar, then walks back to the living room. "Is there any pizza left?"

"Yeah, I put two pieces on a plate in the microwave for you," I answer. Something is off with Ella. She's more subdued than normal. Quiet and somber. "Is your stomach feeling better?"

Ella startles, placing a hand on her abdomen. "Yeah, I guess. Must have been something I ate."

Sitting on the couch, I wait as Ella reheats the pizza, then comes to sit beside me. I chuckle as I watch her cut the slice with a fork and knife.

"What's funny?" she asks before shoveling a bite into her mouth.

"Hopefully you'll find it funny, but I told Oliver to eat his pizza like me, instead of cutting it up. So if he tells you that I taught him that we don't use knives with pizza, or with food in general, that's why."

She smiles faintly. "He's the one who made me cut it in the first place. He didn't want to touch the sauce, and hated the feel of grease on his fingers."

"I think he conquered that fear tonight. Now I think I understand how the sauce got in his hair, since he kept swiping his hand on his head."

"Hair is an excellent napkin," Ella muses with a grin, and I'm thrilled to see a bit of sparkle back in her eyes. Maybe she was just hungry.

"While you're eating, I'd like to explain where I've been for the past two months," I blurt out, suddenly unwilling to wait even a second longer to confess my feelings.

"Alright," she says hesitantly, her eyes darting to the floor.

"I could tell you were uncomfortable with how often I came into the bookstore, so I decided to give you some time. I figured you wouldn't answer a phone call, and I honestly don't care that much for texting, so I didn't contact you that way either. But then life sort of went off the rails, and I didn't come up for air for a few weeks."

"Okay," she whispers.

"No, it's not okay. I should have called. Texted. Showed up here. Something. I should have done *anything* to let you know I never stopped thinking about you." When she doesn't reply, I reach out to grab her chin, forcing her eyes to mine. "Not just the last few weeks, El. I've never stopped thinking of you. You're the last thing on my mind when I fall asleep, you visit me in my dreams, and I wake up with your name on my lips. Always."

"Leo," she says quietly, a sheen of tears glazing over her eyes. "I can't … this is too much …"

"What is too much?" I ask, my eyes pleading with hers. I cup her cheeks in both hands, leaning over to rest my forehead against hers. "Am I too much?"

"No, it's just … I don't know if I can do this right now," she confesses. The words hurt, but simultaneously, she grabs both of my forearms, anchoring me to her. Her mind is at war with her body.

"I'm not asking for everything," I tell her hastily, holding her against me. "One day at a time, baby. That's all I need. Baby steps."

Her breath catches. "Baby … baby steps."

"I just want you. Any way I can have you. If all you can give me is a few minutes a day, I happily accept. I don't care about alone time, or planning dates around Play-Doh and baby bottles. I'm in this, Ella. In whatever way you'll have me." I hold in a breath as I wait for her response, and exhale when she relaxes against me.

"Okay," she whispers, and I lean in to kiss her softly. God, I love how pillowy soft her lips are. They fit so perfectly against mine, and I groan into her mouth. When I feel her tongue tentatively touch my lips, I open, reveling in how she flicks into my mouth. Before I know it, I'm pulling her into my lap, deepening the kiss as she straddles me, wrapping her arms around my neck. I shouldn't let this spiral out of control like the last time. But all the blood leaves my brain for southern pastures, and I almost forget how to breathe, let alone slow things down.

Slipping my hands under the hem of her shirt, I slide them up and down her spine, then move one into her hair. The other hand begins a slow trek around her ribs, until I'm cupping one tit, enjoying how the nipple pebbles under my touch. Her breast feels much fuller than I remember, which I'm sure is also due to age, and Ella moans when I pinch the tip between my thumb and forefinger. I break off the kiss before pulling her shirt up and over her head, then bring her breast to my mouth. Circling the tip with my tongue, Ella's head falls back as she moans again, and I suck aggressively. She cries out, gripping my head and holding it to her, as she grinds down on my hard length. I grab the other breast, giving it the same treatment, as Ella's hips swivel frantically against me. "Are you going to come, baby? Just from me playing with these beautiful tits?"

"God, Leo, yes, don't stop," she moans, and when I nibble lightly on the tip, she tenses, her mouth open with a silent scream, as she orgasms phenomenally. Ella lets out a shuddered exhale as aftershocks rack her body, and I patiently swirl my tongue along her nipple as she comes down from her high. "Holy shit," she pants.

"That was hot," I murmur, switching to tongue the other nipple. "Don't think I've ever gotten you off with just nipple play."

"First time for everything, I guess," she says breathlessly, then gasps when I nip at her again. "Stop or I'll come again."

"Don't threaten me with a good time," I joke. Honestly, as much as I love coming, there's nothing I enjoy more in the world than watching Ella come. I'm not sure what has her all riled up tonight, but I'm not complaining.

"I'd like it if you enjoyed this too," she says.

"Trust me, baby. I'm enjoying this just fine."

"I mean I want you to come too," she says exasperatedly, rolling her eyes. She tries to slide off my lap, but I clamp my arms around her. "How am I supposed to get you off if you won't let me get you in my mouth?"

Fuck. The thought of her on her knees is almost my undoing. "As badly as I'd like that — and trust me, I want that so fucking much — I need to be inside you, Ladybug. Last time was too quick. I swear I can last longer than ten seconds. Frankly, if you put your mouth on me, I'm likely to come in less time than that."

She smiles bashfully. I love this side of Ella, where she knows what she wants, she knows she can trust me, but she still struggles to admit things out loud. But I'm a patient motherfucker, and I just have to wait her out.

Finally, she confesses, "Maybe if I control the pace, you'll last longer?"

"Maybe," I tell her. Hell if I know. "Do you want to stay here, or go to your bedroom?"

"I'd kind of like to stay here. It was always my favorite position with you. When I was in your lap, riding you. I liked having the control, and it always felt really good because you'd hit my clit with each stroke," she explains.

"You're in control, baby. This is your show. I'll do what you tell me to do."

Ella gives me a beautiful smile as she reaches down to untie my joggers. She pulls them slightly so she can pull out my cock, then looks at me. "Will you take off your shirt? I want to see you."

I do as she asks, wondering if she'll finally notice the tattoo over my heart. She's seen me without a shirt on, when I used her shower after Violet threw up on me, but I don't think she looked close enough at the three dates I have over my heart. I have a larger tattoo on my side with the names of each soldier I lost, which is much more obvious. The ones for her are somewhat covered by chest hair as well, which may be why she hasn't commented on them yet. I know Ella, and she won't ignore the fact that she's literally tattooed on my heart.

I wait on bated breath as she stands to push her pants down. She grins shyly as she straddles me again, and I position the tip of my cock at her entrance. Ella exhales as she slowly sits, her heat surrounding me exquisitely, until I fill her completely. My eyes close in bliss, and I'm acutely aware of how perfect it feels with Ella. Even with no other woman to compare it to, I know it'll never be better than this. It's then that I hear her gasp.

"Leo! What is this? Why?" she cries out, and I open my eyes to find her staring at the tattoos on my chest. Her finger traces the three sets of numbers I'd had permanently marked on me only weeks before my last deployment. I'd known then what I know now, that Ella Langley was the only woman for me, and if I couldn't have her, I wouldn't be with another.

When she reaches the end of the first date, I clear my throat. "The day we met."

She continues onto the second date, and I state, "Our first date."

And finally, as she traces the third, "When I told you I love you."

Her body tenses as she hears my words. I didn't phrase it in past tense. It isn't that I loved her. There was never an ending for my love. I've loved Ella since I was barely a man. Through high school, breakups, boot camp, and deployments. I'll love her until my last breath.

I could have added a thousand dates to that tattoo. The first time we kissed, when we had sex, or the first time we danced in the rain. The number of times I called her after I'd lost someone, and she'd patiently helped me through it all. The day I bought her engagement ring, or the time when I went to her dad's grave to ask for his blessing. There would never be enough space on my skin for tattoos, because Ella made every moment of my life that much better.

As her finger gently touches the still recovering skin of the ladybug outline, I let my hand drift up to her hair, pulling a lock behind her ear. She doesn't know I have another appointment scheduled for next week, when I'll be adding the birthdays for Oliver and Violet. "I got that three weeks ago."

"Leo," she says tearfully, her lips only a millimeter from mine. "I have your birthday tattooed on my foot."

"What?" I ask incredulously, pulling my head away from hers. "Seriously? Show me."

"Right now?" she replies, pointing down to where we're still joined. "Do you really want me to get off you to show you a tattoo?"

"Which foot?" I ask, ignoring her rhetorical question.

"Left." I push her slightly to my right, then look down to where her foot is beside my knee. On the outside of her foot, I see a small line of print, featuring my birthday.

I look up at her in wonder, then feel a shit-eating grin cover my face. "I fucking knew you were as gone for me as I was for you."

Ella rolls her eyes playfully. "Uh-huh. That's why you called so much."

Sitting upright, I capture her face in my hands, and wait until her eyes meet mine. "Let's get something crystal clear, baby. I had to give my phone to one of my guys, because I couldn't be trusted with it. I'd have called you nonstop if I thought there was even a sliver of a chance you'd have taken me back. There hasn't been one day, or even one hour, when I wasn't lost for you. There has never been anyone but you."

"Yeah, right," she scoffs sarcastically.

"Baby, I'm not kidding." I pause, letting that sink in. "There's never been anyone else."

"You mean dating, right?" she asks warily.

"No. I mean anyone period. I haven't dated, kissed, fucked, or even looked at another woman since the moment I saw you in the eighth grade. You've always been it for me, El."

Her eyes widen comically. "No one?"

I shake my head. "There will never be anyone who could compare to you. I'll only ever want you."

Ella lurches forward, covering my lips with hers. I wrap my arms around her frame, crushing her body to mine as she kisses me desperately. "Me too. No one else, I mean. I couldn't forget you, and the thought of doing anything with someone else felt so awful. God, Leo, I can't believe we've both been apart this long without —"

I stop her with another kiss, feeling a wild energy inside of me that I haven't felt in a long time. Years, even. I feel like I'm getting my girl back, and everything is finally falling into place. At the ripe old age of thirty-eight.

"I need you to move, baby," I rasp against her lips, aware that our kisses are turning me on a little too much, and I'm liable to embarrass myself if I can't get her off first. As Ella begins to move, I slip a hand between our bodies, finding her clit. I'm only able to strum it a few times before she holds her breath, her walls clamping down on me, and I bury my head against her neck as I groan out my own release.

Perfection. Absolute perfection.

I'm finally home.

Chapter 19

ELLA

Everyone thought I was crazy when I couldn't seem to move on from Leo. How if I'd only just "gotten back on the horse," everything would be fine. Whitley suggested one-night stands, dating websites, and even going to bars to find anyone willing to hook up. She figured if I could have a few male-centered orgasms, I'd be able to get past my memories of Leo.

There was no moving past him. He's been the only one in my heart since I was a teenager. All this time, I couldn't fathom being with someone else, and I naturally assumed he'd had no trouble finding women. To know he couldn't move on from me? God, I feel so much better knowing I wasn't the only one struggling so much.

"Let's go to bed, baby," Leo whispers against my hair. After cleaning up, we'd cuddled on the couch, chatting about our favorite memories from when we were kids. Leo turned on the television for a bit, and I happily snuggled against him as he gently dragged his fingers through my hair. It was peaceful and perfect.

"Mmm-hmm," I murmur, not moving an inch, making Leo chuckle. As I feel him shift to slide an arm under my knees, I smile, knowing he's planning to carry me to bed. I let him, because there's nowhere I feel safer than in Leo's arms, and I know he enjoys taking care of me.

Leo lays me down in bed, then slides in next to me, pulling my back against his front, and I sigh happily. I went years without falling asleep like this, and the wave of peace I feel is so comforting.

Until the last moment before I slip into sleep, when I remember that I still don't know how to tell Leo I'm carrying his child. The wave of comfort is gone, and I toss and turn all night.

"You were restless last night," Leo comments, his voice nonchalant as he sips a coffee next to me at the table. Oliver was so thrilled to find Leo here this morning, and happily ate eggs and toast with Leo while they watched cartoons. Now, as I'm feeding Violet some infant cereal with pureed carrots, I avoid his gaze. I know the even-keeled tone, though. He sounds relaxed, but he's observing everything. Taking in every detail to determine how he should react.

"It happens sometimes," I finally answer. I'm not ready to explain why. I'm freaked about possibly miscarrying, and I don't think I can handle hurting Leo by telling him I'm having his baby, and then ripping that chance away from him. Plus, I'm definitely not discussing this around the kids.

I've seen how great Leo is with kids. He was made to be a father. It's almost as if Oliver and Violet like him more than they like me. Leo's nieces and nephews flock to him, because he has this calming and accepting personality unlike anyone I've ever met. I still haven't forgiven myself for miscarrying years ago, and until I get to a doctor to find out that this baby is real, and I'm not likely to miscarry again, I won't be telling Leo anything.

"You sure you're okay?" he asks, his eyes intense as he watches me. "Seems like you're struggling with something."

I attempt to shrug nonchalantly. "Guess I'm just tired. Maybe you wore me out."

"I highly doubt that," he snorts. "That would involve lasting for longer than a minute."

"I'm not complaining," I reply, happy to have a change of subject. "I'd say we both enjoyed that minute."

He gives me a one-sided smirk. "Practice makes perfect, right? I'll build up to normal at some point."

"What exactly is normal?" I ask.

He laughs. "Not sure. It's been too long, and I'm old now. But I'm cautiously optimistic normal is longer than sixty seconds."

"But if it is the norm from now on, I'm fine with that."

"Good to know."

"My Leo!" Oliver shouts, jarring both of us. I'm still not used to how loud Oliver is in the morning. He's on the floor by the couch, playing with a box of Lego Duplo building bricks. "Can you help me play with my Legos this morning?"

"Only for a few minutes, buddy," Leo answers. "I have to get to work."

I watch as Oliver's face falls, and my heart breaks a little. This sweet boy is desperate for a father figure in his life. I wish I was closer with my brother, and that he recognized how much his nephew and niece need him. I hate that my parents are both gone, because I know they'd be the most doting grandparents in the world.

"Hey," Leo says quietly, rushing to Oliver's side. Crouching down, he looks Oliver in the eyes. "How about I come back after work? I was thinking I could make you guys dinner for a change, and I think I'll need a helper. You up for that?"

"Really? I can help?" Oliver asks, hope blooming in his voice. Emotion fills my heart as I take in the picture before me, and it makes me fall even more for Leo. If this goes badly — again — I won't survive it.

"Of course," Leo replies. He smiles sweetly at Oliver. "Can't lie to my favorite dude. I was thinking about making pizza. Does that sound good?"

"You can make pizza?" Oliver screeches. "I thought it only came in a box!"

Leo looks at me and winks. "Box pizza is really good. But every now and then, I like to make it fresh."

"Do you member my favorite kind?"

"Extra cheese?"

"Yup. I like cheese," Oliver says, grinning. "Can I go back to my Legos now?"

"Yeah, bud," Leo says with a chuckle. "I'll see you later."

I watch quietly as Leo puts his shoes on, then places his dishes in my sink. "You still like sausage and mushrooms on your pizza?"

My mouth falls open in shock. "I can't believe you remembered that. I still like sausage and mushroom pizza, but I'll eat just about anything that I don't have to cook."

"I was thinking I could also make my Nonna's bolognese for the two of us. We can see if Oliver likes it, but if not, I know he'll devour the pizza."

My mouth immediately begins to salivate. "I haven't had her bolognese in so long! You know how to make it?"

He snags a hand around my waist, pulling me against him. "I do. And if I promise to cook and clean up, can I have a sleepover again?"

I can't help the smile that covers my face as I giggle. "Are you bartering with me, Mr. Santo?"

His answering smile is easy, sensual, and borderline wicked. "Maybe. If I do a good job cleaning, can I dirty you up after the kids go to bed?"

Leo doesn't give me time to answer, bending down to seal his lips over mine. I sigh against his lips, allowing his tongue to slide in and circle mine. Standing on my tiptoes, I wrap my arms around his neck, pulling him closer. His hand flexes against my back, and I feel his length grow against my core. He breaks the kiss, moving his head so his lips are next to my ear. "Behave, Ms.

Langley. I promise we'll have more time for making out after dinner."

"Auntie Ella," Oliver whispers, making Leo and me turn toward Oliver. His eyes are as wide as saucers. "Why are you kissing my Leo?"

"Because I like him," I answer simply.

"And I like Auntie Ella," Leo adds in.

"Oh," Oliver says, his brow furrowed in confusion, but he turns to focus on his Legos again.

"He's gonna ask more questions, isn't he?" Leo whispers.

"Oh, one hundred percent."

"Good luck with that, Auntie Ella," he jokes. "You working today?"

"Only for an hour to cover lunch. I take the kids with me. Whitley has Oliver greeting people. He thinks it's a trip."

"I'll call you later. Six okay for dinner?"

"That's perfect." Leo's eyes dart to Oliver, and when he sees Oliver isn't watching us, he gives me a quick, but intense, kiss. I walk him to the door, and he cups my cheek lovingly, but doesn't say a word. As soon as I close the door behind him, Oliver jumps up.

"I don't like you kissing my Leo."

Lord almighty. I pull Violet from her high chair, then motion for Oliver to follow us to the couch. Once Violet is situated on the floor, I turn to Oliver. "I've known Leo for twenty-five years. Have I ever told you that?"

"I don't think so," Oliver replies.

"He was my boyfriend for a long time, Oliver. I loved him, and he was very important to me." I'm still learning how to explain adult concepts to children. How should I get Oliver to comprehend high school sweethearts, why we broke up, and how life will now continue to involve Leo for the foreseeable future?

"Was it like how I love my mommy?" he asks.

"Sort of. Loving a boyfriend or girlfriend is different from loving a mom or dad, but it hurts just the same when that person isn't there anymore. I haven't been the same in the years that Leo and I have been apart. But I'm hoping things are going to be better for us now."

"What if it's not? What if Leo leaves like my mommy did?" His voice quivers on those last few words, making me scoop him into my arms.

"Oh, my sweet boy. Your mommy would be here if she could. She loved you and Violet so, so much. And if Leo were to leave like your mommy … well, I'll still be here. And the three of us will continue to get by like we have for months now. Me, you, and Violet. We'll be alright."

"Are you gonna kiss Leo more now?" Oliver wonders.

"Would it be okay if I did?"

He shrugs. "I guess. You smile a lot when he's here. I like your smile. Can we ask Leo to go to the zoo with us? I think I'd like it more if he came too."

"We can ask him. We'll have to plan it for when we're all off work, so it might not be for a little while. Okay?"

"Alright, I guess," Oliver mutters, his eyes dropping. I smother a laugh. Four-year-olds have no concept of schedules and time. "Can I go back to my Legos now?"

"That's fine. We'll need to leave in about two hours to go help Whitley at the bookstore."

"Can we bring a kitty home for the night?" he asks hopefully.

Crud. He's asked multiple times, and I keep forgetting to grab a litter box, litter, and cat food from the grocery store. "Not today, but the next time we go to the grocery, I promise we'll get some supplies so we can have kitten sleepovers."

While Oliver happily plays with his Legos, and Violet chats with her favorite stuffed animal, I think about which cat I'd be comfortable bringing home for the night, because I know once I allow one to come into my apartment, it won't be going back to the bookstore.

"Where is everybody?" Oliver asks, anger evident in his tone. There's no one to greet, and he's pissed about it.

"I don't know," Whitley says easily. "While we wait, do you want to watch an episode of *Bluey* on my phone?"

"Yes!" Oliver shouts, yanking the phone from her hands. He skips over to the small child-size table I have in the corner, in the children's books section, and focuses completely on the episode, giving Whitley time to grill me.

"So what happened last night? How did he take the news?" she asks.

I sigh. "I didn't tell him."

"What? Why not?"

"I just — I couldn't, Whit," I blurt out, tears filling my eyes. "I haven't even been to the doctor yet. What if it was a false positive? Or what if I miscarry again? I don't know why I did before, and now I'm so much older. It may not even be viable. I can't tell him if I'm just going to have to rip it out of his hands right away."

"Oh, El," she whispers. "You can't think about it that way. You don't know how he'll react, but you're assuming he'll blame you for something you don't control. Maybe you need to give Leo a little more credit."

"But things are going well, and I know I won't be able to survive another breakup with him," I admit softly.

"Every day that you spend more time with him, you're going to fall deeper in love. It's only going to get harder to handle. Plus, the longer you wait? The more angry he's going to be at you hiding it from him," she points out.

"What if he thinks I did this on purpose to trap him?"

"Okay, you're really grasping at straws here. Leo has never accused you of anything like that. I don't know him well, but from everything you've told me, he's got the patience of a saint, and he's incredibly even-keeled. He'd never think so poorly of you."

She's right. I'm so scared to tell him about the pregnancy that I'm looking for any possible reason not to. "I don't know how to tell him, Whit."

She gives me a kind smile, and grabs onto my shoulders, moving me so I'm facing her. "Let's have a little practice. I'll be Leo. You only have to say, 'hey, stud. Thanks for boinking me so good a couple of months ago. Turns out, you dropped some offspring in there. You cool with a lifetime of this?'"

I snort in disbelief. "Incredibly eloquent."

Whitley shrugs. "I mean, you can paraphrase however you want. But the gist is the same. He needs to know, Ella. You can't hide this forever, especially if the boinking continues. He'll figure it out eventually. Now give it a try."

"Okay." Inhaling, I look at Whitley, who nods reassuringly. "Hey, Leo. Remember a few months ago?"

"Do I ever!" Whitley says rambunctiously. "Gave it to ya good, didn't I?"

I giggle. "Something like that. Well, remember how I said it probably was a good time of the month since we didn't use any protection?"

Whitley's eyes bug out of her head. "Oh, shit. Yeah. You know how I like it raw."

"Jesus, Whit. That is not how he sounds."

"How am I supposed to know?" she says, throwing up her hands. "I figure he sounds all growly and alpha with you!"

"Not like that. You sound gross and frat-boy. Leo is a lot more composed."

"Fine," she says with a loud sigh. "Oh, yeah. I forgot I didn't wrap it up. Is that better?"

"I guess," I reply with a huff. "Anyway, I think I'm pregnant, and it's yours."

"See?" she shouts. "Was that so hard? Wait. I guess it was hard, or it wouldn't have worked right."

"Whitley!" I gasp, laughing.

"I guess it probably won't go as well as this conversation did, but I'm superior in all things. What can I say?"

"Your modesty is remarkable," I comment dryly.

"It's a gift." Whitley grins, then sobers. "What would make this easier for you? Is there anything I can do to help?"

"I don't know. I think once I get into see an obstetrician and have them confirm the pregnancy is valid, I'll feel more comfortable. I didn't even know I was pregnant the last time until I was miscarrying, so I guess I didn't have time to wrap my head around it all."

"I think it would have been even worse if you had, El," she replies softly. "Your heart would have gotten even more invested. The guilt you feel now would potentially have doubled or tripled."

"I don't agree. If I had known, I'd have taken better care of myself. I was so miserable I wasn't eating right. I know I had alcohol multiple times, and there were days I barely ate anything at all. That couldn't have been healthy. What if that contributed to the miscarriage?"

"Did anyone tell you it may have been your fault?" she asks pointedly.

"Well, not exactly, but —"

"No, girl. There is no 'not exactly' option here. Either someone told you it was your fault, or they didn't. Here's another time where you're assuming what someone may think. There are a thousand reasons why you might have miscarried. Some of those may have happened at conception. Did you know that? It could have been a wonky egg, or a wonky sperm, and it happened immediately. Would you blame Leo in that situation if a test identified that his sperm was to blame?"

"No, because he had no control over that, if that were the case."

"Yet you blame yourself for what was most likely nothing you could control."

"It's different," I say defensively, even though I have no concrete evidence to back that up. "It's in my body. If something fails, it's on me."

Whitley covers my hands with hers. "No, Ella. It isn't. I know you. I know your heart. You're one of the kindest and most selfless people in this town. A miscarriage isn't something you blame on someone. Now, if you were abusing alcohol or doing drugs, that would be the exception. But you're not that. Yeah, those weeks after Leo left were brutal. I had to remind you to eat a lot. But you still drank a lot of water. You made sure to eat fruit, and you certainly slept a lot. What happened wasn't your fault. I might not be a scientist, and the closest I can get to a medical degree is what I've learned on *The Pitt* and *Grey's Anatomy*, but I know with absolute certainty that it wasn't your fault."

"I don't agree," I rasp painfully, tears pouring down my cheeks.

"I can't make you see it from my perspective," Whitley says with a sigh. "But I think it would benefit you to get in with an OB sooner rather than later, and ask them some of these questions. If they don't give you some peace of mind, then we'll find you a psychologist. You've got a hell of a lot of PTSD from that period in your life. No matter what happens with Leo, or with this baby, you've got a niece and nephew depending on you. It's time you get some closure on what happened back then."

Chapter 20

L + E = ?

Now a routine fixture at Purrfect Books, Leo Santo is clearly all in when it comes to courting Ella Langley again. Is it their sixth relationship or seventh? Honestly, we aren't sure. Sources tell us they've been hot and heavy, with Mr. Santo spending many nights at Ms. Langley's apartment.

A follow-up to a recent story: Marybeth Nix's rug has been recovered, but her flower pot is now missing. It's unknown at this time if Mason is the culprit.

Something is definitely up with Ella.

Whatever it is, she won't talk to me about it. And when I attempt to get her to open up, she manages to redirect the conversation, or we end up having sex, and I forget all about what's bugging her.

While I'm thrilled with all the sex, as well as the fact that my one-minute-man record has now expanded to two-minutes-man, I'm aggravated she won't open up to me. Ella used to tell me everything. I was the person she confided in, and vice versa. I could talk to Alex about military things, and my parents about certain topics, but Ella was who I went to for everything else. My hopes and dreams. Silly stories about my fellow soldiers, and what I feared about deployments. We used to daydream about our future together, down to how we'd pick a house, what we'd like to have in our backyard, and where we'd want to get married.

While I feel like we're in a relationship now, we've never discussed things, and I don't feel any closer to her. Is she closed off because she thinks I'll leave again? Fearful I won't want to raise Oliver and Violet with her? Worried I still have animosity about her ending our relationship all those years ago? I wish she'd talk to me so I could reassure her about everything. I'm in this for the long haul. However she'll have me.

After a long day working at Everlasting, I assume it's Ella calling when my phone rings right when I get into my car, and I'm surprised when I see it's my youngest sister, Arianna, calling.

"Leo, are you home yet?" she asks urgently.

"No, just left Everlasting. Why?"

"I need to talk to you about something. Can I meet you at your house?"

"Sure. Is everything okay?"

"I'm fine."

"Do I need to hide a body?" I joke, then sober when Arianna doesn't laugh. "Ari. You're kind of freaking me out."

"We're all fine, Leo. I promise. I just need to talk to you about something else."

My mind is flipping through a million different scenarios as I drive home, letting out a relieved exhale when I find Arianna already there when I arrive. Jumping out of the car, I'm quickly in front of her. "What's going on?"

Her expression is tense as she studies me. Hair up in a messy bun, she looks somewhat disheveled. Arianna Santo Dixon is never disheveled, yet she stands before me wearing a worn tee shirt of Stone's, oversized sweatpants, and Crocs. "Are the kids okay? I've never seen you like this."

"Kids are fine. I swear. And I have four kids, Leo. I dress like this when I'm dealing with them, because they're all a bunch of feral animals," she snaps as we walk inside my house.

"Alright. Tell me what you need to talk about. Please."

Her eyes flick between mine. "Are you and Ella back together? For real?"

A brick seems to land in my stomach. "For the most part, yes. Why?"

"What does that mean? Either you're together, or you're not," she says impatiently.

"We haven't discussed specifics, but we're seeing each other. I don't think there's anyone else for her, and there definitely isn't for me. But I haven't asked," I confess.

"So there could be someone else in her life?" she asks, her eyes pained.

"Ari, if you know something, you have to tell me," I say hoarsely. I feel my heart rate jump as I consider her words. Jesus. Is Ella seeing someone else?

"I stopped in at Purrfect Books to say hello this afternoon," she begins. "I'd heard you might be seeing her again. Gia said she thought things had gotten serious between you two, and I wanted to extend an olive branch. I know I've never been super close with Ella, and wanted to make an effort if she'd be in our lives again."

"Okay?" I ask warily.

Ari blows out a breath. "She was talking to the gal who works the café. Whitley? Anyway, they were talking about a doctor's appointment Ella had, and Whitley asked if 'the dad' had gone. Leo, I think she's pregnant, and I don't know if it's yours."

My quick heartbeat from a moment ago seems to stop. What the actual fuck? There's no way. "That can't be — no. She couldn't be seeing someone else behind my back. We're together all the time. Us and the kids. There's no way."

"I don't know for sure. Could the baby be yours? Maybe I shouldn't have mentioned it. Your face is getting red. Leo? Are you okay? Leo! Can you hear me?" Arianna's voice seems to echo as I struggle to breathe. I thought everything was going well. We were on the same page. Did I only hear what I wanted to hear again? Is she not as gone for me as I am for her?

What if she is pregnant? It might be mine. Will she even bother telling me? She never told me about the miscarriage. Was that one not mine either? I can't be mad about that. We'd broken up. If she did move on, she was allowed to. But she told me she hadn't been with another man since me. Was she lying?

I can't fucking breathe.

"Stay with me Santo. Sergeant! Stay with me!"

Fuck, am I in Afghanistan? What the hell is happening right now?

I'm not good enough. I wasn't good enough for Ella to stay with me then, I sure as fuck am not now. I should have anticipated this. A good soldier looks at all possible outcomes to a mission. Then again, a good soldier doesn't get half of his squad killed due to impatience and timing.

Probably better if the baby isn't mine. How can I be trusted to be a good dad? I shouldn't be the caretaker for anyone, because I can barely handle myself.

I always wanted to have a family with Ella. It's the only thing I always thought was out of my reach.

"I know you did."

I'm not worth it. No one should love me.

"That's not true, Leo. God, I shouldn't have told you until I knew for sure."

Should have fucking killed myself when I wanted to all those years ago.

"What?!?!"

Shouldn't have let Gia talk me out of it. Had the pills and everything. Would have been better to just end it all. Better for everyone.

"G, you need to get over here. Leo's spiraling, and he's talking about suicide. I don't know what to do."

No one would miss me.

"We would *all* miss you, dammit. Yes, get everyone over here. This is major."

Curling up in a ball on the floor, unaware I'd collapsed right after Arianna said she thought Ella was pregnant, I begin to sob.

"*J*esus, Arianna, you should have told us first before you told him."

"There has to be an explanation. I can't believe Ella would do this." Am I dreaming? That sounded like Dom.

"Who knew she was pregnant before? Did anyone get confirmation?" Luca asks.

"Should we call the therapist he sees?" Shit, Alex is in this dream too?

"Seb already did. He's on his way." Isabella's voice is quiet.

"What about Mom and Dad? Or Nonna?" Why does Arianna sound like she's close to tears?

"No, let's wait to tell them. Leo will be pissed if they get involved." Dom again.

"Leo will be pissed when he figures out we are all here anyway." Alex is right, I will be pissed. Wait. Why are they all talking about me?

"Did he really say he was going to kill himself, Gia?" Was that Hannah? Why the hell is she here?

"Not in those words, but yes. I knew. I felt it and called him. He said it was too hard. I begged him to come home." Dammit, Gianna.

"That's why he suddenly showed up here again? Fuck." Dom's voice is full of pain.

"I'm pretty sure he's awake and listening to all of this." That sounds like Stone.

"Leo? Are you there?" Gianna asks softly.

I open my eyes, finding I'm now on my couch. "Who moved me here?"

"So you remember being on the floor?" Arianna asks, her voice choppy. I open my eyes to find her worried gaze as she chews on a fingernail.

"Vaguely. I guess you all have questions," I comment as I sit up. I hate this. I despise feeling inferior and dependent on my family. I can't stand when my emotions get the best of me.

Gianna sits beside me, taking my hands tightly in hers. "I want to go over some details first, so we know what possibly set off your panic attack. Okay?"

I nod, suddenly so overcome with exhaustion, both physically and emotionally.

"Alright. Arianna asked to meet you here, and wanted to tell you she overheard a conversation between Ella and her friend Whitley about a doctor's appointment, and whether or not a dad would be in attendance. Ella replied that the dad didn't know. Is that correct?"

I nod numbly. Hearing it again is pouring salt into the wound.

"Then you started to mumble things," Arianna says quietly. "I don't think you knew you were speaking out loud. You said you'd always wanted a family with Ella, but that you weren't lovable. Then you said you should have killed yourself like you'd wanted to, but that Gia talked you out of it. Is that true?"

"For the most part, yeah," I murmur. I hear my front door open and close, then see Sebastian and Josh walk in.

"You had pills?" Alex asks, and I nod. "What kind?"

"I'd saved up a bunch of oxycodone pills from multiple surgeries."

"Multiple?"

Fuck. Sighing, I close my eyes. "My left leg, and my knee, are really fucked up. Shrapnel wounds, skin grafts. Debridement. Surgeons tried to revise a scar, but it made it worse. I had five or six surgeries at Walter Reed within a year, and it seemed like every time, my leg got worse. The surgeons in Germany weren't the best with things, as they were just trying to keep me alive."

"You almost died?" Isabella asks quietly.

I nod. "I was in a medically induced coma for a few weeks. I don't remember being flown out of Afghanistan at all, and I barely remember the first month or two in Germany."

"How much time went by before you actually notified us that you were injured?" Dom asks.

"I begged my superiors not to tell you. I knew the fact that half the squad died would make headlines, but didn't think they'd give specifics about which battalion we were from. I figured it was better you thought I was on a mission than at death's door."

"Typical fucking Leo," Alex says angrily. "Assuming no one else can handle things. And then once you were back stateside? How many surgeries did you have where we were clueless?"

"Gianna knew about most of them," I admit, watching her mouth drop open in shock. "When it was supposed to be a simple procedure, I didn't tell anyone. Why stress everyone out when all I was having was an outpatient procedure to remove another piece of shrapnel?"

"Stressing everyone out is what family is for, Leo," Luca spits out. "You're not supposed to handle all of this shit by yourself. You'd be furious if we did this to you."

"So when did you start feeling like you wanted to kill yourself?" Arianna asks.

I look down at my hands, still held tightly in Gianna's. She squeezes them reassuringly. "I'd been back in the States less than a year. The Army discharged me. I didn't know who I was without the Army, and without Ella. I'd figured she'd probably moved on, but I didn't have the balls to ask any of you about her. I didn't have the balls to admit how much I was struggling, how much guilt I had over losing all of my guys. Figured it was better if I just disappeared."

"Did you think we wouldn't support you if you admitted all of that?" Dom asks, and I nod. "I hate that you felt that way, Leo. I can't even imagine how you must have struggled for so long to get to that point. But I want you to hear every word that I say right now: I, for one, will never think less of you for admitting you're struggling or in pain. I'm always here for you. I know you would have dropped everything to help me had I needed it, so you need to know I'd do the same for you. I love you, man."

Each one of my siblings expresses how much they love me, making my eyes fill with tears again. I'm so drained, but also feeling lighter than I have in years because I've finally gotten all of this off my chest.

"This was a crucial part of your progress, Leo," Josh states clearly. "While it may not have come under ideal circumstances, it's still imperative in helping you find peace in the events from your last deployment. We still have work to do, but I'm proud of you for admitting these thoughts to your family."

I nod. "Not that it helps much with Ella."

"Let me ask a few questions," he says. "If she is pregnant, and it's yours, are you happy?"

"Yes," I answer immediately. "Fuck, yes."

"And if she isn't pregnant?"

I think for a moment. "As long as I know she hasn't slept with someone else, then yes, I'm fine with that too."

"What if she's pregnant, and it's not yours?" Josh asks.

"I have a lot of questions. If it's not mine, but it's from before we slept together the first time, then I don't really have any right to be upset. But if she's slept with someone after we were together ..." I trail off. "Well, I'm not sure I have a right to be upset with that either. We never discussed our situation. I just assumed we were exclusive, but we never talked about it."

"Ella has never been the kind of person who would sleep around," Gianna says. "At least not the Ella I knew, and I don't feel that's changed. I truly don't think she'd do that to you, Leo."

"It sounds like you want to be with Ella, no matter what," Josh comments. "Do you think she wants to be with you?"

"I hope so," I answer hesitantly. "I could tell something was off with her. She's been different for a few weeks. If she's known this whole time, why hasn't she told me? Even if it's not mine, I'm struggling with feeling like she's hiding it from me. Does she think I won't want her anymore?"

"It's possible," Josh replies. "We can't be for sure on why Ella has acted the way she has without speaking to her about it. Are you ready to hear her answer, no matter what it is?"

"I guess I have to be," I answer honestly, scrubbing a hand over my face. I'm so fucking tired.

"What can we do to help?" Alex asks quietly.

"I don't know," I reply. Rubbing my eyes, I try to focus my attention on my family, but I can feel the pain of a migraine coming on. I don't get as many migraines today as I did a few years ago, but the aura in my vision tells me this one is going to be a doozy.

"Do you need your meds?" Gianna whispers, and I nod. My twin knows when I'm truly in pain, which is why I've avoided her quite a bit when my leg has really been bothering me. She probably knows it then too, but allows me to maintain a tiny bit of my male dignity by not calling me out on it.

One by one, my siblings head out, until it's only me, Gianna, and Josh. Gianna excuses herself to give me time to speak with Josh privately, and the awkward silence that follows is concerning.

Finally, Josh speaks. "I like to think that I'm fairly prepared for almost every scenario that my clients may bring my way. But I have to be honest, Leo. This is a new one."

"I'm the first guy you've worked with who finds out the love of his life might be pregnant by another man? That can't be right. That shit happens all the time in the Army," I say bitterly.

"Not in your exact situation, and it certainly hasn't involved a panic attack where a client confessed to having suicidal thoughts."

Josh's gaze is unwavering as he patiently waits for my response. In any other situation, I'd be able to out-patience a person, but I already know this man has more patience than me. And considering I'm paying him by the hour, I'd rather not waste my money.

"I guess the panic attack brought back some similar feelings, and my thoughts went right back to that day when Gia called me. I hadn't even intended to answer the phone, but wanted to hear her voice one more time," I admit. "In typical Gianna fashion, she knew I was in trouble and immediately called me. I'm sure you think the twin connection is bullshit, though."

"While there isn't any actual scientific evidence to back up the psychic connection between twins, I'm smart enough to know that some things can't be explained. Many twins describe similar experiences. Whatever you want to call it, what you and Gianna have is an exceptional relationship."

"She's always been my best friend," I say hoarsely. "Not many people have truly accepted me as I am."

"Has Ella accepted you?" Josh inquires.

"I think so. I guess? Now everything is jumbled up in my head, and I don't know what to think. Maybe I made up our entire connection. Where I thought we were moving forward, but she was fighting our relationship. If she is pregnant, and it is mine, why hasn't she told me?"

"She may not be pregnant at all," Josh comments. "I don't want you to get ahead of yourself here. Everything is hearsay until you speak directly with Ella."

"I don't think I'm in a good mental space where I can talk to her. I'll end up yelling."

"It's good that you recognize how you may react. That's growth." Josh pauses when Gianna walks back into the living room. "Do you want someone to stay with you tonight?"

"I'm staying whether he likes it or not," Gianna says pointedly, raising one eyebrow in a defiant gesture that looks so much like our mother it makes me laugh.

"Alright. I'll touch base tomorrow. I'm here to help you work out some talking points, questions, or whatever you need. Once you speak with Ella, I'd like to meet so we can discuss things, and see how you're feeling."

I nod numbly as Josh slaps me on the back, then watch as Gianna walks him to the door. When she returns, she collapses on the couch next to me, resting her head on my shoulder. "I don't care what Ari thought she heard. I know Ella. She wouldn't have cheated on you."

"We haven't laid out any parameters, so she's well within her rights to be dating other people. I'm the one who assumed we were exclusive."

"What if the baby is yours?" Gia asks.

I sigh, closing my eyes as I rest my head against the top of the couch. "Then why hasn't she told me? As fucked up as this sounds, it makes more sense for her not to tell me because it isn't mine. If it is mine, then I have to start asking why she doesn't trust me. Maybe she doesn't see this long term. Or she might not want me in Oliver and Violet's lives. I'm not ready to find out any of those answers."

"Whatever the answers are, we'll get through this, big brother."

I hum noncommittally as the migraine meds finally take me into unconsciousness.

Chapter 21

ELLA

I didn't hear from Leo yesterday evening, which shouldn't be concerning to me, but it is. There have been many days over the last few months where we haven't spoken. But somehow, my gut is telling me this is different.

I tossed and turned all night. I know I need to tell him about the baby, but I'm damn scared. I finally had my first obstetrics appointment yesterday, and got to see the little kidney bean blob on the ultrasound. How the hell had I never known an early ultrasound like that is done via a massive wand that goes into the vagina? Certainly sent up a silent "fuck you" to my sister, who was undoubtedly cackling in Heaven as she watched me freak out about it.

Taking what Whitley said to heart, I confided in the OB about my fears. She was so encouraging. She explained that tons of miscarriages happen with no real understanding, and it doesn't necessarily mean I will miscarry again. She recognized my fear over my age, and said I'll have a few more ultrasounds during the pregnancy to ensure the baby is developing on track. With every passing year, a baby's likelihood of being born with a genetic condition continue to increase. I couldn't care less about that, honestly. A baby with Down syndrome or another genetic condition will still be a complete gift.

So, once I was home from work, I'd waited for Leo to call or stop by. He'd gotten in the habit of eating dinner with us, and more times than not, sleeping over. When I didn't hear from him at all, I wasn't sure what to think. My mind spiraled through a thousand possible options. Maybe he's sick. With family. On a date. With someone else. Having second thoughts about me. Doesn't want the built-in family I come with. Somehow joined the Army again and immediately deployed. Logical? No. But once my brain starts to snowball, everything is fair game.

After basically no sleep, I'm in a foul mood when I drop the kids off at daycare. I've been able to send Violet a few times a week, and she absolutely loves it. As I climb out of my car down the street from the bookstore, I'm unprepared to cross paths with Leo. He looks no better than I do.

"Are you okay? Are you sick? Did someone die? Why didn't you call me?" I blurt out, pregnancy hormones making me instantly on the brink of tears.

"No, no, no, and because I didn't want to," he snaps. His gaze is dark and guarded. He makes a pointed and long look at my belly. "Tell me, Ella. Are *you* sick? Are *you* okay? Do you have anything you *need* to tell me?"

I gasp, covering my mouth with one hand. Oh my God. He knows. "Leo. How did you find out?"

"What the hell does that matter? Is it true?"

I nod miserably, noting the pain that crosses his face. "I should have told you."

"Who else, Ella?" he asks, his voice full of heartache.

"What?"

"Who else have you been sleeping with? That has to be the reason you haven't told me. Because if that baby is mine ..." he trails off, scrubbing a hand over his face, then shakes his head in sorrow, dropping his gaze to my feet. "If it's mine, you must not want it to be with me. I can't think of any other reason why you'd keep me out of the loop."

"No," I whisper. "That's not it at all. I swear I haven't been with anyone else, Leo. The baby is yours."

When his eyes snap to mine, I'm unprepared for the anguish I see. "Do you not trust me? Don't you see how gone I am for you and the kids? How long have you known?"

"A couple of weeks," I admit hoarsely.

"Jesus," he mutters. "I knew something was up, because you wouldn't talk to me. You'd redirect my attention, or you'd seduce me. I guess it's really all my fault. Fool me once, shame on you. Fool me twice …"

"Leo, please," I beg, reaching out to grab his arm. He snaps back like I've burned him. "I need to explain. There are things you don't know."

His eyes fill with intensity as he leans toward me. Dropping his voice, he hisses, "Oh, about the other baby you lost? Was that one even mi —? You know what? I can't be around you right now, Ella. I need some space. I need to clear my head before I say something I can't take back."

Speechless, I watch through tear-filled eyes as Leo stalks down the street. Somehow I manage to walk to the bookstore, and as soon as Whitley sees my tear-streaked face, she runs from the café. "What happened? You look like you've seen a ghost!"

"Maybe I have," I whimper, falling into one of the plush chairs I have by the romance book section. One of our regular cats, Honeycomb, immediately jumps into my lap to make biscuits. "Leo knows. He knows everything, Whit."

"What?" she breathes. "Oh, El. What happened?"

"I don't even know! He didn't call me last night, and when I ran into him walking from the day care, he got snippy with me. Asked me if I had anything I needed to tell him. Then asked who else I was seeing, because it couldn't be his, since I'd have told him by now."

"Well, you kinda had that coming," Whitley says with a

soothing voice. "I know that's hard to hear, but I've been telling you since you took the test to talk to him about it."

"I was going to tell him last night!" I cry out, throwing my hands up in frustration. "But he didn't call!"

"Why didn't you call him?" she asks, and my mouth drops open in shock. Whitley rolls her eyes. "For fuck's sake, El. You're allowed to call the man."

"I guess I felt like it was best if I let him do all the contacting. I didn't want to force myself on him, after how I ended things years ago."

Whitley sighs. "Or you were afraid of something like this happening, so you took yourself out of the equation."

"How so?"

"You didn't want to contact him, risking an argument, so you've waited until he's made the first move. Honestly, you're pretty much like that with most situations. I think I call you more than you call me."

"That can't be true. Can it?" I think back to the last six months. Granted, I've been caught up with raising two kids, so reaching out to people hasn't been a priority. But even before that, did I sit around and wait for people to call me? Am I that bad of a friend?

"Listen, it's not a big deal. I think some people have the personality trait where they flourish in being the one to reach out to others. You're not that way, and that's okay. Your strengths lie in other areas. But it does help to explain some of your behavior with Leo this year." Whitley hands me a box of tissues, and I dab at the never-ending wetness on my face. "I love you, El. You're my best friend. And I know life has dealt you one hell of a curveball this year. But I'm going to give you a reality check here with some harsh words. Leo has put in the effort. You haven't. You need to think about why you've chosen to do this, because I really don't believe your reasoning of keeping the ball in his court."

I spend the entire day floating through my work responsibilities as I try to wrap my head around the things Leo and Whitley said. The only real conclusion I come to is that I've hurt Leo again, and probably so much more than the last time. But I don't know how to make things better.

Five minutes before closing, the door slams open, and Gianna stalks in. Fury envelops her as she approaches me, and I reflexively put up my hands in a defensive gesture.

"What the hell is wrong with you?" she snaps. I open my mouth to reply, but no words come out. She's right. She's completely right. "God, I feel like such a fool. I've been pushing you two together for months! I seriously can't believe this."

"Believe what?" Whitley asks, coming to stand beside me. She crosses her arms over her chest, giving us the look of a unified front, but I know my best friend. If Gianna lunges toward her, Whit will fold like a towel.

"How long have you been hiding this? What's your plan here? I just don't understand you, Ella. Were you acting all these years, floating through life as a ghost? Did you really ever love Leo? Because I can't believe you did, if you'd hide a pregnancy from him." Gianna mirrors Whitley's posture, staring defiantly at the two of us.

"Of course, I love him," I murmur, but no one hears me when Whitley jumps to my defense.

"What the hell is your problem? You remember how she was when Leo left the last time. She barely brushed her hair for months. Have you seen her on a date? God knows that stupid website would have published that shit immediately." Whitley pauses, then smirks at Gianna. "How's your grandmother, by the way?"

"Why?" Gianna asks warily.

Whitley smiles maliciously. "No reason. Saw her walking out of Norma Binnington's house last week, and not even an hour later, that new article about Ella's niece and nephew popped up on the site. Same thing happened two weeks ago with the image of Leo leaving Ella's apartment one morning. Pretty convenient that news seems to travel like that, isn't it?"

"My grandmother is not publishing *The Eagle Has Landed*!" Gianna shouts, her eyes wild.

"She may not publish it, but she's certainly helping with the content," Whitley replies.

"There's no way! Do you know how many times that website has published awful stories about my family? Why would she partake in that? Why would —" Gianna stops, her eyes snapping back to mine. "No. You're not getting me off topic."

"I didn't do anything," I say with confusion.

"The baby is Leo's," Whitley snaps, drawing Gianna's attention again. I feel a bit of hysterical laughter bubble up my esophagus. It's like I'm not even here. "I'm her best friend, so I would know if she was dating anyone. She's been in love with that man for as long as I've known her, and that's not any different today."

"Then why hide your pregnancy? Why do that to him? He had to hear it from Ari, El. Because she overheard the two of you" — she points back and forth between us — "talking about how the dad didn't know about the baby yet."

"Because I wanted to get to my first appointment before I told him," I interject.

"Why?"

"So I could make sure I wasn't going to lose it again," I blurt out.

Gianna's eyes widen. "Again? Again! Ella! When were you pregnant?"

I collapse in the chair as fresh tears erupt. I'm so damn sick of crying. "After we broke up. I didn't know I was pregnant until I was miscarrying. I tried to call Leo, but he didn't answer. I figured he was already deployed and on a mission, so I didn't leave a message, and he didn't call me back."

"So you worried you might miscarry this time?" Gianna asks, and I nod. "One miscarriage doesn't mean they'll all end that way.

Just like one pregnancy doesn't mean you'll have no trouble getting pregnant. Fertility is a fickle bitch."

"I know that now," I whisper. "But I couldn't tell Leo. He's been through so much, and I know he's always wanted a family. I couldn't dangle it in front of him, and then rip it away right afterward."

Gianna watches me thoughtfully. "What do you think he'd be doing with Oliver and Violet?"

"Oh, I mean, that's different."

"How?" she asks.

"They won't be his biological children," I answer.

"They're not biologically your children either, but I know you treat them like they're yours," she points out.

"She's got you there," Whitley murmurs.

"I don't know how to explain what was going on in my head," I say exhaustedly. Slumping in the chair, I throw my arms over my face. "Leo was born to be a dad. You should see him with Oliver and Violet. He's a natural! They gravitate toward him. Violet only smiles for him. Has he told you that? I couldn't tell him we were having a baby unless I was absolutely sure this one was sticking. I can't give him anymore grief."

"I'm probably going to regret saying this, but there are no guarantees this pregnancy will stick," Gianna says quietly. I feel her crouch next to me, patting my knee reassuringly. "But I know my brother. He'd much rather be with you, supporting you through whatever may come with this pregnancy, than on the outside looking in. He was devastated when he thought you were with someone else, Ella. I've seen my brother at his lowest, and this was on par with that. He just wants to be with you."

"I told him I haven't been with anyone but him! Why didn't he believe me?"

"Because you weren't upfront with the pregnancy either, so you may not have been truthful about any other partners. And, as he so eloquently pointed out, you two hadn't set any parameters for your relationship. So you'd be well within your right to sleep with someone else."

My face screws up in distaste. "Gross. I could never. I haven't even been on one date since we broke up! Why would I ever lie about something like that? He's the only man I've ever touched, and the only man I've ever loved. I'll never be with anyone else."

"You're all I've ever wanted, Ladybug."

Hearing Leo's voice, I jolt, standing suddenly, and knocking Gianna over. Whirling around, I find Leo by the door. I don't think. I just run, launching into his arms. "I'm sorry. I'm so sorry. It's your baby, I swear. I just didn't want to tell you if I'd miscarry again. It's only you, Leo. It's always you."

"I know," he says quietly, burrowing his head against my neck. "I'm sorry too."

I begin to cry in earnest, ignoring the soft conversation happening around me. I vaguely remember hearing Oliver and Violet's names, but can't register what was said. Leo starts walking, through the front door of Purrfect Books, and down the block toward my apartment. I grip him tighter, ignoring everything around me.

"I'm not going anywhere, baby," Leo whispers, squeezing me against him.

"I'm scared," I confess softly, and he kisses my shoulder in response. The warm late-June breeze flutters across my skin, and I'm glad I didn't need a coat today, so I can be as close to Leo as possible.

Five minutes later, after climbing the stairs to my apartment and unlocking the door, the two of us are sitting on the couch, me still in his lap. When I attempt to move, his hands latch onto my thighs. "No. I need this connection. Please?"

Unable to verbally respond, I simply nod. He sighs loudly, then says, "Tell me about the miscarriage."

I take a deep breath before launching into the three months between our final breakup and when I'd ended up in the emergency room. He added in the detail of Arianna also being at the hospital that day, which explained how he knew about the miscarriage. "Why didn't you tell me you already knew?"

"I had no way of knowing if the baby was mine," he replies. "You'd called me, but I couldn't jump to connect the two. Since you didn't leave a message, and I never heard anything else, I assumed you'd moved on."

"It was only a few months after you left, though," I press.

His eyes close in anguish. "I couldn't think about that, Ladybug. I was struggling. I couldn't think about how you'd possibly moved on. It honestly didn't occur to me that it might be my baby. If I had known, I'd have been back here on the first fucking plane to make sure you were okay."

"I'm sorry," I whisper, so ashamed at my part in all of this. I hate knowing how much I've hurt him.

"You did what you thought was right at the time. But I appreciate your apology. I'm sorry that I ignored your concerns back then. I could have spent more time listening to you, and then we may have worked together to find a solution."

I shake my head. "I'm not sure it would have been that easy. Regardless of us discussing the problem, we still lived a couple thousand miles apart. We basically had two options: either I move, or we break up."

"Why do you think we couldn't stay together?" Leo asks. "I'd have chosen that over breaking up."

"Because you deserved to find someone who wanted the same things as you. I knew I wouldn't be happy with anyone else, but I also knew I couldn't leave Eternity Springs. So, I figured breaking up at least allowed you to move on, and find a woman who could be exactly what you needed." I drop my gaze from his, embarrassment seeping from my pores. Saying it out loud makes me realize how unbelievably dumb I was.

"Do you like it when people make decisions for you, El?" he asks, and when I don't respond, he snorts. "That's what I thought.

You assumed what I wanted, what I needed, and didn't bother to actually ask me about it. You thought I wanted a family, and there must have been some age limitation on things where you couldn't participate in that?"

"Obviously not, when we lived in separate states," I snap.

"It doesn't matter."

"Yes, it does!"

Leo grabs my face tenderly in his hands, forcing my eyes to his, as he rests our foreheads together. "No, baby. It doesn't matter. All I've ever wanted is you. Kids or no kids, it wouldn't have mattered to me. You're it for me. And now I get to raise Oliver and Violet with you, *and* we're having a baby? I'm so fucking happy. Well, I guess that's if you'll still have me."

"If I'll *still* have you?" I ask incredulously.

He smiles sheepishly. "A relationship is between two people. I realized last night that we never discussed exclusivity, or any parameters of our relationship for that matter, and I was so aggravated with myself for not laying it all on the line. You deserve to know exactly where I'm at, and —"

"I love you," I interrupt, watching a huge grin bloom across his face. "I love you so much. I know it's cliché, but I don't know what I'd do without you."

"I love you too," he says quietly. "It's only ever been you."

Chapter 22

When Ella leans forward to cover my lips with hers, we both sigh. I thought I'd lost her. I worried the baby wasn't even mine, or that she wanted it to be someone else's. I was a nervous wreck that she'd force me out of Oliver and Violet's lives, and then I'd be completely alone again.

Well, not alone. I know I'm so fucking fortunate to have the family that I have, and there are definitely enough nieces and nephews to go around. But any man will agree that it's different when it's the love of your life. When it's your children. And yeah, Ella was right. I have always wanted a family. But if it wouldn't be with her, then I didn't want it.

"Leo," Ella mumbles against my mouth as she wraps her arms around my neck. "Please take me to bed."

"My pleasure," I reply, grabbing Ella's ass as I stand, striding quickly into her bedroom. I shut, and lock, the door, mostly as a precaution in case Whitley shows up with the kids. That first night was too close for comfort in my mind, and I'd rather not scar them for life by having them witness me rutting into their aunt on the couch.

I drop Ella onto the bed, then follow her down, taking her lips in a deep and scorching kiss. She wraps her legs around my hips, and my cock hits her core perfectly. I don't think I'll ever get enough of this woman. I've been obsessed with her for over half of my life, and I don't see that changing anytime soon.

Suddenly, I dislodge myself and jump up.

"What?" Ella yells. "Get your ass back here!"

"Wait! Does this hurt the baby? Do you need to be on top?"

"Does it hurt — Jesus, Leo. You just scared the crap out of me," she says with a giggle. "No, I doubt it does. According to my app, the baby is only the size of a plum."

"I have no idea how big that is, so that measurement doesn't help."

She giggles again. "Two to three inches, Leo. Not big. I'm not even really showing yet."

"How far along are you?" I ask as I gingerly cover her body with mine again, but put the bulk of my weight on one forearm.

"Eleven or twelve weeks. I wasn't really tracking my cycle, so they're guesstimating it based on the size of the baby."

"So when is the baby due?"

"They were careful to tell me it's an estimate, but as of right now, it's mid-to-late January."

Guess that'll be the best Christmas present I've ever gotten. "You know you're gonna need to move in with me, right?"

"What?" Ella asks with a laugh.

I nod my head around her bedroom. "This is a great apartment, but you're already capped out on room. Where will the new baby go? And where will I go?"

"This bed does fit two people, Leo," she remarks dryly.

"Har har. I come with things, Ladybug. And I already have all the bedrooms. It makes more sense from a logistical standpoint for you and the kids to move in with me. You know Oliver will be on board."

"Only because of the bunk beds," she retorts with an exaggerated eye roll, but I see the smile she's struggling to hide.

"I'd like to think he'll enjoy living with me too." I certainly hope so, at least. Hell, I'll probably have an easier time convincing Oliver to move in with me than I will with Ella.

Ella shifts beneath me, pushing her groin against mine. "Can we maybe discuss this a little later? I'd really like to get you to take off your clothes now."

I chuckle as I lean down to peck her lips. "Oh? You're sounding incredibly needy, Ms. Langley."

"I am," she sighs dramatically. "I'm aching, Leo."

Well, shit. Far be it me to keep my woman unhappy. Jumping up, I rip my shirt off, then dance around as I try to remove both pant legs simultaneously. I lose my balance, fall backward against the door, then jump forward until I can fall onto the bed again. Ella's laughter reverberates around the room. "What the hell was that?"

"I may have misjudged my ability to disrobe as quickly as I thought I could," I answer sheepishly. Before she can say anything else, I grab hold of the waistband of her shorts, yanking them down, happy to see I managed to grab her underwear as well. I lean forward and place a gentle kiss against her abdomen, and hear Ella's quick intake of breath. Kneeling beside the bed, I grab her ankles, manhandling her to the edge of the bed. "Thighs open, baby. I'm starving."

"Oh, my," she whispers, as I lean forward to drag my tongue through her wetness, from bottom to top, then swirl it around her clit. Ella grabs a handful of my hair, shamelessly gyrating against my face, as I draw figure eights with my tongue around her pussy. So close, but not right there, and I feel how agitated Ella gets. When I slowly slide one finger inside her, she moans rather loudly. "Leo, you're killing me!"

I chuckle against her, making her entire body shake with the movement. I know she wants to come. But I also know the edging makes the orgasm worth the wait. Honestly, it's kind of a metaphor of the two of us. If I knew we'd get here today, I'd do everything the same with Ella. I wouldn't mind the years-long breakup, if it meant we'd find our way back together again. I'd wait forever for her.

When I barely crest my tongue over her clit, Ella whimpers, attempting to control my head a la *Ratatouille*-style, by grabbing my hair. A sheen of perspiration covers her body as her legs quiver around me, and she grabs one breast roughly. Deciding enough is enough, I suck hard on her clit, then add a second finger inside her channel. When my fingers rub against her G-spot, Ella screams out her orgasm, her thighs clamping down on my head so I can't move. Not that I would. I'm perfectly content where I am, eating her out, knowing I'm the only man who has ever done this. Who will ever do this.

I quickly bring Ella back up for a second orgasm, then patiently stroke her through the aftershocks. I could get her off a bunch more, but tonight, I want the rest of her orgasms to be on my cock. And when I notice the floor-length mirror opposite the bed, I know exactly what I want to do.

Ella is smiling peacefully as she comes down, and I maneuver her into my arms. It's not the easiest moving her when she's basically dead weight, and she slurs, "What we doing?"

"Got an idea," I grunt, finally sitting at the foot of the bed, her in my lap. Her head lolls against my shoulder, and her legs fall on the sides of mine. "Need you to focus, baby."

"Mmm-hmm," she murmurs, but she jolts when I reach around to pinch both of her nipples. "Oh! They're super sensitive now."

I laugh against her neck. "Well, that explains the time I got you off just by sucking on them."

She giggles breathlessly. "That was such a good orgasm, too."

"Noted."

"So, why are we here —" Ella gasps, her posture straightening when she sees how I've positioned us to face the mirror. I watch as her eyes dance leisurely down our bodies, and she reaches a hand around to grab onto the back of my head. "*Oh.* Are we going to watch?"

"We are," I answer simply, tweaking her nipples again. She shivers as I drag a fingernail across each diamond peak, and I keep my eyes on her as I nibble on her neck. "Put me inside you, Ella."

She silently does what I've asked, positioning the head of my cock just inside her pussy, and then she slowly sinks down. So. Fucking. Perfect.

"God, baby. You were made for me," I groan as Ella slowly begins to move. I drop my hands to her waist, helping her speed up, but she slaps my hands away.

"I'm in control," she snaps. Fuck, it's hot when she gets brazen like this. I slide one hand up to bracket her neck, while the other finds her nipple again. Her head drops back to rest on my shoulder, letting me whisper in her ear.

"You like taking what you want, baby?" She nods restlessly. "You enjoy when you're in control, but I've got my hand around your neck?"

"I love when you do that," she whimpers.

"I know you do. Do you like when I fuck into you like this?" I ask, as I jam my hips into her ass, making her cry out. "Do you really want to be in control, or do you want me to get you off as many times as possible?"

"That, that! I choose the second one!" she moans. I let go of her nipple, dragging my hand down her body to strum her clit. It only takes a few seconds until she seizes around me, her walls clamping down so hard that I almost come myself.

I get her off a fourth time in the same position, flexing my hand on her neck just slightly, and feel a wave of wetness coat me as she comes. I stand and turn, tossing her onto the bed, then pull her until she's on her knees. Bending, I swirl my tongue around her back hole. Ella inhales harshly, her body stiffening, but then she relaxes against me. I circle her clit with my finger in the same pattern, and get her off for her fifth and sixth orgasms.

Spinning her so she's facing the mirror again, I climb onto the bed behind her, then deftly slide my cock back inside her. My injured calf aches, but I force my brain to refocus. I've got the love of my life exactly where I want her, and I'll be damned if I'm stopping because of a muscle spasm or cramp.

Ella lets out a guttural groan as I begin a punishing pace, only pausing to grab a handful of her hair. I only vaguely recognize her seventh orgasm, which sets off my own, and I come with a loud grunt. Pulling out, I paint her back and ass with my cum, then drag my fingers through it. Marking her. "Fuck, that's hot."

"How caveman of you," she murmurs. "Marking me for all to see."

"No, baby. This is for my eyes only. I know one day you'll wear my ring, and everyone will know you're spoken for," I answer confidently.

I collapse beside her, noting her amused expression. "Leo, I'm pretty sure the whole town knows I'm spoken for, with or without jewelry."

I pretend to ponder her statement. "How about a forehead tattoo? That will tell everyone in neighboring towns that you're off the market as well."

"I didn't date anyone when we weren't together," she points out, raising her head to rest against her bent arm. "What makes you think I'll suddenly go after someone else now?"

"The tattoo won't be for your benefit. It'll be for everyone else."

"How so?"

I lean forward and kiss her softly. "So I don't have to kill anyone who talks to you. I know how to avoid jail, Ladybug. But my brothers will try to help, and at least one of them will break under the pressure. Luca doesn't look good in orange."

Ella lets out a loud cackle. "Why not Alex or Dom?"

"I highly doubt that Alex breaks. And if Dom did end up in prison, he'd make someone his bitch immediately."

The following morning, under the guise of having breakfast with the kids, I drive all of us to my parent's house.

"Leo, what are you doing?" Ella asks, panic evident in her tone. "No! I'm not ready. I need to put on better clothes, and bring your mom flowers, and get the kids cleaned up. This can't happen right now!"

I look over at her outfit. She's wearing shorts, flip flops, and another one of my old tee shirts. Not a lick of makeup on her face, but she's glowing. She looks stunning, happy, and maybe a little bit deliciously fucked. Whitley kept the kids all night, and I kept their aunt up all night. I'm proud to say I've graduated well past the two-minute-man mark of the past.

"I think you look gorgeous." Grabbing her hand, I bring it to my mouth, kissing it. "Besides, they want to know the real you. Not some perfect version of you. They're going to accept Oliver and Violet as their own, and they won't care what they're wearing either."

"Is it just them? Or your grandmother too?" she asks worriedly.

"Oh. Uh, pretty sure everyone will be there, actually," I say nonchalantly.

"What?!?" she shouts, making Violet cry. Ella immediately unhooks her seatbelt to kneel on the seat and see into Violet's rear-facing car seat. "I'm sorry, baby girl. It's okay. Auntie Ella was being silly."

"Mmm-mmm," Violet says, and I watch in the rearview mirror as she reaches up to touch Ella's face. "Mama. Mama."

Ella gasps, then begins to cry as Oliver chimes in. "Can I call you Mama too?"

"You can if you want, buddy," I answer, reaching to rub Ella's neck as I pull into my parent's driveway. Seeing the number of cars on the street tells me everyone is already here, and I assume we were given an arrival time later than everyone else. Can't have the threshold performance if someone isn't in attendance, I guess.

As I throw the car into park, I pull Ella into my arms. She blubbers into my shoulder about not replacing her sister, and how are we to explain the dynamic in our household once the new baby arrives. "If they want to call you Mama, let them. You are the mother figure in their lives, baby."

"It feels like I'm somehow stealing her thunder," she murmurs, raising her head to meet my gaze. "Like I'm taking over when she did all of the hard work."

"I'm sure my parents will tell you that every stage of childhood involves hard work. Ember handled the first few years, and now we've got the rest. It doesn't make you any less of a mother simply because you didn't give birth to them."

Her face screws up as she starts to cry earnestly. "That might be the sweetest thing you've ever said to me. Thank you."

"I want to call you Mama, Auntie Ella," Oliver announces. "I miss my Mommy, but she gave me to you, and so I want to call you Mama. She's my Mommy, and you're my Mama."

Craning my head around to smile at my favorite four-year-old, I chuckle when he gives me a huge grin. "You're pretty smart, kiddo."

"It's cuz I drinks all my milk," he replies confidently.

"Must be. Ladybug, do you remember the deal with my parent's front door?" I ask cautiously. Her eyes widen.

"I completely forgot about that! Do I have to carry you? I remember hearing about Gianna doing that with Travis." Ella swipes hastily at her face to scrub away the tears, then takes a cleansing breath.

"No, it's just the Santo kid that does the carrying. So you're safe."

She looks confused. "What is the problem with that? Surely all the guys managed it."

"Alex and Dom didn't, until they did it with Natalie and Kate."

"Really?"

"Yup."

"So you carry me over, and then the whole family knows we're soulmates? Does that mean they won't give me any shit over the breakup?" she asks hopefully.

"I don't know about that. There's bound to be some ribbing from at least one of my siblings." I give her a big smile. "Gia's on your side, and I bet Ari and Belle will be too. My brothers will probably be dumbasses."

Ella opens her mouth to reply, but stops when my door is pulled open with gusto. I turn to find Sebastian, his face tense. "Dude. Your brothers just found out your grandmother has been involved in all the stories on *The Eagle Has Landed*. You better get in there before Nonna murders one of them."

"There's no fucking way she's involved! How can that — wait." I pause, looking at Sebastian as I unbuckle my seatbelt and step out of the car. "Why would Nonna murder someone?"

Sebastian gives me a pointed look. "Have you met your grandmother? If anyone is getting hurt this morning, it's one of your brothers. She will take them down, one by one, and still sit peacefully for brunch."

"Leo, your grandmother scares me," Ella whispers from beside the car as she takes Violet out of her car seat. "Are the kids safe here?"

I scoff. "No one is going to murder anyone. I think."

I pull Oliver from his seat, then wait for Ella to round the car. Sliding my arm around her, we march toward the front door, where the majority of my family awaits. "Everyone still alive?"

"For the time being," Dom says ominously. He looks back into the house, then back to us. "She ran off with Sebastian's daughter. We can't kill her in front of the kids."

"She ran?" I ask.

He rolls his eyes. "Figure of speech. She ambled slowly with her walker, but conveniently kept Camila behind her so we couldn't take her out."

Our dad snickers. "She's going to make you pay for those comments."

Dom shrugs. "She literally had that website print a story that Katharine was cheating on me with my own brother. Nonna is lucky I didn't smother her as soon as I saw her."

"They printed my high school picture before anyone even knew I was with Luca," Hannah comments.

"They're the ones that busted my romance book club," Isabella adds. "We had to shut it down because of too many people showing up uninvited."

"I really miss that club," Arianna says with a pout. "It made for great foreplay with all the phallic shaped items we'd make to go along with the book."

"I could do without that being broadcast to your parents, Princess," Stone mutters.

Dad groans. "I really don't want to hear any of this."

"*The Eagle Has Landed* is responsible for Abbie running away from home when an article hinted that Natalie and I were in trouble," Alex growls.

Natalie pats him on the arm. "In their defense, we were in trouble."

"The whole town didn't need to know that, though," he replies. "That stupid website has brought a lot of pain on all of us, and I'm really pissed that Nonna was involved."

"Has she always been involved? When did the articles start? Does anyone know? All I can remember is it's been quite some time," Ella asks quietly. When everyone turns to look at her, I notice she visibly shrinks against my side. "I wonder if something was a catalyst. Like maybe the articles helped her cope, or gave her a purpose."

We're all silent as everyone thinks back to the beginning. *The Eagle Has Landed* used to be the town website, welcoming tourists and new residents with good information on amenities, restaurants, and special events. Then it suddenly turned, going full-on gossip site. But when?

My mom gasps. "Oh, no. It was right after Nonno passed away."

My eyes flutter closed as I think back to that time. Our grandfather, Nonno, was the perfect match for our grandmother. He quietly brought her back down to earth when she was so busy reaching for the stars, she forgot to keep her feet on the ground. They balanced each other incredibly well, because she brought him out of his shell. When he passed after a long battle with cancer, we were all worried Nonna might die of a broken heart.

We're all somber as we think back to that time. Was that what kept her going? Helping someone — or a group of someones — write blind items and Santo-centered articles focused on gossip? "I really hope this isn't true, because if it is, l feel like we failed her. We could have done a better job of helping her."

"How would we have helped her? We didn't even know she was struggling," Gianna interjects. "And everyone was so young. We wouldn't have known how to help her. We were all just kids."

"Let's get this show on the road," Dom says with a loud clap. "Carry your girl over the threshold so we can go yell at Nonna."

I turn to Ella. "You ready for this?"

"Do I have a choice?" she asks quietly.

I lean down to kiss her temple. We're crossing the threshold one way or another. I don't care if I have to catapult us through the doorway, then turn so I take the impact, but I'm getting us through there. "Of course, Ladybug. This doesn't actually impact us in any way. I'll give you a full disclaimer though: if we don't at least attempt it, my siblings will bring it up incessantly."

"So, are you carrying me like a bride, a sack of potatoes, or can I climb on your back?"

"Whichever you'd like."

Gianna squeals. "No one has tried the sack of potatoes technique before! You should totally go with that one."

I look to Ella, and she shrugs. "Whatever gets this done the quickest."

Gia takes Violet out of Ella's arms, then ushers Oliver to head into the house. Without a second thought, I bend down, grab Ella's legs, then throw her over my shoulder. Pain shoots through my injured calf, but I ignore it as I strut through the doorway. I let Ella slide down my body as I set her feet back on the ground, then kiss her hard. "Told you it would be fine."

"Am I allowed to say that your family is weird?" she asks in a teasing voice.

Stone walks by, slapping me on the shoulder. "I'll add you to the spouse group chat here in a sec."

"Me?" I ask, confused.

Stone stops, staring at me. "No, dummy. Her. We all married into this nonsense, so we need a non-Santo chat so we can complain without any of you hooligans chiming in."

The Santo Curse Is Broken

For anyone not local to Eternity Springs, here's a quick rundown of the curse called the Santo Threshold. Eldest child Alex jokingly bestowed a curse on all the siblings, stating they had to carry their one true love over the threshold of their parents' home. After multiple attempts were made with zero success, the curse took hold.

Then Gianna Santo carried Travis Anderson across.

Luca Santo carried Hannah Beauregard.

Arianna Santo carried Stone Dixon.

Dominic Santo carried Kate Reynolds.

Alex Santo carried Natalie Jackson.

Isabella Santo carried Sebastian Garcia.

And now, finally,

Leo Santo carried Ella Langley.

Is the curse fully broken because all seven Santo children found their true loves? Or will the curse carry on to the next generation? No one knows, but we'll be here to cover it when the first Santo grandchild finds love!

Chapter 23

I'm ridiculously giddy about being added to the Santo spouse group chat. While I'm not technically a spouse, I'm optimistic that's where we're headed. Plus, it'll be nice to chat with everyone else who isn't familiar with some of the unique Santo idiosyncrasies. Granted, I used to be. I felt like one of them for years. But feeling a sense of kinship with the spouses will help me become more comfortable with the entire family.

"Are we going to go yell at Nonna now, or bring her in here to stand trial in front of everyone?" Leo asks. I look around, noting how fired up all of the Santos are, especially the guys. I'm honestly shocked Nonna Santo was attached to the website. They've posted some incredibly distasteful articles over the years.

"I think she should face everyone," Dominic says, then turns to Alex. "Do you think my kids and your kids can corral all the littles downstairs for a bit?"

Alex sighs, then looks to his wife, Natalie, who giggles. "Abbie has been anti-babysitting for a few months. We'll have to barter something."

"I'll handle it," Natalie says as she repositions her toddler on her hip. "Fortunately, Abbie rarely says no to her baby brother."

I giggle as I look down at Violet. Her eyes are locked on Leo, but then she looks up at me, and gives me the biggest gummy smile she's ever given me. I gasp, then immediately tear up. It's been such a long year for this beautiful girl, and I was incredibly worried she wouldn't bounce back. I was determined to let her work at her own pace, and I'm so glad I did.

"Someone was looking for her Mama," Leo whispers as he circles his arms around both of us. "Hard to believe she's going to be one soon."

"The daycare said she pulled up on the table yesterday to stand, like she was ready to start walking. She's barely crawled for that long. I'm not ready for her to walk yet," I confess.

"Better babyproof everything. This kiddo looks like she'll require padlocks with fingerprint sensors on them," Leo comments. Violet is certainly smart, and has already gotten into quite a bit of trouble with what she finds while crawling. I can see her observing something, working out the variables, and then finding the solution to give her what she wants. It's pretty interesting watching how her mind works.

"Uh-oh," I hear from the side of the great room, and I look to find Nonna standing with Dominic. "Guess I'm finally in trouble."

"We'd like an explanation, Nonna," Arianna says.

"Let's wait until all the kids get downstairs," Dom says hastily, as two older girls, who I assume are Dominic and Alex's oldest daughters, begin to round up children. When one puts her arms out to Violet, I reflexively try to pull Violet closer to me, but my girl lunges for the new person, happily clapping as she's carried into the basement.

"She'll be okay," Leo whispers in my ear.

"I know. But it'll take some getting used to. I've been all she's had for quite some time."

"She's had me for months, baby. You haven't been alone for months, you're just finally realizing we've been a team for a while." He rests his chin on the top of my head, and I reach up to hold onto his forearms. I never thought of it that way, but he's right. We have been a team.

"Alright, Nonna, spill," Alex says, his voice booming around the room. "Why did you partake in all of this? You're responsible for some incredibly awful articles that went out about this family."

Nonna looks around the room, and smiles. "It began as a way to pass the time. When Nonno died, I was lost. When Norma asked if I'd like to help her one week, I figured, why not? Tourism is the bread and butter for Eternity Springs, and it could potentially bring more clientele to Everlasting as well."

"Why did the website suddenly switch to more gossipy articles?" Hannah asks, sitting in Luca's lap.

"Around thirteen or fourteen years ago, there was a lascivious situation involving the man who portrayed the Easter Bunny, the woman who played Mrs. Claus, and the guy who ran the local theater. They were caught all together, in the buff, in the town gazebo. Mrs. Claus was married at the time, and her husband showed up at the Easter Bunny's church the following Sunday morning. Made a huge uproar right in the middle of the service! A fight broke out, and someone knocked over a candle. The resulting fire destroyed a huge portion of the pulpit. The original article stated the church would be closed for renovations, but the comments went wild with gossip about the actual reason the church caught fire. Norma decided to write a follow-up article with all the sordid details, and it actually broke the website. From that moment on, *The Eagle Has Landed* was all gossip."

"But why participate if you knew it would hurt any of us?" Isabella asks quietly.

Nonna shrugs nonchalantly. "It didn't start out that way. But then we felt it was best if we shared the story of Sara's death —"

"Not cool, Nonna," Alex snaps. I remember when his first wife, Sara, passed away. It was such an awful time for the entire family. Their two kids were still so young, and Alex was deployed at the time. It took a full week before anyone could get word to Alex.

"It wasn't meant in a salacious way, Alessio," Nonna replies, her eyes pleading with him. "The article was all about what a joy Sara was, and how the entire community could step up to help you and the children in your time of need. And again, the traffic to the website was remarkably high. In fact, Norma tracks the data, and whenever there's an article featuring one of you, the website gets more visitors."

"So you figured you'd continue to capitalize on us?" Gianna says angrily.

"In my defense, I didn't write the articles. I only supplied a small detail, usually just the headline, and Norma ran with it. Like the article about Dominic and Kate. I never suggested there was anything going on between Kate and Alex. That was all Norma. I stopped talking to her for a few weeks after that. I was very aggravated at her spin on things."

"A few weeks? Wow, Nonna," Dom says sarcastically. "How did you ever manage that?"

"Watch your tone," Mr. Santo says deeply. "You can be angry, but you will not disrespect your grandmother."

Dom growls in response. "Why not? She disrespected us! How would she feel if she'd seen articles about Nonno up there, based on nothing but gossip and vague details? What if someone suggested Nonno had stepped out on her? None of you would have accepted that. But it's okay if it's us?"

"I've spoken to Norma about this, actually," Nonna says. "It's why there haven't been as many articles as of late. Have any of you noticed? Only a handful within the past few months. And no one knows about Ella's pregnancy yet."

I gasp. "How did you know?"

"Shit," Leo whispers. "That's probably partially my fault. When Arianna overheard you and Whit talking, I spiraled. All of my siblings ended up at my house, so I'm guessing one of them told the rest of the family."

"I most certainly did not know about a pregnancy," Mrs. Santo says, tears filling her eyes. She approaches me, grabbing my hands. "A grandbaby? Really? And we get to have Oliver and Violet, too?"

"Told you," Leo murmurs.

"Oh, hush, you," his mom scolds. "Let go of her so I can hug her, please."

Leo removes his arms from me, and I'm engulfed in Sofia's embrace, then immediately pulled into her husband's arms. Suddenly I'm passed around the room, getting congratulations from the entire Santo family. Last, I reach Nonna. When she hugs me, she whispers, "I found out from Norma, but I told her not to post it. She had a source at the obstetrician's office."

"It's okay," I mumble. "I'm not hiding it any longer."

She pulls away from me. "But you were hiding it originally?"

I nod. "I was worried about miscarrying, and didn't want to tell Leo unless I was sure the pregnancy would stick. I thought he'd been through enough, and I didn't want to give him good news, and then yank it back."

She smiles sympathetically. "I understand that. I had a miscarriage before Leo's father was born. It was incredibly difficult to stay calm through the pregnancy with him. I was so scared the same thing would happen. Whenever you're feeling exceptionally anxious, you reach out to me, okay?"

"And me," Gianna pipes up. When my eyes meet hers, I see the sadness blanketing her face. "Not many people know this, but I've had two miscarriages."

"What?" I breathe. "When? Why didn't you tell me yesterday? I'm so sorry, Gia."

She looks to her husband, Travis, who nods reassuringly. "Two years ago, and around four years ago. It was so emotionally traumatizing that we decided we'd be happy with being a family of three. And I didn't bring it up yesterday because that would have been adding salt to the wound. I was supporting you, and telling you my story would have made it all about me."

Walking to Gianna, I pull her into a hug. "I'm so sorry I wasn't there for you during those times."

She nods as she sniffles. "It's okay. I can understand what your mind has worked up now, and I think it's helped me see things you may have felt all those years ago when things ended with Leo. But I'm glad you're back in both of our lives now."

I smile as I step back. "Me too."

Nonna grins triumphantly. "See? This is good. *The Eagle Has Landed* worked its magic."

"How do you figure?" Dom asks.

"Look around the room, Dominic." Nonna points at each couple, including her son and daughter-in-law. "Ten years ago, none of you were happy. You may have been in a relationship, but it didn't fulfill you as your partner does now. Gossip articles were an odd choice for pushing you in the right direction, but it worked. I get to watch my favorite grandchildren be happy, and all of my great-grandchildren grow up in the town that I love. What a life I've lived of one hundred years."

"You're not one hundred, Nonna," Luca says. "Not even close."

"Eh," she says, waving her hand in dismissal. "Semantics. I don't do math."

"Explains why she always asks me if Carson is going to middle school yet," Gianna whispers. "He's six. Middle school is in five years."

I snort as G links her arm with mine. She walks me back to Leo, who looks adoringly at me. "Brought your baby mama back to you."

"Thanks," he replies, pulling me into his arms again.

"Will you all be mad at your grandmother for long?" I ask.

He shakes his head. "Doubtful. We all know Nonna. She's not a malicious person. I believe her when she says she provided a detail or the headline, and her friend ran with it. I'm glad she had a purpose after my grandfather passed away, but I'm also glad that we're all married now, so hopefully the articles are few and far between."

"We aren't married, Leo," I remind him.

"Eh," he says, mimicking his grandmother with her wave. "Semantics."

Three hours later, after an amazing brunch at Leo's parents' house, we're back at my apartment. I'm suddenly melancholy, assuming Leo will leave to go back to his house, but he surprises me again. "Where are your suitcases?"

"In my closet?" I reply, confused. I follow him into my closet, then watch as he grabs handfuls of clothes on the hangers, tossing them onto the bed. "What are you doing?"

"Moving you out of here. Grab a suitcase, and go fill up whatever clothes Oliver and Violet need. I've already asked Alex to bring over some boxes so we can take all of the toys back to my house."

I stare at him incredulously. "Moving me out of here?"

"Uh-huh."

"Were you going to bother asking me?"

He stops, giving me a big grin. It's a grin I've seen so many times in my life. It shows a dimple in his right cheek, and his eyes sparkle with mirth. "My Ella. My love. My Ladybug. I'm packing up your shit, because you *are* moving in with me, so we can raise all three of *our* kids in the same house. Now please, go pack. I've got a surprise in the backyard for Oliver."

He spanks me softly, making me squeal, then laughs as he turns around to continue loading things into the first suitcase. I turn to walk out the door, saying, "You really have a way with words."

He grabs my hand, yanking me back into his arms, then kisses me passionately. When he ends the kiss, I'm breathless. "I love you more than life itself, baby. I can't go one more night without you in my bed. In our bed. In the home that I built for you, because I remember every detail you ever told me about what kind of home you'd want. Those two matching rocking chairs on the front porch? Yeah, I got those so we can sit together and watch the sunrise. Please. Move in with me."

"You built that house for me?" I whisper, fresh tears filling my eyes.

"I did," he answers tenderly. "I surrounded myself with every memory of you."

"I love you so much," I breathe. "No one will ever love you like I do."

"I know," he replies with a smile. "You're my home, Ladybug. I love you, too."

We kiss, a soft and tender kiss full of longing, and I feel like my heart is singing. This is where I've always been meant to be.

"Oh," Leo says, pulling away from me slightly. "It's also worth mentioning that I've ordered more mirrors for our bedroom, so we can watch as I rail you from every direction."

Good God. I squeeze my thighs together, even as my heart skips a beat at his words. "Okay, I *guess* I'll move in with you, but it's mostly for the mirrors."

He lets out a loud chuckle. "That's the spirit."

*B*y dinnertime, we're officially moved into Leo's home. I should have known it wouldn't be only Alex that showed up to pack things. Eight members of the Santo family packed up my entire apartment in less than two hours, delivering everything to Leo's soon thereafter. We'll have to go back to decide what we want to do with the furniture, but all of our things are safely inside Leo's.

We passed Jeremy on one of the last trips down to the street, and Leo waved cheerfully at him. "Guess who got the last laugh? Gonna go fuck my woman at our house now. Bye, Jimmy!"

"His name is Jeremy," I say, laughing as Leo pulls me outside.

"No one fucking cares what his name is, Ladybug," he says huskily, dipping me into a kiss. "He doesn't matter. No one matters but you, me, and the kids."

Back at the house, after picking up nine large pizzas from a local pizza place, I watch as Leo's family sits around his living room, inhaling pizza and joking with each other. What a wonderful group to be part of. I know if Ember were here, once she got over her initial thoughts, she'd be right in the mix, taking digs at the older Santo brothers, and sharing parenting tips with Leo's sisters. I miss my sister so much. I miss the inside jokes I had with her, how she made me feel, and how much she loved her babies. While I'm not close with my brother at all, I know he's created his own family among a large group of friends in Denver, and I'm happy for him. But this? I need this. Being part of the Santo family is exactly what my soul needs.

"You good, baby?" Leo asks quietly, putting an arm around my stomach, and pulling me into his body.

"Yeah," I reply simply. "Just watching your family."

"Our family."

I smile, loving that Leo knew exactly what I was thinking. "Our family."

"Come outside for a sec?" he asks, and I nod. He grabs my hand, walking quickly out his back door and into the yard. His surprise for Oliver was a large wooden swing set, on which Oliver played for two straight hours while we unpacked, then collapsed in complete exhaustion across Luca and Hannah's laps. Violet seems to have fallen in love with Dominic, being completely unwilling to leave his arms all evening, leaving me child-free for a few hours.

"I know Oliver loved his surprise, but I also have a surprise for you," Leo says, his voice low and tentative. He grabs both of my hands, walking backward until we're in the middle of the yard. It's the twilight hour, when the sun is behind the mountain peaks, leaving the beautiful silhouette of the mountains to the west, and a smattering of stars already glow in the sky. "Do you know the first time I realized I loved you?"

"Not exactly, no."

He smiles warmly. "It was in Mrs. Wickman's biology class, our junior year of high school."

My mouth drops open. "What? Why?"

"Most of the girls in that class were grossed out by everything, but especially when we had to dissect things. But not you. When other girls were shrieking and crying about the poor life of the worm or frog, you snatched the scalpel right out of my hand and attacked the thing with gusto. It was absolutely mesmerizing," he boasts.

My face screws up in a grimace. "Why? I hated doing that stuff."

"I know you did. I'm pretty sure you told me multiple times how much you hated doing it, especially the worm one, because you are not wriggly critter friendly in any way." He chuckles when I nod emphatically. "It was the drive. You were determined. You hated it, but you persevered. I fell in love with you right then. I knew that, if I had you as my partner, I could achieve anything, and be happier than I could be with anyone else. I knew you'd push me to try my best, but love me through my worst, because that's the kind of woman you are. Every accomplishment I've ever made has been because I knew you had my back."

Tears block my vision as I give a watery giggle. "I've always felt the same way about you. You pushed me out of my comfort zone a lot, but I knew you'd catch me if I fell. And for the record, I'm pretty sure I fell in love with you that same year, when you made me stop my dad's car so you could go rescue the tortoise that was in the middle of the road."

He laughs heartily. "I forgot about that! At one point, I did actually like animals."

A movement out of the corner of my eye catches my attention, and I turn to find the town marmot, Mason, hanging out on the top of the swing set. "I don't think I'm that surprised he's already up there."

Leo looks up, swearing. "That fucker has Luca's hat!"

"Motherfucker!" Luca shouts from the back door, running toward the swing set. "I set it down for two fucking seconds!"

"Was he in the house?" I muse, laughing as Mason dangles the hat just out of Luca's reach. "Does anyone know where his lair is? Must be lined with all kinds of treasures."

"I bet he has fifteen or twenty Denver Wolves hats by now," Dom says, smiling from the door. He raises an eyebrow to Leo. "You do the thing yet?"

"No," Leo replies, irritated. "Mason and Luca interrupted us."

"You were interrupted by a hat-stealing marmot," I say, giggling. "Wait, what are you — oh my God."

Leo slowly lowers himself to one knee, holding a velvet box. "Ella Taylor Langley. I love you with every fiber of my being. There isn't anyone on this planet who will ever love you the way that I do. I promise to fulfill all your pregnancy cravings, massage your feet whenever you ask me to, and hold you every night when we go to sleep together. But even more, I promise to support your dreams, listen to your worries, and help you survive any storm that comes our way. I love you, Ladybug. Will you marry me?"

"Yes," I whisper, dropping to my knees and throwing my arms around Leo's neck. I sob into his shoulder as his family hoots and hollers from the back porch.

"Give me your hand so I can put my ring on there," Leo murmurs. I sit up, extending my hand, then watch as he places a ring with a white gold band and a beautiful solitaire diamond onto my ring finger. "My brothers told me to throw this away, or sell it, but I never could. I think I knew we'd end up here. It sat in my sock drawer all these years, patiently waiting until you came back to me."

"Leo," I whimper, tears cascading down my cheeks. He wipes them away, then leans forward to kiss me softly.

"Worth the wait, sweetheart."

Chapter 24

LEO

SEVEN MONTHS LATER

"This is bullshit," Ella snaps.

"I know," I reply.

"Bullshit! Bullshit! Bullshit!" Oliver shouts. Neither of us bother to correct him, because frankly, it is bullshit.

Ella is forty-one weeks pregnant, and our child is happy to stay holed up in her uterus. Ella isn't dilated, effaced, thinned out — whatever the hell that means — or anything. And as I'm tying her snow boots onto her feet, because we just got a foot of snow, I agree with everyone. It's bullshit.

"Bah-sit. Bah-sit." Violet toddles over to us, beaming to show off her six teeth. "Dada! Bah-sit!"

"I'm not even mad. Let her say it," Ella says nonchalantly. "It's all bah-sit."

"Bah-sit!" Violet yells jubilantly, holding her sippy cup in one hand as she throws her other fist into the air.

"God I love this family," I murmur, laughing.

"Easy for you to say," she snaps. "Your child keeps using my bladder as a punching bag, I can no longer sleep unless I'm sitting upright, and my acid reflux is ruining everything. Why do women have more than one child? And why didn't my sister warn me about this shit?"

Still at her feet, I rub her calves slowly. I've learned there is a fine line between what I'm *allowed* to say, and what I *want* to say. Hormones have wreaked havoc on Ella, especially in the third trimester, and I've found it's best to remain silent in a lot of situations. I'd rather her get mad at me for silence than begin crying because I've said something stupid.

Ella reaches up, dragging her hand through my hair, then exhales loudly. "I want to meet this baby. I'm sick of them turning away during the ultrasound. You were so excited about the surprise, and I thought I could enjoy it too. But now I'm pissed off, and I want to know. Pink or blue? There's only so much yellow and green clothing we can buy, Leo. I'm done."

"I know, baby," I say quietly, leaning into her hand. It centers both of us to be touching in one way or another. It's grounding, like a gentle reminder that we can accomplish anything because we're a team. A core unit. "Let's drop the kids off, then hopefully we'll get some good news from the OB."

Ella nods, but her breathing catches as a borderline sob tries to break through. "Do you think we can just tell them they need to induce me today? I don't think I can go much longer."

I nod. "I have every intention of pushing for some good news. At the very least, I'll be bringing in my mom, because no one wants to deal with her when she goes full momma bear."

Ella smiles faintly. "I do love it when she gets a little feral."

I push up to brush a soft kiss across her lips. "I think that way about you as well."

"Really?" she asks, her eyes getting a little glimmer back in them, and I nod. A few months ago, a visiting pediatrician saw Violet, and aggressively told Ella that Violet's speech was delayed because we were the problem, since we hadn't switched her from a bottle to a sippy cup fast enough. I've never seen Ella turn so fast on someone before, and she had the man cowering and apologizing profusely in remarkable speed. Needless to say, we were thrilled when the guy left Eternity Springs. I've never been prouder, or more in awe of Ella.

"Are we going to Nani's?" Oliver asks excitedly.

"We are," I answer, rising to stand so I can help Ella up. She's perfectly capable of getting up from a chair, but I'm honestly loving taking care of her. "I think Carson may be coming to hang out after school as well."

Carson and Oliver have become best buds. While there are a couple of years between them, they bonded over their love of *Bluey*, and they both really enjoy helping my mom in the kitchen. Both Oliver and Violet have sets of their clothes at my parents' house now, and are all too thrilled to be welcomed into the Santo family. Meanwhile, Violet has become my dad's shadow. I don't think he'll ever admit it, but Violet is his favorite grandchild. There's something about her sassy personality that won him over immediately. I'm sure he's going to get a kick out of how she tries to pronounce bullshit, because she will undoubtedly perform for him as soon as we get there.

An hour later, after dropping the kids off, we're on our way to the birthing center. Ella shifts awkwardly in the passenger seat, pressing on her protruding belly. "Are you okay? Contraction?"

"No, I don't think so," she murmurs. "Some weird pressure. I'm just uncomfortable."

"What if the OB says you're in labor?" I joke. "You know, you probably are. We didn't put the bag in the car."

"Don't tease me," she mutters. "All I need is you, my phone, and a charging cord. I bet whatever your sisters told me I needed to have I won't ever use."

"Well, a lot of that came from Arianna. She's always been a massive over packer."

"Whitley didn't help much either. I shouldn't have trusted her, since she's an emotional basket case as well." Whitley recently found out she's also pregnant, from a fuck buddy situation, and the guy immediately said he wanted nothing to do with the baby. Not surprisingly, my parents basically adopted her, telling her they'll be the family she needs. Whitley's parents are both gone, and as an only child, she gratefully accepted the welcoming gesture from my family.

Thankful for the expectant parents parking right in front of the birthing center, I jog around the new SUV to help Ella out of the car. While neither of our cars were in dire need of an upgrade, we chose to get a larger SUV for Ella, as she'll be most likely to have all three children at once for the time being. Since all will be in full car seats for the foreseeable future, Ella's new car will be the family car. I sold my car, and took over driving her older SUV. It made the most sense for both of us to have SUVs for our larger family.

We're whisked into an exam room as we wait for the OB. Doctor Morales has delivered quite a few of my nieces and nephews, and it's surreal she's now delivering a child of mine. But once the heart rate monitor is strapped onto Ella's stomach, I see the immediate concern on the nurse's face. "What is it?"

Ella's hand blindly reaches out to grab mine as we wait for the nurse to respond. "I need to get Doctor Morales. I think it's safe to say you'll be delivering this baby sooner rather than later."

A moment later, the doctor strides in, grabbing the ultrasound machine. After squirting a glob on Ella's stomach, she applies the wand, gazing intently at the screen. She nods once, removes the wand, then wipes off the gel. Turning to us, she says, "The baby's heart rate is decelerating. Usually that means there is a decrease in oxygen due to the umbilical cord being compressed, or there may be an issue with the placenta. Whatever the case, I'm not taking any chances. As long as you agree, I'd like to do an emergency c-section right now. It's time to meet your baby."

In shock, Ella nods numbly, then turns to me, bursting into tears. "I wanted the baby out, but not this way!"

"I know, sweetheart," I whisper, slowly stroking her spine.

"Doctor Morales wouldn't do a c-section unless it was absolutely necessary. I'll be with you every step of the way, alright? It's going to be okay."

We're ushered into a birthing room, where Ella is handed a gown. Once she's undressed, nurses arrive to quickly get her ready. The monitors are again attached to her belly, an IV is inserted, and she's given a catheter. She's administered medicine meant to relax her, and I step out to call my parents to let them know that they can start the Santo phone chain. We decided a month ago that my mom would also come to the hospital, as we felt having a mother here would be moving for both of us. I know if Ella's own mother could be here, she would be, and I'm thankful my mom can step in. Gianna will be taking Oliver back to her house, while Violet stays with my dad.

When I'm given scrubs, booties, and a hair net, I find myself chuckling. When I catch Ella's eyes, I shrug. "Guess I was right about not putting your hospital bag in the car."

"Gia already texted me to say she'd grab it on her way to get Oliver, and she'll give it to your mom."

"I was only gone for a couple of minutes. You discussed that with Gia already?" I ask.

Ella cocks an eyebrow at me. "I texted her as soon as you said it wasn't in the car, Leo. Did you really think we wouldn't have a plan for everything? The Santo women could undoubtedly rule the world one day."

I grin, leaning down to kiss her softly. "Kinda love that, baby."

I'm suited up when a team of nurses come in, ready to wheel Ella into the operating room. "Dad, you wait here."

"What? No!" I blurt out. "I have to be with her. Is this normal? Why keep the dad out of the room? This is bullshit."

Ella snorts. "Bullshit. Bah-sit. Bah-sit! Oh, fuck. I think the relax-y drugs they gave me have kicked in a little."

One nurse laughs. "We're not keeping you out of the room, Dad. Just until we get Mom situated, and the spinal administered.

Once we begin the procedure, you'll be brought in. I promise you won't miss the birth of your baby."

"Alright, I guess," I mutter. I look down at Ella, smiling happily up at me, and I'm momentarily struck speechless. She's about to give birth to our baby. While this might be the first baby born of our blood, it's our third child. But, regardless of the number, this is still a brand new experience for both of us. I bend down to kiss her, letting my lips linger on hers for a few moments. "I love you, baby."

"I love you," she coos, reaching up to pat my cheek a little too harshly. "Goodness, you're hot. Do you know how hot you are?"

"Those meds kicked in fast," I comment.

"They did. I like them. Is this what weed is like?" Ella says, then gasps, her eyes opening comically wide. "Oh! Is this what it's like to take gummies? I think I would like gummies."

I stifle a smile as I shake my head. "I'm not sure if a gummy gives you this much of a high, Ladybug."

She waves gaily at me as they wheel her bed out of the birthing room, and then it's quiet. Disturbingly silent, to the point where all I can hear is my own breathing and my quickly spiraling thoughts. What if something happens to her? We aren't married yet. Ella was adamant that we not marry until after the baby was born. She wants a ceremony in our home, with just us and the kids, but was clear she needed to wear a dress and not feel like a beached whale — her words, not mine. If something happens to her, what happens to Oliver and Violet? I'm suddenly furious with myself for not making her write things down. Would I have any claim to them? What if the baby survives, but Ella doesn't?

"Leo," I hear quietly, and I turn to find my mom standing at the door. Without a word, I stalk toward her, and she opens her arms. I cling to her for a moment, needing the support more than I realized. "I know. It's going to be okay. Don't let your brain get ahead of your heart."

"I'm scared," I confess, my voice barely above a whisper.

"That is a very acceptable feeling to have right now. Put your trust in Doctor Morales. We've trusted her with so many of our family members, and she's yet to let us down," Mom says softly, her voice soothing me perfectly.

"It's hard for me to trust others when it involves my heart," I blurt out. Throughout the entirety of Ella's pregnancy, I've consistently worked with my therapist to combat the negative self-talk I'd gotten into using as a defense mechanism. Ella attended quite a few sessions with me, to work on our communication, and to bring as much closure as possible for our breakup from years ago. I feel stronger today than I ever have, and I think it's a combination of Josh's therapy and Ella's love that have made me the man that I am. Do I still feel a sense of guilt over the soldiers I lost in Afghanistan? Absolutely. That'll probably never go away. But consistent therapy, as well as connecting with other veterans in Sebastian's Rocky Mountain Range Riders Motorcycle Club, have allowed me to find some semblance of peace. The guys at RMRRMC have helped me to see that my guys in Afghanistan wouldn't have held me accountable for what happened. They encouraged me to reach out to every surviving soldier, and I did. Each man confirmed that what happened wasn't my fault. I'll still grieve the lives lost, and feel pain for the families that had a part of their hearts die off that day. But I no longer allow it to control my life.

"I'm so proud of you, *polpettino*," she whispers. Yes, on occasion, my mother calls me her little meatball. She has given all of my siblings nicknames. She calls Gianna her *patatina*, which means little potato. Most of the others got cute nicknames, whereas we are basically what she craved during pregnancy.

"Leo? You can come back now. Doctor Morales is ready to make the first incision," the nurse calls from the hallway.

"Go," Mom says, squeezing my arms. "I'll be right here. Give Ella a kiss from me. And for what it's worth, I think it's a girl."

I nod, then dash after the nurse. She takes me first to a sink, having me scrub from my fingertips to my elbows, then I'm putting on a mask, and escorted to Ella's side. She turns her head once I'm seated, a peaceful smile on her face. "They gave me more drugs."

"That's good, baby." I chuckle. Her eyes lose focus as her head turns to stare at the ceiling, but I'm laser focused on everything going on around us. An anesthesiologist monitors Ella's vitals from behind her head, while two nurses get a warming station ready. Before I know it, Doctor Morales announces she's about to cut into the amniotic sac.

"Any last guesses on gender and weight?" she asks.

"I said boy and eight pounds even," Ella murmurs.

Another nurse says nine pounds, while the anesthesiologist says eight and a half pounds and boy. I'd told Ella all along I thought it was a boy, but I change my answer. "Girl, seven pounds, twelve ounces."

Absolutely no clue where I get those numbers. I don't even know what the average weight is for a baby at forty-one weeks. Maybe I'm too low? Who knows.

An ear-piercing and shrill cry fills the air, and it might be the most beautiful sound I've ever heard. Doctor Morales looks over the sheet at me. "Well, Dad? Want to come and cut your daughter's cord?"

Holy shit. I have another daughter. I nod, unable to speak, and stand on shaky legs as I step toward the obstetrician. I'm given a set of scissors, told to expect it to feel more rubbery than I think it will, and then I'm cutting through it. I watch as the nurse whisks my daughter away to the warming table, where she's suctioned, wiped off, and officially weighed.

"What's the weight?" Doctor Morales calls out, and I find I'm still standing next to the table.

"I don't know how he did it, but Dad was spot on. Seven pounds, twelve ounces," a nurse replies.

"Well, I'll be damned," Doctor Morales says with a laugh, as she works on Ella's abdomen. "You missed your calling, Leo."

I turn to Ella, dropping back into my seat, then pull my mask down so I can kiss her. "It's a girl, baby. We have another daughter."

"I'm so happy," she sighs. "Penises scare me."

Honestly, that's fair. Every single one of my nephews has peed on me more than once.

"Dad?" A nurse motions for me. "Want to come hold your daughter?"

I eagerly go to where my girl is bundled up in a blanket, hat with a big pink bow on her head, and gingerly scoop her up. Wow. "This is surreal."

"Come on," the nurse says, grabbing me by the arm. "Go introduce her to her momma."

Once I'm seated by Ella again, I hold our daughter by Ella's face. Ella whispers to the baby, but I don't lean forward. I want this moment to be about them. When Ella's gaze meets mine, I smile. "What shall we name her?"

"I was thinking since we already have a Violet, that we name her Rose," Ella says softly, her eyes darting down at the beauty in my arms. "And if it's okay with you, I'd like her middle name to be Twyla. After my mom."

"I think Rose Twyla is perfect," I say hoarsely, my eyes shining with emotion. As if she knows we're talking about her, Rose opens her eyes. "Hello, my sweet Rose. My *piccola coccinella*."

"What is that?" Ella asks.

I gaze adoringly at the love of my life. "It means my little ladybug."

"Ba-ba," Violet says, pointing at Rose.

"Yes. Baby. Baby Rose."

"Ba-ba Rose."

"Yes, *fiorellina*. Baby Rose." Violet beams at me, loving her new nickname of little flower. A few months ago, on a completely random day, I began calling Oliver *lupacchiotto*, which means little wolf. He took to it naturally, immediately growling, and thought it was mostly in reference to his Uncle Luca being an alumni for the Denver Wolves NHL team. In reality, I thought it suited him, and had such fond memories of all the nicknames my mom had for us kids growing up. I want my kids to experience the same thing.

"Mama, will Baby Rose come home with us today?" Oliver asks.

Ella giggles lightly. "No, Rose will stay with me here today, but we'll both come home tomorrow."

"I can't wait to show her my swing set," Oliver gushes. "When will she be allowed to play on it with me?"

"I think it'll be quite a bit of time before that happens, *lupac-chiotto*," I tell him, kissing the top of his head. "I think Mama will need Rose to grow up a bit before she's allowed on the swing set."

His face falls. "Bummer. Uncle Luca showed me how to put bubbles on the slide, and it makes it really fast! I was excited to show the baby."

Oh, my brother is fucking dead. "Uncle Luca should have thought about if that was a safe choice."

I watch as Ella picks up her phone, and when I catch her eye, she rolls her eyes. "Sorry. I'm warning Aunt Hannah that Uncle Luca is about to get a visit from Daddy."

Oliver's eyes light up. "Do you think Caleb knows about the bubbles on the slide?"

Luca's son Caleb is only a little bit younger than Oliver, and I find myself grinning wickedly. "Do you think we should go tell him? And you know what? I think we should go get a gallon-size container of slime to bring to Caleb. You know how much he loves slime."

"That's a great idea, Daddy!" Oliver exclaims happily.

"Aunt Hannah is not going to agree," Ella comments.

"Her husband threw down the gauntlet. It's really his own damn fault."

Ella sighs. "I'll try to remind her of that when she shows up and asks for your head on a platter."

I grin at my Ladybug, my little flower, Violet, and my little ladybug, Rose, all cuddled together on the hospital bed. "As long as I have the four of you, I'm happy."

Ella beams at me as I sweep Oliver into my arms, then perch on the edge of the bed. A year ago, I had nothing. Now I have the most perfect family, with the four people I love most in this world. I don't know what I did to deserve this, but I'll never take it for granted. Everything up to this moment was worth it. They're all worth the wait.

Chapter 25

ELLA

ONE YEAR LATER

STONE DIXON RENAMED THE GROUP SANTO
SURVIVALISTS

Me: Santo Survivalists? Really?

Stone: Travis has a thing for alliteration.

Travis: Hey! That wasn't my suggestion.

Stone: You were pretty excited about it
when Natalie brought it up.

Travis: Sigh. I guess I was.

Kate: We are surviving the Santos children.
It fits.

Me: Well, I'm still honored to be included.

Sebastian: It's calm in here. Don't let them
add you to the entire family group chat. It's
absolute bedlam in there.

Natalie: How has she not been added in
there yet? She's been a Santo for
MONTHS!

Me: I think Leo threatened everyone.

Arianna: He did.

Hannah: I hate to tell y'all this, but I'm pretty sure Luca is adding her now.

Natalie: I'm sorry, girl. Come into this chat when you can't handle them … and always remember to mute the group! Those fuckers start talking, and your phone will pretty much burst into flames because of the chaos.

Me: That has to be an exaggeration.

LUCA SANTO ADDED ELLA LANGLEY TO SANTO SHENANIGANS

Alex: All I'm saying is, whichever one of you assholes has decided to hide pickles in our houses, once I find you, you won't like the consequences to your actions.

Dominic: I thought we figured out it was Luca?

Leo: No one admitted to anything.

Luca: And I refused the lie detector test.

Isabella: Who has a lie detector test?

Arianna: Jesus. Who do you think?

Alex: Since none of us have actually seen it, I think Leo is bluffing.

Me: I've seen it.

Leo: I love you, Ladybug. And I'm sorry I couldn't keep you out of this chat any longer. I've been outvoted.

Me: It's okay. Now that Rose is one, I'm sure I can handle this group chat.

Leo: Famous last words.

Luca: SEE? I fucking told you guys he calls her Ladybug!

Hannah: Honey, it's not that big of a deal.

Kate: I think it's adorable.

Natalie: Have you really seen the lie detector test?

Sebastian: Does anyone know how to administer it?

Leo: Obviously.

Stone: All of this because of a pickle.

Arianna: Hey, Hannah, did you ever track down that missing hat of Luca's? From when he won the Cup?

Hannah: No. That stupid marmot has a hidden cave somewhere full of his spoils.

Alex: He stole underwear from someone in this family, right?

Arianna: Me.

Kate: He's gotten a couple of my bras, I think.

Me: How on earth is this marmot getting into your houses?

Kate: I had them air drying outside.

Arianna: Umm … I'm not sure I want to ask why.

Hannah: I totally want to know why.

Dominic: The sun is a natural stain remover.

Leo: What kind of stain did you need to remove?

Dominic: There were … multiple stains.

Sebastian: Good God.

Stone: Did it work?

Dominic: Did what work?

Alex: The sun, dumbass. Did it remove the stains?

Kate: We don't know, because Mason took off with them.

Isabella: Mom's birthday is coming up. Who wants to host?

Luca: Not us. We hosted for Dad's birthday.

Alex: I'm renovating our kitchen cabinets right now, so we're not able to host.

Natalie: Is that what we're calling it now? Renovating?

Alex: Sunflower, I was giving us an out. Throwing me under the bus right now? Not cool.

Leo: No one comments on him calling Natalie Sunflower, but I'm not allowed to call my wife Ladybug?

Travis: We never said you weren't allowed to call her that. It's just cute. And sweet. And very un-Leo-like.

Isabella: We can host, but that means we won't host Christmas.

Dominic: Actually, I wanted to run it past everyone. I thought we could do Christmas at Everlasting this year. There's too many of us to handle at Christmas. We can just open up one of the large banquet rooms, then have the meal catered so none of us have to cook.

Kate: None of "us" have to cook. Okay.

Dominic: Katharine, go ahead and read Alex's last text. It also applies here.

Hannah: It'll be really easy to plan for that at Everlasting.

Arianna: I'm fine with that.

Arianna: Can any of you babysit on Saturday?

Arianna: Seriously? No takers?

Arianna: My kids are gorgeous, loving creatures. Your nieces and nephew.

Leo: With all due respect, Ari, there's four of them. We all have kids. It becomes a basketball game with only one ref.

Arianna: Yet I seem to handle taking on your kids just fine.

Me: You've never babysat mine.

Arianna: Because you won't let me.

Leo: It has to be a safety hazard for one woman to have seven children by herself.

Arianna: Stone is there too! He's not completely incapable.

Stone: Thanks, Princess. I appreciate the vote of confidence in my ability to adult around children.

Sebastian: Is there an actual ratio for adults-to-children in these situations?

Me: Yes. Depending on the age, it's usually something like one adult to fifteen children. The younger the kids, the lower the ratio.

Leo: Did you know that info, or did you google it?

Me: Both?

Hannah: I love that you're not sure of the answer.

Alex: I've found another pickle. STOP HIDING FUCKING PICKLES IN MY HOUSE, LUCA

Luca: I swear it wasn't me this time!

Sebastian: Christ Almighty. I just found a pickle behind Isabella's coffee cup in the cabinet.

Natalie: Guys! I saw Mason, and I'm following him into the forest. Maybe I'll find his lair!

Alex: Baby, that's not a good idea. Are you alone? Not cool.

Luca: I don't think she's alone. I'm fairly positive Hannah is with her.

Stone: Arianna snuck out ten minutes ago.

Leo: Do they have a separate girls chat?

Dominic: Obviously. We have a chat as well.

Dominic: Also, I can't find Kate.

Leo: Ella isn't answering my texts or calls.

Sebastian: How the fuck did they all skip out at the same time, without us noticing?

Leo: We were too busy talking about pickles and lie detector equipment.

Leo: I wish I could leave this chat, but I know you'll just pop me right back in here.

Alex: If we all have to be in here, you do as well. Honestly, we're lucky Mom, Dad, and Nonna aren't in here. They never shut up.

Nonna: Clearly I shut up just fine, Alessio. I've been silently reading this text chain for months.

Nonna: Your wives just sent me a picture of them beside a marmot burrow.

Nonna: They've found Mason's lair.

Nonna: Oh my.

Luca: What?

Dominic: Nonna, spit it out! Katharine won't answer my calls.

Nonna: There are pups.

Alex: Come again?

Nonna: You have children, Alessio. Clearly you understand the concept of procreation.

Stone: I think what he's trying to say is, where is Mason's wife, partner, spouse, etc.?

Leo: I think she means Mason is the mother.

Travis: For fuck's sake. No one ever checked to see if Mason was male or female?

Sebastian: I don't know about you, but I'm staying the hell away from a feral marmot. I don't care if it's a male or female.

Luca: Well, I fucking care! That fucker has taken so many of my things.

Hannah: Relax. I got your hats back. Most of them. I left one. She seemed pretty attached to it, and one of the babies was napping in it. Quite cute, actually.

Me: That was so exciting! Is this typical for a Santo event? Sneaking out to track down a wild animal?

Leo: I wish I could say no, but there's really no telling with this family.

Leo: Welcome home, Ladybug.

Me: This is the best day ever! Can we get a pet marmot?

Leo: No.

Me: Aw, shucks. Why not?

Luca: I've got a connection who can get you a boatload of guinea pigs if you're interested.

Me: Ooooooo! Guinea pigs!

Leo: No.

Natalie: Let's all get guinea pigs! We could have little piggy play dates!

Hannah: You should see the setup Luca's friend Jax has. There's an entire room in his apartment for his piggies.

Kate: I'm totally on board with the guinea pigs.

Isabella: Me too!

Gianna: Why did I wake up to one hundred text notifications?

Me: Why the hell are you napping right now? You missed all the fun!

Stone: I just found another pickle. What the actual fuck.

Luca: Okay. That one was me.

Stone: So you've pickled my house, AND you suggested we should all get guinea pigs?

Stone: Payback is a fucking bitch, Luca.

Dominic: Never a dull day in the Santo Shenanigan group chat.

Leo: I apologize now for what my wife just sent all of your spouses.

Travis: Seriously? You can buy actual outfits for guinea pigs?

Sebastian: Christ Almighty. We're never going to talk them out of it now.

Leo: Gianna, why were you napping the entire day?

Leo: And why were you napping most of yesterday?

Leo: And why did you get sick right before we met for lunch two days ago?

Me: GIANNA SANTO ANDERSON do you have something you would like to tell the class??

Gianna: Well, we'd hoped to wait until Mom's birthday to tell everyone, but I guess now is as good a time as any.

Gianna: I'm four months pregnant.

Dominic: That's amazing!

Alex: Congratulations, sis. I'm so happy for you.

Natalie: Another Santo baby!

Kate: Putting it out there now, I think it's a girl!

Hannah: I'm so excited for another little one to love on!

Me: Rose literally just turned one, Hannah.

Hannah: I said ANOTHER. There can never be too many babies to cuddle.

Arianna: Agreed! Congrats, Gia!!

Leo: Sometimes I hate this twin connection we have.

Sebastian: Even through text?

Leo: It works across the country, Seb. Our connection is weird.

Leo: You got something else to share, sis?

Travis: We're excited to announce that there will be TWO babies joining our family later this year.

Leo: It's a boy and a girl, isn't it?

Gianna: It is. Can you believe it? Almost forty and pregnant with twins.

Me: Is Carson excited?

Gianna: Over the moon … except for the baby sister part.

Leo: He'll get over it. I managed it just fine.

Gianna: I was born like five minutes after you, Leonardo. Stop acting like you made this big sacrifice.

Me: I really love this group chat.

Leo: I really love you, Ella Santo.

Me: And I really love you, Leo Santo.

Luca: (gushing) Aren't you guys the cutest! Now can someone go help my wife bring home all of my Denver Wolves memorabilia that Mason stole from me?

Luca: Please?

Luca: Anyone?

Arianna: I will.

Arianna: But you're babysitting my kids this weekend.

Alex: I fucking love this family.

Nonna: There will be more Santo babies.

Alex: Not from me.

Dominic: Or me.

Luca: We're cool with two.

Isabella: I will not have another baby. Pregnancy wasn't for me.

Leo: Shit.

Me: Oops?

Gianna: ARE WE PREGNANT AT THE
SAME TIME, ELLA?

Me: The more the merrier, right?

Epilogue

ELLA

ONE YEAR LATER

"Mama."

"Yes, Rose."

"Cake?"

I sigh, looking down at my daughter's cherubic face, her large brown eyes staring up at me with so much hope. Hope for sugar. "No, baby. Not yet."

Lips turning into a frown, she harrumphs. "No. Cake now."

I fight to hide my smile as she crosses her arms in obvious frustration. "We have to wait for Oliver to get home from school before we can have cake. It is his birthday cake, after all."

"Cake?" Violet asks hopefully, skipping into the kitchen. At three and a half, Violet is the spitting image of her mother. It gives me peace to know that, while Ember is no longer here, I get to watch the very best parts of her grow up every day. Even now, as Violet gives me an innocent smile, I see my sister shining back.

"Not yet. Daddy will be home with Oliver soon, and then we can have cake."

It's Oliver's seventh birthday. My sweet nephew only asked for two things for his birthday. He wants to have his best friend Carson over for a sleepover, and he wants cake right after school. I know there will be years where birthday requests are much more involved than this, or when extracurriculars take so much time that we'll barely see Oliver. He's already showing amazing prowess in the peewee hockey program Leo and Luca got him into, and he loves the elementary STEM and Pokémon clubs that meet each week after school. Honestly, Oliver has a better social life than I do.

"Ladybug?" Leo calls from the door. Brody, the surprise mic-drop baby that we didn't anticipate, squeals in happiness, his arms and legs flailing against me. I can already tell this boy is Leo's mini-me. Brody isn't happy unless he can survey his surroundings. He's an observant one, content to watch the world around him.

"Cake!" Rose says gleefully, clapping her tiny hands together, then looks up to Violet. "Oli cake!"

As Leo and Oliver walk into the kitchen, the girls surround Oliver excitedly. Violet shouts, "Happy birthday, brother!"

"Bird-day cake!" Rose adds, her voice growly and intense. "Cake now, Oli."

Leo approaches me and kisses my cheek. "There's a familiar looking woman in the driveway who yelled that she's still mad at me for almost running over one of her mini highland cows twenty years ago. Any idea who that may be?"

I gasp. "Ally is here? No way!"

He gives me a big smile. "She'll never let me forget about that, will she?"

Squealing, I run outside to find my favorite cousin, Allyson Sterling, smiling widely at me. Wearing worn jeans, boots, a faded blue tank top, and a cowboy hat, Ally looks exactly as she always has. A little sliver of my childhood in Silver Mist Falls. At three years my junior, Ally was always my favorite cousin to pal around with on her family's ranch, Sterling Falls Ranch. It was always me, Ally, and Ember. The three musketeers. We knew from early on she was destined to take over running the ranch. Not only is it in her blood, but the ranch, and the town of Silver Mist Falls, are in her soul.

"What are you doing here?" I gush, sweeping her into a big hug. Ally laughs as she returns the hug tightly.

"I can't come to celebrate my favorite cousin's birthday?" she answers.

Pulling back, I raise an eyebrow. "I thought I was your favorite cousin."

Ally shrugs, then gives Brody a big grin. "Cute kids trump childhood friendships, El. You should know that. But seeing this little one means I should probably specify that it's my favorite seven-year-old cousin's birthday, because aren't you just the cutest thing in the whole wide world?"

I laugh. "That's fair. They are pretty cute. Especially this one."

I hear Ally's intake of breath as she looks over my shoulder. "God, she's a little Ember."

I feel a tug on my heart as I watch Violet confidently walk up to Ally. "I 'member you."

"Oh yeah?" Ally asks with a chuckle.

"Uh-huh. You have all the little cows."

"I do. I have quite a few animals," Ally says.

"What else?" Violet asks, as Oliver ambles up, swinging his arm around his sister.

"Well, I have quite a few horses, some normal size dairy cows, a herd of chickens —" Ally stops when Rose claps wildly.

"Chickens!" she bellows.

Ally looks to me, biting her lip to keep from laughing. "I have chickens. Do you like chickens?"

"Yes," Rose answers. "Cute and yummy."

"Well, that's an interesting take," Ally replies.

Leo laughs as he sidles up beside me, wrapping his arms around my shoulders. "There may be a slightly violent tendency in this one. We're working on it."

"Unless you're bringing me one of the animals," Oliver blurts out, "I would like to have my birthday cake now."

"Cake!" Rose screams, throwing a fist into the air.

"Any chance the cake is sugar-free?" Leo murmurs against my ear, making me shiver. "I don't think this one needs more ammunition."

As Rose follows Oliver back into the house, by jumping every step, I shake my head. "It's going to be a long night."

Seven hours later, after what could possibly have been the longest bedtime ever, all four kids are asleep in their rooms. Oliver still sleeps in the boys room, and he loves having Carson over for sleepovers. Thankfully, the sleepover is tomorrow night, as tonight is a school night. While we initially thought about allowing Violet and Rose to share the girls room, we decided against it. Violet still has difficulty falling asleep, and we wanted her to have her own space. Violet took over the girls room, and we renovated another bedroom for Rose. If the girls choose to share a room down the line, we'll deal with it then.

Brody occupies the last bedroom, but Oliver has made it very clear he expects to share a room with his little brother at some point. I'd feared having a six year age gap between the oldest and youngest would be difficult, but Oliver has surprised me at every milestone. He's all too engaged with his siblings, and loves every moment.

"Whew," Leo says with a loud exhale as he hands me a longneck beer beside our fire pit. Sitting beside me in a rocking chair, he clinks his beer to mine before taking a long swig. "Took Violet forever to fall asleep tonight."

"Too much excitement," I murmur, closing my eyes as I rest my head back. "Rose had trouble too. Oli's birthday, too much sugar, and Ally surprising us. Their little brains can't process it all."

"Shit, I'm sorry," Ally says as she walks out to join us. "I should have let you know I was coming."

I shake my head. "It's not a big deal. They would have been overstimulated even if you weren't here. In case you missed it, the girls are big fans of cake."

"You don't say," Ally says with a giggle. "They're a hoot. I wish we lived closer so I could see them more often."

Silver Mist Falls sits just about due west of Eternity Springs, but because of the mountainous terrain, it takes two hours to get there. It's a quaint city located just south of bustling Interstate 70, thrown in the midst of all the well-known skiing and winter sports locations. With no major ski resort in town, Silver Mist Falls manages to maintain its small-town charm, while pulling in tons of tourism to keep the businesses going.

"How's ranch life?" Leo asks easily, stretching over to pull my chair closer to his. Wrapping an arm around my shoulders, he mindlessly twirls a lock of hair around his fingers. I lean into his hand, finding peace in the feeling of his metal wedding band hitting my warm skin. We were quietly married in this backyard with only our kids, Travis and Gianna, and Leo's parents in attendance. I'd invited my brother, but he never answered me, and I haven't spoken to him since. I won't force someone to be family for me. I married into the best family, and the rest of the people I've chosen to surround myself with make up for everyone else.

"Ranch life was going well," Ally spits out, her gaze darkening. "We were doing just fine, until Dipshit McGee rolled into town and started making a fuss about things."

"Dipshit McGee?" Leo asks dryly. "Please tell me that isn't someone's actual name."

"No," she mutters. "Although I think it sounds better than his actual name."

"Oh, a *man* is causing problems," I tease.

Her eyes are full of annoyance as she glares at me. "Of course it's a man. Whenever someone causes drama in my life, it's always a fucking man."

"Alright. Who is causing drama this time?" I ask.

Ally blows out a breath, the breeze forcing hair out of her eyes. Resting a boot against the edge of the fire pit, she audibly growls. "This rich asshat rolled into town a couple of months ago. Drove a Benz right onto my ranch and had the absolute audacity to tell me he wants to buy it. Then the asshole had the *nerve* to be offended when I told him to get the fuck off the property!"

"Woah," Leo murmurs. "Why did he want to buy it?"

Irritation wafts off Ally in waves. "Does that really matter? Why does any entitled prick want to do anything? Because he *can*. Because it'll satisfy some innate need to take something from a woman. And probably because he also propositioned me the night before, and then he was butthurt about it."

"Wait," I interrupt. "He propositioned you? Did he take advantage of you?"

"No, nothing like that. We were both at the Timberline Tavern. I didn't know who he was. Just that he cleaned up nice. When he whipped out his black Amex, I knew he was above my pay grade, and I got out of there. Then he shows up at the ranch the following day, dressed to the nines in a bespoke suit, and told me he was buying the ranch out from under me."

"Ally, are you having financial troubles?" Leo asks bluntly. "For him to specifically state that he's going to buy it out from under you makes me think he knows you're in trouble."

"Not really, no," she murmurs. "Granted, it's been a rough year. Tourism has been down, and we haven't booked as many weddings we usually do. But we've been doing okay. I've never talked to anyone about struggling."

"Have our other cousins?" I ask. Ally's dad and my mom have another sibling. Our Uncle Jesse is the youngest, and always resented Ally's dad, Boone, for inheriting the ranch. When Boone had a stroke ten years ago, Ally took over the reins, much to Uncle

Jesse's dismay. He has two sons, Dean and Walker, who both always seemed to walk a line between sniveling asshole and good guy. "If you've ever mentioned anything to Dean and Walker, I wouldn't put it past them to start shit."

"Could there be a connection between them and Dipshit McGee?" Leo asks, making me giggle. "What's the guy's name?"

Ally sighs, a sound full of resignation and exhaustion. "Cole Cunningham."

Leo whistles low. "Damn. That's not a dipshit, Ally. Not many men out there can call themselves billionaires before the age of forty. And he's made quite a name for himself in commercial real estate. Not that I'm saying he has any right to tell you he's going to buy your land, but you've got the best acreage in Silver Mist Falls. He'd be an idiot not to offer."

"Well, I don't want his offer! I want him to leave my town!" she seethes. "He's everywhere I go. He wants horseback riding lessons and to host small dinner parties at the ranch. He shows up at town hall meetings, and even when I'm at the grocery store. He's every-where, Leo. And he's so damn happy all the time. Who the hell smiles nonstop? And does he sleep? I get texts at all hours of the night."

"How'd he get your number?" I ask, intrigued.

I notice a slight blush creep up her neck, only barely visible in the light from the fire. "A mistake on my part, before I realized who he was."

"So change your number," Leo offers up, his fingers finding the back of my neck to rub gently. I fight the urge to close my eyes in bliss.

"Like you changed yours when you guys broke up?" Ally asks defiantly.

Leo raises a brow. "Exactly. I didn't, because I still wanted her. Seems to me like you want this dude reaching out to you."

Ally stands in anger, her breath coming out in quick huffs. "I absolutely do not! I want to keep my life as simple as it's always been. Me, my friends, my animals, and the ranch. That's it! He can fuck right off, and I won't care! I'm going to bed."

As she flounces off, Leo chuckles. "Is it bad that I'm looking forward to watching this play out?"

"Why?" I ask.

He smiles sheepishly. "I don't know Cole Cunningham. I've heard of him, obviously. And I think Dom's met him once or twice when they've been at conferences together. But the one thing I know about the man is he gets what he wants. Since there isn't anyone I know as stubborn as your cousin, this is going to be a battle of wills. Unless she blatantly tells us she's changed her phone number, I'm going to assume she subconsciously wants him to contact her."

I turn toward him, laying a hand over his heart. I smile, knowing I'm covering all the tattoos he has for me, including where he added the birthdays for Oliver, Violet, and Rose onto the wings of the ladybug. "You know, I guess that's why I never changed my number either. I was there, patiently waiting for you."

His hand covers mine, clasping it tightly against his chest. "We were always meant to be, Ladybug. It just took us a little bit of extra time to find each other again. But that brings up a question. Do you remember when we made wishes?"

I nod. "Mine came true. Did yours?"

His face breaks into a beautiful smile. "It did. I wanted to have a family with you."

"I wanted to marry you." I beam. "Who'd have thought we'd be here today? Married with four kids, you finally have that wood-working business with Alex, and the bookstore is actually in a good financial place."

"When we're a team, we can achieve anything," he murmurs, leaning over to kiss me. "Any idea how soundly your cousin sleeps? I'd like to make you moan a little, if that's okay."

"She sleeps like the dead," I whisper, even though I really don't know. And honesty, I don't care. When my husband wants to make me moan, I'm all too willing to give him what he wants. "Take me to bed, husband."

If you're not ready to say goodbye to Leo and Ella yet, be sure to grab this special bonus scene!

Want to start over at the beginning? Grab Worth it All for free, featuring Travis and Gianna, then head into Worth the Risk featuring Luca and Hannah!

Looking forward to my new series, where we'll find out about Ally and Cole? Sterling Ranch Falls is coming Fall 2026! Go pre-order When Starlight Falls today!

Acknowledgements

When I first began writing this series back in the fall of 2022, it was originally going to be a hockey series centering around Luca Santo and his crazy band of bad boy hockey teammates. But honestly, can you even imagine Luca without his meddling sisters, Mason the marmot, or Nonna butting her head into things? Or the epic sibling group chats?

I'm so glad that I had an epiphany in the summer of 2023 telling me to have Luca play hockey, but also be from a large Italian family in a small town west of Denver. I began picking out their names and careers, and almost immediately knew the toughest two to write would be Leo and Alex. Alex is clear: still grieving his dead wife, and unable to move on, even when his perfect match is right in front of him. But Leo's story was a little murky in my mind. He's the smartest, the stealthiest, and the one who knows everything. I knew he'd be injured, but I was unsure of how badly I wanted the injury to be. And the part about him being discharged because of the injury? That's a true story, folks. The Army doesn't care. When you're no longer good for them, they'll toss you aside.

I'd originally planned for Leo to be the grumpy, silent type. Just let anger overwhelm him. But, as it is with so many of my characters, he wasn't on board with that. Oh, he definitely has angry moments. But he's also sarcastic, loving, and undoubtedly the most patient character I've written so far (but Gabriel Campos is right up there too!). I absolutely love how he turned out.

I can't believe I've come to the end of Eternity Springs. Seven books, because we can't leave out Gianna and Travis in the prequel of Worth it All. I struggled writing the epilogue for Leo and Ella, mostly because I just don't want to say goodbye to these characters yet! I almost think I should keep writing things in Eternity … hmmm.

So, the first thanks I'm giving is to my friend Matt. He had firsthand experience with an IED in a war zone, and all the injuries that came with it … including the honorary discharge within a year. Thanks, Matt, for telling me all about it.

Thanks to my husband for answering the rest of the military questions, like when I asked him how veterans feel about the VA, and his response was, "Oh, we all think the VA sucks." So there you have it.

I'd like to thank my two children, one of which found an image on my phone of a crocheted peen today, and asked me what it was. After I said it was nothing, he replied, "Really? Cuz it looks like a dick to me." And that's how I found out my 11-year-old has learned some slang for penis.

On the business side, I'd like to thank Luna Literary, for being an amazing PR company to work with. Colby and Jamie for doing their things on TikTok so that I can stay off of there, and Morgan for all the amazing Reels. My editor, Brenda, for always rooting for me, and helping calm me down when I'm weeks behind schedule.

To my PA, Morgan: you're such an amazing cheerleader. I'm so thankful for you. Now don't bug me about an accidental/surprise pregnancy for a couple of books.

Lastly, to my wonderful group of friends who've supported me in this gig while also doing their own author thing. Tamara, Catie, Becky, BJ, Alina, Breanna, and Nikki, you're so amazing. Thank you for listening to me vent, being ready to set fire to the world, and letting me be part of your lives. I love you all.

Forever Series

Forever Sunshine

Forever Yours

Forever Ours

Forever Mine

Forever Us

Forever Together

Eternity Series

Worth the Risk

Worth the Trouble

Worth the Vow

Worth the Test

Worth the Heat

Worth the Wait

Mile High Sports Series

Blue Lines and Lullabies

Forecasting the Forward

Paws on the Playbook

Cooking up a Curveball (Summer 2026)

Sterling Falls Ranch

When Starlight Falls (Fall 2026)

About the Author

Jennifer was born and raised in Ohio, but currently calls Colorado home. A lifelong lover of romance books, Jen felt pulled to write stories with older characters, because "old farts" deserve love too. Jen prides herself on delivering realistic characters that struggle with normal problems. She spends most of her free time within her zoo: two kids, two dogs, and two cats! When not containing the chaos, Jen can be found lounging on her covered porch devouring books on her Kindle.